Man Hunt

Unzipping her skirt, she let it slip over her hips
on to the floor, so that she was wearing
nothing but skimpy underwear that matched
the elegant bra. She slipped her underwear
over her slim hips, noticing her pants were
damp, then placed them near her bra. She
bent to his ear so that her words could barely
be heard. 'I'm real. You can smell me. You like
me so much you want to taste me. Think of
me writhing under you as you explore me
with your tongue. Imagine asking me to do
anything you like. Anything at all.

Man Hunt
Cathleen Ross

BLACKLACE

Black Lace books contain sexual fantasies.
In real life, always practise safe sex.

This edition published in 2006 by
Black Lace
Thames Wharf Studios
Rainville Road
London W6 9HA

Originally published 2001

Typeset by SetSystems Ltd, Saffron Walden, Essex
Printed and bound by Mackays of Chatham PLC

ISBN 0 352 33583 1
ISBN 9 780352 335838

Chapter One

Angie stood in the train station wet with arousal. Her blood tingled and her nipples hardened when she spied the ebony-haired man. He was tall, and was wearing faded jeans and riding boots. 'I want you,' she whispered, 'and I always get what I want.'

She liked the way the stranger wore his dark hair unfashionably long. By his dress, she guessed he could be a jackaroo from one of the northern cattle stations, but Australian men always dressed down and looks could be deceptive.

The train station was crowded and there were lots of men to choose from, but Angie wasn't interested in just anyone. She'd marked out her man and started walking towards him. I want to feel your cock inside me, she thought.

The stranger turned her on because he walked with an air of assurance and strength. She welcomed the challenge of making him her slave.

She followed him to the train, the adrenaline from the hunt sending tingling sensations to her nipples. When she glanced down, she realised there was no disguising the height of her arousal through her shirt. Already the

1

filmy wetness rubbed against her thighs and her breath quickened, to match the pace of her heart. When she reached Sydney it would be dark, but providing the stranger played her game, Angie knew she would be satisfied.

Angie had spent three years studying catering, and due to her study commitments she'd experienced a sexual famine. Right now, Mr Feast was boarding the afternoon train for Sydney. The same train that Angie intended to catch.

The train was old, one of the last ancient variety to survive modernisation. Angie was pleased because the separate compartments offered privacy.

Grabbing hold of the railings, she pulled herself up the metal train steps and walked along the corridor, searching each cabin for her man. The separate compartments teemed with occupants but her stranger was not to be found.

'Now, where have you gone?' she said, looking around. Then she noticed the train door that separated the carriages swing closed, and she realised he'd chosen the last carriage to find a seat.

Her pulse racing, she opened the carriage door and stepped across the rickety compartment. A snatch of denim caught her eye. 'I've got you,' she said, with fierce determination.

She pulled aside the cabin door, and was delighted to discover they were alone. Quickly, she surveyed the door handles. She noticed to her satisfaction that they could be lashed shut.

Her stranger was already seated alongside the window with his eyes closed, unaware of what was in store for him. Placing her bag on one seat, Angie settled down near to the doors, her body hot with anticipation. Her stranger stirred but his eyes remained closed.

In frustration, she picked up a discarded newspaper and turned to the employment section. There were

2

plenty of jobs advertised but they all had the same thing in common. Experience wanted.

Her eyes were drawn to the personal section, caught by one of the ads. *WANTED lap dancers, blonde girls, sexy bodies wanted. Make real $$$.* That's what I'd like, thought Angie. She circled the advertisement. She knew she would enjoy dancing semi-naked but not for a group of men.

An audience of one would be more exciting, under certain circumstances. Circumstances involving the leather belt around her waist, along with the corset and stockings she wore under her wrap-around skirt, and the handcuffs she kept in her duffle bag for special situations. Angie believed in always being prepared.

There was a low groan, then a shudder, as the train slowly pulled out of the terminal and gained momentum, until the rhythm of the train throbbed pleasantly under Angie's thighs. Their journey had begun.

'Looking for a job?' asked a deep, husky voice.

Angie turned to the stranger in the carriage. He had slid far enough up the seat to look over her shoulder at the newspaper.

In repose, his sun-tanned face had held a look of peacefulness. She knew she could change that. Angie had learnt from past experience that lust did strange things to men. Timing was everything.

'I'm just looking at what's available in Sydney,' she said, taking her time to answer his question.

He gazed at her and Angie knew she had piqued his interest. There were two types of men, according to Angie. Men who would run the moment sex was mentioned, and men who were trapped by their desire.

'Funny place to start,' he said, moving closer, and she smiled, knowing her stranger belonged in the latter category.

'But the most interesting,' she answered. Holding his gaze, she folded the paper and put it by her side. A

3

sharp jerking movement, accompanied by a screech from the train's wheels, pierced the air as the train, building speed, turned a curve. Vibrations thudded through the vinyl seat. Angie enjoyed the sensation. The air in their cabin was thick with tension.

From the way his gaze devoured her, she knew he was assessing her for potential. 'Going to Sydney for a holiday?' he asked.

'No, I'm going to study, plus maybe do a bit of part-time work.' Carelessly, she flicked her blonde locks behind her ear and uncrossed her legs so that the split of her wrap-around skirt opened to expose the slim line of her thigh.

His eyes darted downward and Angie barely suppressed a grin, knowing her seduction was going to plan.

'A girl like you wouldn't have any trouble getting something.'

She noticed the way his Adam's apple moved up and down as he swallowed, and she enjoyed the hot caress of his eyes.

She looked at her watch. There was just over an hour to go before the train pulled into Central Station, Sydney. She longed to imprison him, to writhe over him and explore his lean, hard body.

'Do you know Sydney well?' she asked.

'Well enough. When the country gets too monotonous I go to Sydney for a little relief. If you know what I mean?'

'Uh-huh.' She nodded, understanding him only too well. The rhythm of the train created a gentle rocking movement and the vibration was pleasant against the sensitive skin of her bare bottom.

He was handsome and roguish, qualities that instantly aroused her. She noticed from the indent on his left ring finger, where his wedding ring had been, that he was probably planning some light entertainment, not realising he would get more than he ever anticipated on the train.

'What kind of work are you looking for?' he asked.

'I haven't made up my mind yet. I'll have to see what I can get when I'm there,' she said, opening her legs further, inviting his glance. Her sex was throbbing pleasurably, craving attention, her clit-hood piercing making its presence felt.

'I noticed you circled the lap-dancing ad. Ever done it?' he asked, his voice low and husky.

'No, but I'd like to,' she answered directly. She watched him intensely, waiting to see if he'd snap up the bait she was dangling.

His tanned skin was flushed with arousal at the throat. 'You know, I reckon in that little skirt, if you just pull it up a tiny bit, unbutton your top a little, you'd make a great dancer.'

'You *want* me to dance for you?' she asked.

A look of raw lust crossed his features. She realised he thought he had just got lucky. Her nipples tightened in anticipation at having this hunky stranger as her sex slave. She imagined him tied, fully excited and waiting to fulfil her desires.

He glanced at his watch. 'The train will be in Sydney in about fifty minutes. Why don't you come stay with me? I've got a room booked in one of the good pubs.'

'I've got other plans,' she said coolly.

The train shuddered to a stop. Their shoulders touched momentarily. The heat from the stranger's shoulder seared through her shirt and her nipples ached to be sucked. She looked at him, eyes wide, sending unspoken messages of seduction, willing him to lose control. She was resolved to have him her way and the danger of discovery made her more excited than ever.

His disappointment at her refusal of his invitation punctuated the silence as he looked around the carriage.

Angie waited, noticing the way his pants strained at the zip.

Winding some of her blonde hair around her index finger, she gazed at him. Break, damn you, she thought.

The train started moving again. The rhythmic rocking sent primeval messages through her body, and she knew the seat was damp from her juices.

'I'd like to see you dance,' he said. His eyes moved from her face to her breasts and stayed there. 'You've got a great body. Pity we're on this train.'

'Oh, I don't think that's a pity.' He was so close she could reach out and stroke his muscular thigh. Trace her thumb over his bulging jean-clad cock. But she could not afford to give in to her lust. Not yet.

'You mean, you want to dance here?' he asked, the tone of his voice full of surprise and possibilities.

'Why not?' she challenged, waiting to see whether his desire for her would overrule his common sense.

'Because anyone could come in. I don't want to get arrested.'

'Pity,' she said, shrugging her shoulders. 'I've got a cassette player in my duffel bag.'

'What are you? Some kind of professional?' His eyes narrowed suspiciously.

'Of course not. I'm moving to Sydney and I brought all my gear with me. Anyway, I haven't asked you for any money and I don't want any.' Flicking her hair away from her face, she leant forward. 'I think you're the kind of guy who would appreciate something different.'

She watched as perspiration beaded on his brow. 'Seeing you dance would be nice in that little skirt of yours,' he said, his voice dropping an octave.

Angie stretched her long legs in front of her and folded her arms across her lap, feigning boredom. She could see, from the expression on his face, that he wanted her. Now it was only a matter of time.

'Dancing without it would be better,' he added, smiling and looking roguish.

I've got you, she thought. I can imagine your cock thrusting inside me.

He rose to his feet and walked over to examine the old sliding doors. Closing them, he wiggled the handles. 'You know? I think I can tie these handles together and pull down the blinds. No-one would see us then.'

She shrugged. 'If that's what you want.'

He quickly stripped his belt from his waist to tie it securely around the handles. 'We don't have any more stops until Sydney. Going to dance for me?'

'Now that depends on how well you behave yourself.' She stared at him, knowing the balance of power had tipped in her direction. He'd secured the doors. All she needed was to secure him.

'Just a little dance. I'll sit right here, keep my hands to myself.'

'I'll dance for you but on one condition.'

'What's that?'

'That you do exactly as I tell you. Don't move unless I let you.'

'I'll keep my hands on my lap.' He settled on the carriage seat, leaning forward, palms pressed together expectantly.

'Not good enough. See those baggage rails? I want to tie you to those.'

'Never done bondage,' he said, but his eyes gleamed and Angie knew he was intrigued.

'And you never will, either, unless you agree to exactly what I want.'

He stopped silent for a moment and shifted uncomfortably in his tight jeans. She slowly undid two of her shirt buttons, so that her cleavage and lacy corset showed clearly.

'Bossy little miss, aren't you?' he said, his gaze glued to her large, but firm, breasts.

7

'Do we have an agreement?' she asked, all senses tingling, knowing that one of her most erotic fantasies – that of having a handsome, powerful man tied to do her bidding – was about to come true. Unlike other women, boring sex did not exist for Angie, because she lived out her fantasies.

When he nodded agreement and offered his hands to be tied, her excitement teetered on the brink of orgasm. She knew he had lost all reason and she wanted to feel his hard cock inside her.

'This better be good, otherwise I'm gonna be the boss and I'm thinking your sweet, peachy arse could do with a spanking.'

'Settle down. You're going to like this.'

She extracted her cassette player from one of the bundles and flicked on the switch. The music let out a steady throbbing rhythm. She slowly slid her skirt above her stocking line and unclicked her stocking from each suspender. Curling the stocking around her fingers, she advanced towards him, moving her hips to the beat, preparing to tie him up.

Suddenly he leant forward and his hands dived under her skirt, wrapping on to her bottom like plastic.

'Mmm, no panties and wet pussy,' he growled.

'Quit it,' she said, pushing him away, but he leant forward to caress her again, his fingers nudging against her piercing.

'God, you feel good,' he groaned. For a moment Angie wondered which way things would go. There was no going back now and she hoped he would let her tie him up. Already his hands and fingers were searching her outer wetness, and Angie almost gave in to the pleasure of his touch. Pressing her hands firmly against his shoulders, she pushed him away.

'This will be more fun for you if you let me tie you. I'll make it last much longer.'

She watched the shadow of the hunter move across

his features, before lust compelled him to submit to her wishes. He leant back, licked his fingers, and then held out his hands to be bound.

'Think I was wrong about you,' he said.

'Oh, how's that?'

'You done this type of thing before. Look at that piercing you've got. You're certainly no innocent.'

'Lift your arms up.'

Angie climbed up on to the seat, her legs astride his face as she secured his hands to the overhead railings. She ran her hands over his broad shoulders, feeling his muscles tighten in response to her touch. He groaned, breathing in deeply and pressed his face in to her skirt.

She stepped down, pulled his shirt from his jeans and unbuttoned it, to reveal a tanned muscular chest, lightly covered with crisp dark hair.

Her insides liquefied as her eyes moved from his handsome face to his broad V-shaped torso. The intense feeling of desire set her throbbing between her legs. 'You want me to dance dirty?' she asked huskily.

'Yes. Wriggle that pussy in my face.'

She smiled, dipped one finger inside herself then traced her fingertip along his lips. 'I'm wet for you. Be good and you'll be tasting more of me soon.'

He breathed in heavily, his tongue tracing his lips for her essence, and groaned in pleasure.

Angie's eyes narrowed. 'I like it that you want to taste me. I'm going to peel myself open and let you thrust your tongue inside me.'

'Come on, you dirty bitch,' he urged. 'Don't tease me. Either let me suck you or sit on my cock.'

She looked at him. He was downright sexy and he was all hers to torment. 'I call the shots,' she said. 'I'll let you shove your cock inside me when I'm ready.'

Hips moving to the beat of the music, she sat astride him and slowly unbuttoned the rest of her shirt, letting it slide off her shoulders to reveal a lacy cream corset.

9

He strained forward to suck on the rosy nipples that peeked above it.

She leant backward, teasing him, laughing, before running her hands over his chest, arousing his nipples with skilled fingers until they were hard and tight. Taking one nipple in her mouth, then the other, she sucked, then nibbled, doing to him the things she knew he wanted to do to her, but could not unless she let him.

She could feel the hardness of him, straining through the coarse denim of his jeans. She moved her hand downward, stroking him through the fabric, her fingers tracing over his rigid cock. A thrill of excitement shot through her when she realised, from the size of him, that she was not going to be disappointed.

'You're huge. I want to explore you,' she said, her voice breathy with excitement.

'Please.' He nodded, his mouth open, panting short hot breaths of lust. His eyes never left her face.

Slipping her fingers under the waistband of his jeans, she enjoyed the sensation of his smooth skin and the way it stretched tautly over his washboard abdomen. A fine trail of body hair ran from his navel downward and she ran her fingers over the hair, pulling it lightly between her fingers, following the intriguing pathway.

'Unzip me, baby,' he demanded hoarsely.

'When I'm ready,' she said.

Her eyes met his and she watched as a tear of perspiration ran down his brow. She bent to lick it, tasting him, enjoying the sensation of tongue-to-skin contact. 'You're delicious. I want to taste every inch of you,' she said, determined to savour him. That was the wonderful thing about bondage. Give a man the upper hand and everything was all over in minutes.

'Fuck me,' he begged. 'Let me shove my cock inside you.'

With no further stops until Sydney, the train gathered

momentum, the pistons turning frantically, building speed.

Moving to the beat of the music, pressing rhythmically against him, she slowly peeled the delicate corset straps from her shoulders and pushed the lacy bra cups from her breasts. Fondling her nipples, she smiled with delight when he lunged forward hungrily, trying to take her nipples in his mouth. The muscles of his arms bulged. The stockings dug into his wrists, leaving a crimson line.

'You moved again,' she said, teasing him, leaning slightly out of his reach. 'Every time you disobey me, you have to wait a little longer.'

'Come on, baby,' he begged. 'Take it out of my jeans. I can't wait any longer.'

One of her hands stroked his cheek. His skin was damp with desire and he was so darkly handsome and desirable, she needed to see his cock and feel its hardness in her hands.

Reaching down, she unzipped his jeans to release his engorged member. It stood stiff, thick with blood, anticipating attention. She ran her hands lightly over his penis, noting with satisfaction that her index finger and thumb could not meet when she circled his shaft.

Teasingly, she leant back and folded the waistline of her skirt so that it became minuscule, the hem stopping just short of revealing her sex. 'This short enough for you?' she asked, noticing with pleasure the intensity of his stare. Reaching upward, she held on to the overhead baggage rail and slowly pulled herself to a standing position, positioning herself so he could peek under her skirt.

The train jerked suddenly, flinging her hips forward. Her sex pressed against his open mouth, the metal stud vibrating against his teeth. The heat from his lips sent a thrill through her body, with the intensity of an electric shock. 'Oh, that was good,' she sighed.

11

It would be so easy to sit on him and fill herself with his engorged cock, but she was on the edge, and she loved the intensity of balancing near the peak of orgasm.

Her stranger groaned as she pulled away, his lips gleaming with her juices. 'You're good, real good, but don't stop there.' He nodded, keeping his eyes pinned to the level of her skirt.

She climbed down. 'Lift your hips,' she ordered.

'About time, bitch,' he said. She smiled then pulled his jeans down to his ankles. She knelt, knees either side of his legs, careful not to touch his cock.

'Suck my nipples,' she ordered, wanting to feel his hot tongue running over her tender peaks. She closed her eyes in pleasure, her head tilted back as he sucked, then licked the stiffened tips of her breasts.

Instinctively, she positioned herself just above his penis and he bucked to meet her. 'Come on, you dirty bitch. I want to shove my cock inside you.'

She kept herself positioned above him, not letting him make contact. 'You're not allowed to move unless I tell you,' she ordered again, relishing her control of this powerful, sexy man.

'You want this as much as I do,' he growled.

Pulsing to the beat, she allowed her wet pussy lips to lightly graze across his tip. Groaning, he bucked upward in anticipation.

'Uh-uh, you're not listening.' She laughed mischievously. 'You have to keep perfectly still.'

'Sit on me, baby.'

'Patience. You'll enjoy it all the more,' she said, as she unbuttoned her skirt to reveal a downy, blonde pussy.

She noticed that his eyes were riveted to her perfectly shaped sex, with its gold stud, trimmed hair and small pink inner lips. His muscular arms strained at his bonds, until the veins stood out on his forearms.

'You're beautiful,' he moaned, his voice hoarse with desire.

Suddenly the handles of the cabin door rattled. 'Hey, open up,' called a male voice.

'Suck my nipples again,' ordered Angie, ignoring the intrusion.

'Are you crazy? Someone's trying to get in. Untie me,' implored her stranger.

Angie reached over and turned up the volume of her cassette player, until the throbbing sound of the music filled the cabin.

'Do as you're told. Suck me.'

The cabin doors shook violently. 'Hey, let me in,' yelled the would-be intruder.

Ripples of pleasure radiated upward from Angie's sex. She moaned and arched her back. The doors rattled again, the handle twisting violently. The danger of discovery increased the potency of her excitement.

The doors stopped rattling, and the unwanted intruder fell silent.

'Untie me. I'll do anything you want,' her stranger pleaded. 'Someone's going to burst in here.'

She nodded, enjoying the moment. 'Yes they could,' she agreed. 'That's what makes it so good,' she added throatily.

Ignoring his plea, she pressed her breast into his mouth, enjoying the feeling of being devoured, while she used the hard knob of his cock to stroke her slippery cleft. It slid readily between her lips, slick against the silky wetness, until the head of his cock met the heat of her clit. Slowly, but with skill, she guided it over herself. The eroticism of the moment left her gasping.

But she did not want to explode just yet. This occasion was delicious. She wanted to savour her handsome captive. From the second her hand wrapped around his cock, he stopped protesting.

Her eyes met his, his expression intense. A pulse beat at his temple. 'Quit playing with me.' He groaned, but he was not in any position to make demands.

'I said I'd dance,' she said, with a lilt in her voice. She laughed mischievously. 'If you behave yourself I might do more than dance.'

Listening to the throb of the music, she pulled herself backward and rotated up his body, pulsating her sex in his face to the beat of the music.

Straining at his ties, he tried to grab at her with his hands. 'Finish me off, baby, I can't take any more. Sit on me. I'll do anything for you,' he said. His voice was hoarse and impatient.

Ah, the sound of a sexy, powerful man begging. She smiled, looking down at him. This was turning out to be more fun than she had expected. The best was yet to come.

'Oh, I'll fix you up all right but first you'd better make me happy.'

'Make you happy?' His eyes grew wide with alarm. 'What do you want?'

'Don't argue and do what I say,' she said, opening her pussy lips. She noticed her clitoris pop out, ripe and red, needing to be sucked.

She watched as beads of perspiration gathered at his temples. He was so hot for her he was melting.

He licked then sucked on the delicate folds before finding her core. Angie felt a volcano building up inside her. He had the most firm, sensual mouth. Full, generous lips. A mouth made for sucking pussy. First he nipped at her bud, then sucked it between his lips. She edged forward slightly and his long tongue probed inside her like a delicious cock. A fireball built in the base of her spine and sped up her vertebrae, exploding in her head until her senses dissolved. Her hands, the knuckles white with intensity, gripped the overhead bars as she arched her back.

'Yes, yes,' she groaned, as he licked furiously up and down the cleft of her sex, concentrating on the piercing

14

above her clit. She came really hard, her cries intermingling with the heady throb of the music.

Head spinning, she looked down at him with satisfaction. 'From the moment I saw you, I knew you'd be good at sucking me,' she said. 'But now I need your thick cock.'

The combined pulse of the music and rhythm of the train vibrated through her. Suddenly the cabin was plunged into darkness as the train entered a tunnel. 'Sit on me, baby,' he urged, his voice urgent through the darkness.

She climbed down on shaky legs, feeling her way over his broad chest, smelling his musky scent, and lowered herself down on to his lap. By the end of the tunnel, she had taken him inside her. She could feel herself stretching to encompass him.

'Thought we were never going to get to this,' he said.

Moving in time to the beat of the music, she moaned and pressed her hands against his firm chest, savouring the feeling of the crisp body hair.

'Untie me, baby, so I can touch you,' he begged.

She shook her head, enjoying the sensation of having him exactly where she wanted him. She wanted the feel of him filling the very core of her. He had staying power and she was delighted her instinct for picking the right man had proved fruitful.

He bucked vigorously, close to his own satisfaction, but Angie needed him to serve her a little longer. 'Don't move,' she ordered, determined to control him to the end.

'You dominating bitch.' He groaned. 'You've had your turn.'

'Do as you're told,' she demanded, and leant forward to take his face in her hands. Kissing him deeply, she thrust down on him, the scent of herself on his lips added to the intensity of the fucking. The sensation of

15

his lips, the taste of herself on his mouth made her call out in pleasure.

Her cries were matched by renewed hammering at the train doors. 'Open these doors,' yelled a male voice.

Her stranger groaned as he thrust into her and Angie felt him tense. She ground down on him, faster and harder, enjoying every second of his pumping cock. Despite the urgent threat of discovery, he did not ask her to stop and she sensed he was beyond caring.

The voice at the door grew louder but her stranger was lost in his ecstasy as Angie consumed him. His head thrown back, his eyes closed, he roared as he came, adding to the cacophony of sound.

Sated, they sat staring into each other's eyes, their hot breath intermingling as the train slowed its pace.

'What's your name?' he panted. 'I want to see you again.'

He was good, thought Angie. No, he was better than good, but all good things had to come to an end and now that her head had stopped spinning, she knew it was time to leave. 'You don't need to know.'

A fist hammered at the cabin doors again.

The stranger's eyes opened wide in alarm as he looked at the shaking doors. 'Hurry up. Untie me before someone breaks the door down.' He tried to grab at her with his restrained hands. The weave of the stocking pulled tight, threatening to break.

'I told you not to move,' she said.

'Enough of this game, you mean bitch,' he growled.

Angie carefully manoeuvred herself out of his reach. Climbing off him, she reached for her shirt, did up the buttons, then put on her skirt.

'Hey, what are you doing? You have to untie me,' he said. He struggled with his bonds as the train slowed but the bonds only pulled tighter, making them impossible to undo.

16

'Why? You look great as you are,' she said.

He struggled furiously and his wallet slipped from his jeans. His wedding ring fell from his wallet on to the floor and rolled under the train seat. Angie picked the ring up and placed it next to him. 'Wouldn't want you to lose this,' she said with a smile.

The hammering continued and the doors shook.

'Quit hammering. I'm opening the door,' she called.

Turning off the music, she picked up her bag and unstrapped the door. Perfect timing, thought Angie, as the train slowed to a crawl into Sydney's Central Station.

'You can't leave me here like this,' implored the stranger, writhing and twisting, trying to free himself. 'I don't want them to find me like this. Untie me!' he roared, glaring at her furiously. 'Wait until I get you.'

She looked at him and smiled mischievously. 'You already have.'

Face dark with anger and straining at his bonds, he looked like a dangerously virile pirate, and she certainly did not intend to unleash him.

'You forgot rule number one. If you touch a lap dancer, she just gets up and walks away.' Angie slid open the train doors and smiled sweetly at the shocked look on the face of the train conductor outside her cabin.

'Bitch!' the stranger roared.

'That's right,' she called back. 'I'm a man-hunting bitch, who always gets what she wants.' Angie laughed then jumped off the slowly moving train. It was time to start her new life in the hospitality industry in Sydney.

Chapter Two

'What makes you think you're suitable for a placement at Hotel Desire?' thundered James Steele, the head of the Hotel Training Academy where Angie had been a student for the past month. He leant back on his chair, folding his arms behind his head. His dark eyes narrowed and Angie knew she was undergoing a not-so-subtle sexual appraisal. Her nipples tingled, responding to the caress of his eyes.

Although he dressed conservatively, Angie sensed a dark side to her teacher, a brooding shadow of the unknown, and though common sense told her not to tackle him, she could never resist a challenge. Instinct warned her that his poised self-assurance was a front that hid a wilder nature. The tingling that started at her nipples spread lower.

'I think I can handle anything that comes my way,' she said, looking at him directly.

'Really. Anything?' he questioned. 'I only send special students for work experience to Hotel Desire. Students who can cope with the demands of some very wealthy and unusual clients.'

She watched as James Steele unbuttoned his expensive

suit jacket with beautifully manicured fingers. On his left hand he wore a curiously ornate gold ring, with a coal black stone that glowed when it caught the light. The suit jacket fell open, so that it no longer constricted his broad chest.

He caught her observing his every movement and smiled momentarily, his white teeth wolfish against his pale features, but his smile didn't reach his eyes.

A surge of pleasure shot through her as she sensed an unspoken challenge. He was curiously abhorrent, yet attractive at the same time, and Angie found this juxtaposition of feelings puzzling. He was handsome with short, dark, cropped hair, clouded dark eyes full of sexual secrets, and a straight patrician nose, which contrasted with a slash-and-burn, sensuous mouth. Yet despite his good looks, she did not like him. After a month of lectures and intensive work experience at one of the Academy's hotels, Angie had learnt that James Steele was a demanding taskmaster.

He wore an intense expression and though his eyes burnt through the thin layer of her summer dress, she knew he would be difficult to bend to her will. She was used to being appraised by men, but this man was different. There was an element of arrogance about him combined with sheer hulking masculinity. The hunter in her reared its head, yet while she wanted him for her next conquest, she sensed he was dangerous.

At five foot ten, Angie stood taller and stronger than most women. The combination of her height, waist-length blonde locks, large blue eyes and curvaceous lips kept men doing a double take when she walked past. But it was the cat-that-got-the-cream expression which she carried around with her that turned their heads.

Only this time she was at a loss. This was not going to be a simple tie-up-and-leave-'em seduction because, effectively, James Steele was her boss, and she wanted the work experience placement at Hotel Desire.

For as long as she could remember she had wanted to run her own hotel, but not just any establishment. She wanted to manage something special, like Hotel Desire, and the only way to find out how the hotel achieved its international five-star status and a celebrity guest list was to work there. James Steele had the power to grant the work experience placement, so for now she'd have to play his game. Whatever that was.

'Hotel Desire takes the best.' He raised his eyebrows. 'What makes you think you have what it takes to work there?' he asked, his face grim.

'I topped my catering training college and won the scholarship here —'

'I think we both know I'm not talking about marks,' he interrupted sharply. 'The type of person suitable to work at Hotel Desire is not an academic. Have you ever worked for wealthy people?'

Angie shook her head.

'The wealthy can buy anything they want. Anything! Do you understand what I'm saying?' He looked at her, his eyes hooded with secrets.

Angie shivered. Though it was a hot summer day in Sydney, the sun seemed to have retreated behind a cloud.

'No, I don't think you do. I don't think you have any idea what goes on in Hotel Desire, or what's expected from the staff who work there.'

'I know what I read,' she said, angry that he seemed to be discounting her so easily.

'Ah, the tabloids. Celebrities from all over the world flock to stay there because we ensure complete privacy. Do you think we'd be foolish enough to let in the paparazzi? The tabloids only guess at what goes on there.'

Angie could see her dream dissolving before her eyes. 'I'm not as naive as you think,' she said, determined to push her point.

'This is a special placement. I'm looking for a sophisticated student. A sybarite. Someone used to the needs of the wealthy. Someone obedient, yet unshockable.' James stood and walked over to her, standing close, so that she could feel his breath on her face.

'You don't have an obedient nature. You proved that at your last work experience placement. I have just read the hotel manager's report on you and I intend to reprimand you.'

He cupped his hand under her chin and Angie fought the desire to push him away. A strange tingling had started in the pit of her stomach, and she wondered just what he meant by reprimand.

She did not intend to be subservient to any man, yet he had her in a difficult position. From everything she had read and heard, no other placement would suit her, except Hotel Desire.

'You do realise that in this business you have to start at the bottom,' he said. His hand slid slowly down from her chin, lightly grazing over her throat, and came to rest on her shoulder. 'Wherever I decide to place you next, you'll start as a maid. Serving others. Obeying their every wish.'

'I know how to obey orders, when I have to,' she said.

'Hmm, I wonder.' His fingers caressed her shoulder. His voice was deep and had a wonderful quality that reminded her of rich, dark chocolate.

Angie liked the feeling of his firm touch on her shoulder and her nipples hardened in response to his close proximity. Slowly, seductively, he ran one hand down to her aching breast and caressed the tip.

'Perhaps,' he said, breaking his touch. 'Perhaps you could be trained to serve, but you will have to prove it to me.'

She looked at him as he walked to the window, standing in front of it, blocking the light, so that the features of his face hardened with the darkness. She blinked again, trying to focus. He moved from the window to sit behind his desk and light again flooded the room.

'Lift your skirt.'

The order had the effect on Angie's senses that was intended. Shock, closely followed by intense desire, burnt through the layers of her resistance.

James Steele carried an air of authority and the tension in his private office was suddenly electric.

'Staff from the Meriana Hotel have complained you don't follow orders,' he said. 'Perhaps you care to explain your misdemeanour before I punish you.'

Angie knew the complaint had come from the hotel, where she'd just completed her work experience. The head bitch had obviously complained, so Angie did not intend to elaborate. Seeing as James intended punishing her in a most unorthodox way, he had obviously heard the complaint in vivid detail.

'I'd hardly call being late with the housekeeping round a misdemeanour.'

'That wasn't the nature of the complaint,' James said. 'Using your hotel key to gain access to a hotel client's shower was a breach of hotel regulations.'

'Cleaning bathrooms was part of my housekeeping duty,' she answered back.

'Not when the client was in it. When you represent the Academy on work experience, you do what you're told, if you intend to graduate.'

'Or what? Are you going to spank my bottom like a naughty girl?' she couldn't resist taunting. 'Is that why you want me to lift my skirt? Or don't you know what a woman looks like?'

'You're slow to take orders. I don't like to be kept waiting.'

The authority in his voice was intensely exciting. The man had the strength of a footballer but the face of Adonis, and the combination of the two intensified her

22

desire, until the very air in his private office seemed honey-thick with sensuality.

Slowly, but with deliberation, she unzipped her skirt until it dropped to the floor, her shirt barely covering her bikini thong.

'I said lift your skirt, not drop it to the floor,' he said coolly in his mesmerising voice.

Challenging him was probably not a good idea, and Angie knew she was risking her scholarship, but her desire for James grew every second she was in his office. She would do more than lift her skirt, then see how he handled the situation. 'I've never been good at taking orders. Perhaps you can teach me how,' she taunted, boldly unbuttoning her shirt, revealing firm, tanned breasts, her nipples taut with desire.

She saw his wonderfully pale skin flush deeply, highlighting the blackness of his hair until in her hedonistic state of euphoria, he became the intense colours of desire. Black for control; red for passion.

'Bend over the desk.'

A shiver of excitement set her body tingling on the edge. Shucking off her shirt, she stood facing him in nothing but her thong, watching the colour of his face burn deeply to his throat. He wanted her to be subservient. Well, she would give him more than he bargained for.

'Make me,' she challenged. Silence filled the air with electric tension.

He walked towards her, so that she could feel his hot breath on her face. 'You want me to, don't you?'

'Yes.'

He ran one of his hands over the curve of her face, down over the soft skin of her throat. His fingers moved still lower to linger on her breast, slowly flicking over her nipple until she wanted to cry out with pleasure. His touch was delicious, and when he stood close she could smell the crisp freshness of his scent edged with musk. The arousing aroma combined with the eroticism of his touch made her throat go dry.

Suddenly he held her close, with his body pressed hard against hers. One of his hands circled her waist, the other held firmly on to her wrist, pushing her arm behind her back, so that she arched into him. 'You're enjoying this, aren't you?' he said.

Head spinning with desire, her lips opened and, pinioned by his hold, she ground her pelvis against him, in answer to his question.

'Yes, I think that's exactly what you like, but I have something else in mind,' he said.

When he let her go, her curiosity overcame her disappointment as she watched him unlock an ancient Korean chest in the corner of his office.

Her breath still coming in hot pants from his ministrations, Angie observed as James opened the cupboard and extracted a whip with several leather tails, and a small bottle of something that looked like oil.

'Bend over the desk.'

'No. I want to take my punishment face to face.'

Walking towards her, he placed the whip on the desk and opened the bottle, pouring some of the oil into the palm of his hand. 'That's your problem. You want to give the orders but in this business you have to learn to take them.'

Rubbing his hands together, he lubricated them with the oil and began massaging her breasts until pleasure made her dizzy with longing and a burning sensation pulsed in the very core of her. Angie closed her eyes and sighed, wondering where he would touch her next and when he would use his whip. The anticipation was exquisite.

She heard the soft pop of a cork and felt a cool dribble of oil seep its way between her breasts, pool slightly in her navel and then run freely on to the top of her thong. Opening her eyes she saw that the oil had stained the fabric a vivid scarlet and Angie knew it matched the colour of her vulva. She was ready for him.

Subservient to the pleasure of his touch, she allowed him to turn her and bend her over the desk, ready for whatever he had in mind.

The softness of the leather tickled the sensitive skin of her thighs. He ran the tasselled whip over her skin, nudging her legs apart. One hand massaged her back, moved sensuously over her shoulder, down her arm, before slipping to cup her breast. The pleasure was intense and she tightened and contracted her inner muscles, wanting him to enter her.

'A beautiful woman who loves sex is rare,' he said. 'I've desired you from the moment I saw you.'

A thwacking sound split the air and she cried out as the leather hit her backside. Pressing one of his hands on to her back to stop her moving, he continued to stroke her bottom with the soft leather tassels, until the sensation eased to one of pleasure. She could feel the fabric of his trousers against the back of her thighs, but she could not tell if he was hard.

'Stay where you are,' he ordered, taking his hand from her back, and again she felt his voice held a hypnotic quality. One of his hands slid down her back and under her thong and he proceeded to search along her slippery cleft, massaging the moistness, opening her to his touch with two very capable fingers. 'You like that, don't you?'

Angie opened her legs further, to give him access to where she needed him most, and when he brought the whip down again, it delivered a stinging sensation, which may have been slightly unpleasant if it hadn't been accompanied by the intense pleasure of his fingers. His thumb, which had entered her to the hilt, rhythmically moved inside her like a small penis, while his index and middle finger had found her hooded clitoris and the small gold stud adorning it. Moist with her juices, he

25

slid his fingers over her clit and Angie pushed towards his hand, wanting more.

'Yes, yes,' she moaned, arching her back.

'Close your eyes,' he ordered, and she obeyed because his touch was exquisite and she did not want him to stop. He seemed to have the rare ability to balance pleasure and pain, with pleasure just tipping the scales. The effect was intensely erotic.

'My beautiful Angie, you were made for this,' he said. He brought down the whip on her sensitive buttocks, just hard enough to make her arch and moan in pleasure as he increased the intensity of his fingers. His fingers found her clit. They slipped and rubbed in an upward, rhythmic motion and she clenched her pussy tightly on the thick base of his thumb.

The waves of pleasure started in the small of her back and she knew that very soon she would rocket into an uncontrollably violent orgasm. The eroticism of waiting for the whip to fall kept her on the edge, the complex signals of pain converted to intense pleasure by the exquisite manipulations of his fingers.

She could not hold back. She wanted to come but, to her disappointment, he withdrew his thumb and fingers. Opening her eyes, she tried to turn to see what he was doing.

'Keep your eyes closed,' he ordered. 'The pleasure of the unknown will add to the experience. This is a test of your obedience. Open your eyes again and I'll stop.'

The last thing she wanted him to do was stop now. Every part of her ached for release. Her nipples were tight and swollen; her clit sought deliverance. If he left her on the edge of orgasm, she would ache with frustration. She surrendered to his order, her eyes tightly closed. In the few seconds it had taken to come to the decision to obey him, he had changed his technique.

He lifted her further on to the desk and parted her legs, so that she was fully exposed to him, then pulled her thong aside. She felt his hot breath against her downy pubic hair and suddenly he licked her, in one long slow movement that started from her anus then moved in between the delicate swollen lips, until his tongue replaced his fingers. Firm and pointy, it nestled against her swollen bud, oscillating with an intensity all of its own, rubbing against the metal stud.

Writhing in pleasure, she arched her back until it ached, allowing him access to her. Something large was inserted into her pussy. At first she thought it must be him, but realised that was impossible, given that his tongue continued to lick the sensitive tip of her bud. Then she realised the handle of the whip had another purpose. The texture was different from a penis, slightly rougher, not the silky softness of skin, but it was a snug fit, moving in and out, and the feeling was intensely pleasurable, like being fucked and sucked at the same time.

He matched her rhythm perfectly and the slick moistness of her entry allowed him to push the whip handle deeper in and out and in and out again. He built the rhythm faster and faster, sucking her clit between his lips, like the top of a lollipop.

Somewhere in the back of her mind she knew she had bent to his will. She had wanted him to have sex with her but he had not even removed his clothes. Yet she could not stop. She was so aroused, he could do anything he wanted with her.

The muscles in her back strained, her legs and buttocks tightened and she cried out in pleasure as each orgasmic wave hit her, building in sensation and power. The colour red flooded her mind as her sex clenched down on the whip handle and she wanted to pull away, but he held her down. His hand hard on the flat of her back, he continued to suck her and thrust the whip handle. The tension inside her swelled to a frightening height of pleasure until she exploded again, the intensity

27

of her orgasm leaving her weak and pliant, lying across the desk gasping for air.

He stood and walked round to face her. She could feel his hot breath on her face and smell her scent on his lips. 'You're mine, Angie. I can do whatever I want with you, and I intend to tame your wild spirit,' he said, his voice harsh with command.

She struggled to rise but he pressed his hand on her back to keep her still. It was infuriating to be held down by him. Why hadn't he taken her? She realised the reason for her feelings of ambivalence towards him, and she had learnt to trust her instinct. His mask of normality hid something menacing, something strange that she did not quite understand. James was different from other men.

'I have another student interested in working at Hotel Desire. Isabella di Bellini.'

She glared at him, her mouth hardened at the thought of Isabella di Bellini. She struggled to move but, with his hand on her back, she had no strength. Physically, he had established control, and mentally he was manipulating her, by setting up a competition for the work experience placement with a woman she disliked.

Isabella was as darkly exotic as she, Angie, was blonde. When Isabella had swept imperiously into the college she had complained at the top of her voice that she could not possibly fit her designer wardrobe into the small closet in her room at the college.

Her family had a string of small hotels along the east coast of Australia. Isabella was determined to get management experience in a top-class hotel in order to upgrade her family business at a later time. Nouveau riche, she wasted no time in finding out who came from money and who did not. Those who did not, like Angie, she did not bother with.

Slowly, James's hand moved from her back. He walked to the door and turned, his arms folded, his eyes lingering over her prostrate form, casually appraising her.

'Isabella has a more malleable nature and would be suitable for Hotel Desire, but she lacks imagination. I haven't made up my mind as to which of you I will choose. I shall be watching you over the next few days and then I will decide. You or Isabella. Don't disappoint me,' he said, before walking from the room, leaving her to heave herself from his desk, her muscles weak, her strength sapped.

'You don't really think he's going to choose you?'

Angie looked up from her lecture notes, which she had been studying outside the lecture theatre, to see Isabella di Bellini dressed in the shortest, fringed mini-skirt Angie had ever seen. Although most of the students attended the college lectures casually dressed, Isabella eschewed jeans, preferring the latest designer garments, the more figure-hugging the better. She had added large gold earrings that dangled when she laughed or tossed her thick dark curls from her face – something she did frequently in the presence of the opposite sex.

'I beg your pardon?' Angie asked, though she knew Isabella was talking about the work placements, which were going to be announced at the lecture today.

'James won't choose you for Hotel Desire,' said Isabella, her eyes narrowed to dark slits.

'And just how do you know that? The placements haven't been announced yet.'

Isabella smirked. 'James told me you wanted to go there. But now he knows I'm interested too.'

A lurch of disappointment hit Angie, though she made sure her expression did not change. She had watched all week, gritting her teeth as Isabella flirted with James, making her availability obvious. While she, Angie, found James extremely attractive, the lesson in dominance in his office had left her feeling cautious. She

29

wanted this placement badly, but she was not going to crawl to James to get it.

'James wants someone special for this placement. Someone sophisticated. That's why he's chosen me for Hotel Desire.'

'You already know?' Angie asked, surprised.

Isabella smiled slyly, refusing to answer.

'Hi, Angie.'

Angie bit her tongue to refrain from asking further questions Isabella obviously wasn't going to answer. She turned to smile at Jacob Hamilton, one of the students making his way towards her. He was well built and handsome with curly brown hair and twinkling blue eyes. Angie had noticed him on her first day, finding his clean-cut boy-next-door appeal refreshing.

'Hi, Jacob,' she replied, standing to join him and walk with him into the lecture theatre. 'I'm going to sit down the front today.'

'Sure,' he replied, good-naturedly.

She led the way, anxious to keep the frown from her face. Isabella had got to her and now Angie felt more determined than ever to get a placement at Hotel Desire. And she knew exactly what she wanted to do to get it. She had a little surprise in store for James.

She sat adjusting her skirt, her legs crossed in front of her, waiting for James to start the lecture.

Today's lecture was on the requirements of work experience in the hotel industry, and the location of each work placement was going to be announced. There were twenty students and Angie noticed they were all on time, because a good placement could mean a top job at the end of the course.

The buzz from the students dropped to complete silence when James Steele entered the room. Dressed in a black suit, James stood surveying his audience, looking sexy and utterly masculine. Angie, primed for her performance, fought a primeval fantasy to strip him down and take him in front of the audience. His dominance had annoyed her, though at the time she had not seemed to be able to do anything about it. Today was different, however, and she had a more subtle way of attracting his attention.

When James began outlining their duties, Angie caught his eye, smiled, and opened her long, shapely legs in invitation. She wore no underwear, and she noticed he faltered, his eyes transfixed by the ripeness of her exotically shaven sex, displayed so casually before him.

She could tell from the dark flush that tinged his complexion that the effect on him had drained the words from his speech. She watched as he strode to the other side of the lecture theatre, coughed and fought to regain his equilibrium. Angie waited patiently, knowing that like a bee to enticing pollen, he would return.

Lips parted, eyelids heavy with the pleasure which seeped like thick honey through her veins, Angie leant back farther. Her long, lean legs opened pleasurably, the cool air caressing her thighs. Excitement moistened her inner lips and she longed to stroke and open herself further for his gaze.

The bench-style seats provided her with privacy from all except the lecturer, because the front bench tabletop opened only at the front. Her fellow students sat beside and behind her, oblivious to the little show she was conducting. If James wanted a sybarite, he had come to the right person.

Slowly, she rolled the hem of her skirt until it met the tops of her firm tanned thighs. From across the room James's eyes met hers and he walked towards her, lured by her silent siren call. Though James kept talking, his voice dropped an octave when she opened her legs still further. Very slowly, she rocked her hips, enjoying the stimulation provided by her piercing. The dark flush that had tinged James's cheeks spread down his throat, and he momentarily put aside his notes to pour himself a glass of water.

Heat flooded her pussy, which was now moist and swollen. A heady sense of power intensified her pleasure when she realised he was no more immune to her charms than she was to his.

Smiling at him, she leant her head against the lecture bench behind her and her hand crept down to gently rub the gold stud. The sensation, like that of a moist tongue, radiated upward, so that her nipples swelled in response.

She watched with pleasure trying to see if a bulge was forming in James's trousers, but he placed his lecture notes in front of him and continued to talk, though his eyes were continually drawn to Angie and her silent manipulations. Her breath came in short pants and she teased and played with herself in front of him, knowing that she was safe from his hypnotising touch.

Once the placements were done, she would not see James until he visited each student. Hotel Desire was a longer visit because it was situated on an island in tropical North Queensland. If James wanted her, he had more chance at the isolated Hotel Desire. She knew she was playing with fire, teasing this dangerous man, but danger fuelled the heat of her desire.

She longed to caress her nipples. The tips rubbed against the silk of her shirt. James walked closer. He appeared to be mesmerised as she lubricated her fingers with her juices, sliding them up and down, over and around her clitoris. The thought that twenty students were concentrating on his every word, while he in turn stood mesmerised before her, filled her with a heady euphoria.

The deep tone of his voice broke off with a sigh, and she could sense a potent silence filling the air. Pleasure filled her until she was almost ready to burst. With her middle finger and thumb, she opened herself like a split peach, then gently rubbed the stud with her index finger.

She watched in satisfaction as James swallowed hungrily, his Adam's apple moving up and down in response to her teasing. He wanted her as much as she wanted him. For a moment James looked away to address a student's question but his gaze soon returned to her. Masturbating in front of an audience had always appealed to Angie and the danger of discovery fuelled bubbles of excitement to flood throughout her, so that her skin tingled with pleasure. She loved the way she was surrounded by young nubile students while she was open, wet and needing to be filled.

James coughed, his face tinged with perspiration. He began naming the students and their work assignments, but he was clearly having difficulty reading off his list. Angie, in a state of sensual euphoria, listened for her name to be called. If he wanted her alone, let him come and try to seduce her at Hotel Desire. She was a huntress, a seductress, not like Isabella di Bellini. She wanted him on equal terms, away from his power base in the city. From the way he looked at her, he wanted her too.

'Hotel Desire,' rasped James, coming to stand directly in front of her, his face full of erotic hunger.

Angie stroked faster, her eyes glazed, lips parted, hips arched.

'Angie Masters,' he said.

Eyes fixed on his face, she climaxed, unable to delay the pleasure further. Biting hard on her bottom lip, she forced herself to remain silent as delicious warmth flooded her body. Her hips shuddered and she fought to suppress a primeval groan. James stood in front of her, only inches away as she came.

His eyes narrowed, his face darkened and his teeth gleamed white. The ecstasy of orgasm exploded again and for a moment they seemed alone together. The lecture room faded and the voices of the students became distant. There was only him and her. His expression was hungry, his face wolf-like and, as her orgasm faded, she wondered whether once on the wild island paradise she would be the hunter or the hunted.

Angie checked in her bags at Sydney Airport and examined the screen displaying incoming and outgoing flights to check the time of her flight to Brisbane. She hoped her plane would leave on time because the schedule for the connecting flight to the tropical Island of Desire was tight.

She wondered whether James Steele had intended to place her at Hotel Desire, or whether her performance had assisted in his decision making. She would have to wait until he came to Hotel Desire to find out.

The side of her nature that encouraged danger had hoped that she would be called to James's office for a 'please explain' session followed by fast and frenzied sex. Instead, James had stormed from the lecture theatre, his expression dissatisfied and angry, with a tearful Isabella di Bellini in tow.

Angie walked to the security gate and placed her bag on the X-ray conveyor belt, feeling frustrated and needing sex, wanting James more than she cared to admit.

The loud sound of an alarm jolted Angie out of her daydream as she walked through the security gate. Frowning, she looked around, trying to work out what had set off the alarm. Dressed only in a strappy, diaphanous blue summer dress and leather sandals, she could not work out why the alarm had sounded.

'Step this way, miss,' said the security guard. Angie glanced over and found herself looking up into the face of a giant of a man with cerulean eyes. Her heart started to thump in her chest, though not from fear.

The blood coursing through her veins made her tingle pleasantly and she realised that, although she had a plane to catch, there was no point in telling him her genital piercing had set off the alarm. Let him find out for himself.

She stepped towards him, taking in his attractive, even features, his chunky ready-for-action build and large hands. Hands that could perform the most exquisite search of her body.

She liked the way he stood a head taller than she did, and in her present state of excitement this tall well-built man was having a dramatic effect on her senses. He had thick, blond, closely cropped hair, a straight nose and broad cheekbones. Her gaze dropped to his mouth, and she admired the curves of his full lips. There was no doubt he was born with a mouth made for sucking, and she hoped he knew how to use it.

She waited while he ran his metal detector over her breasts and abdomen. The machine buzzed loudly the lower it went and a slow throb pulsed repeatedly where she needed him most.

'Are you wearing anything metal under your dress?' he asked.

'I'm not wearing anything,' she replied. A small smile creased her lips as she met his eyes in challenge. 'Nothing at all.'

He looked at her sharply and she smiled in response. 'Look for yourself,' she said, lifting her arms so the curves of her breasts pressed against the bodice of her summer dress.

Frowning, he ran the metal detector over her again and the machine screamed the lower it went. A vein pulsed in his temple and Angie noticed to her satisfaction that he was starting to feel the strain.

'You realise it is a federal offence to carry a weapon on board an aircraft?'

'Now where on earth do you think I'd conceal a weapon?' she said. She reached behind her to gather her long, blonde locks and coiled her hair into a bun, then pirouetted tantalisingly in front of him so that her curves strained against the thin fabric of her summer dress.

The hunger of desire crossed his handsome features. 'You're hiding something,' he said, the timbre of his voice deep with authority. 'This machine only responds to metal.'

'So search me,' she challenged. 'See if you can find what's making your machine hum.'

He stood inches away and the tension vibrated between them. She noticed the small creases on either side of his mouth deepen. He was sexy and she wanted to feel his hands search her; first over her clothes, lightly lingering on her breasts then, finding nothing, he'd strip her down . . .

'There's nothing in her hand luggage.'

Angie turned to face an assistant who returned her handbag from the X-ray machine.

'Handbag's clean,' repeated the assistant to the security guard.

Silence punctuated the air between them and Angie waited for the guard to come to a decision. He was in his early twenties yet he carried an air of authority that she found intensely exciting. Authoritarian males turned her on because she liked to break their rules.

'Come with me,' he ordered.

Angie looked at her watch, noticing she had 40 minutes until her flight. 'Where are you taking me?'

'I'm detaining you.' The guard ushered her into a small room which held a table and chairs. 'If you want to make your flight, you'd better explain what's setting off the metal detector.'

Angie shrugged. 'How should I know? I already told you I'm not wearing anything except my dress.'

'You do realise, if you don't cooperate, you can be detained and searched by a female officer.'

'What's the matter?' she said, her disappointment acute. 'Afraid to search me yourself?'

'You'd like that, wouldn't you?' He walked towards her, looking into her eyes so that Angie could see in close detail the tension in his face. His uniform strained at the shoulders where his muscles bulged, restrained yet dangerous. 'You want me to touch you?' he asked hoarsely.

'I think you'd do the job more thoroughly than a woman, don't you think?' she said, tempting him. 'I think you'd be better at exploring whether I have anything hidden under my dress.' She started stroking her nipples seductively with her index finger and thumb so that they rose stiffly to greet her touch. 'You might even find what you're looking for.'

The sharp intake of his breath cut through the silence like a knife as his gaze dropped from her face to her breasts following her manipulations.

Looking down, she realised his evident arousal matched hers. She cupped her breasts so that they strained against the thin fabric of her dress. 'I'd like you to do this to me.'

He groaned and his breath came hot and hard against her face. 'It's illegal for me to search you without a female present,' he said, obviously struggling between his professional duty and raw, male lust. Angie judged, from the perspiration beading at his temple, that lust would win.

'Some rules are made to be broken,' she whispered. She took his hand and sensuously rubbed her thumb over the sensitive skin of his palm before placing it on her breast. 'See, nothing metal here. Nothing except me,' she said, pressing his palm over her nipple, which peaked eagerly at his touch.

'This is against regulations,' he said huskily, in his clipped guard way of talking.

She took his free hand, pressing it against her other breast, and he began to massage them, his eyes closed as if savouring a delicious moment in time.

'And is this against regulations too?' she asked, slowly removing one shoulder strap and then the other, so that the bodice of her dress dipped revealingly.

At the sound of her voice, he opened his eyes and she noticed a dark flush deepen the tan of his face when she revealed the curves of her breasts. His hot breath fanned her face, the fight between following rules or passion won by lust.

'I like breaking rules,' said Angie. She turned and pressed her stomach and breasts against the cool wall and looked at him over her shoulder. 'Aren't you going to frisk me?'

He groaned and moved closer, so that his breath caressed the soft skin at the nape of her neck. She felt him run his fingers through her hair, untying the knot, letting her hair flow free.

He had the wonderful firm touch of a professional masseur as he ran his hands through her hair, expertly over her shoulders, down her back, cupping her waist then moving lower, stopping at her buttocks where he lingered, rubbing her erotically through the thin fabric of her dress.

'You're not wearing panties,' he sighed as he bent to nuzzle her neck, so that she could smell his clean yet intensely male scent.

'Nothing at all,' agreed Angie. Her breasts felt full and heavy and her nipples ached to be stroked again. 'Do you still think I'm hiding something?'

'You'd be surprised what we find hidden on people's bodies. I'll have to keep searching,' he said, as he moved lower, running his hands over the backs of her thighs until they struck the delicate skin behind her knees. Angie shivered in pleasure as he stroked his knuckles back and forth. Instinctively she opened her legs; his touch was so enjoyable.

'Turn around,' he ordered, and when she did she

found him kneeling at her feet, ready to explore her further.

'Found what you're looking for?' she asked.

'Not yet,' he answered, and he pressed his palms against her shins and slid them upward until the tips of his fingers disappeared under the silky fabric of her dress.

'Don't stop there,' she urged, needing him to explore her further.

But he did not need any encouragement. His firm hands were already stroking the smooth skin of her inner thighs, so that any thoughts she might have had of James dissolved.

His mouth soon followed his fingers, alternately sucking then nipping the delicate skin of her inner thigh in a maddeningly erotic way, so that Angie bit her lip to stop herself crying out. What she wanted was the hardness of him inside her, but he seemed to be taking his time, enjoying his thorough exploration of her most sensitive erogenous zones.

When he raised her dress above her thighs, he stopped and whistled softly at the sight of her shaven sex. 'You are one hot babe.'

A soft moan escaped Angie's lips when he pressed his mouth over her sex, lapping over her silky outer lips. 'Open your legs,' he ordered. Angie did not need to be told again as she arched to meet his exploring tongue, which he slid into her, until she gasped in pleasure.

'Wow,' he said softly. Using his thumbs, he gently parted her sex to reveal the gold stud shining like a jewel.

His face had the expression of a boy opening a brand new toy. 'No wonder you set the machine off.'

'Don't stop now,' she said urgently, on the edge of coming, needing his mouth, his lips and his cock.

'I knew you were hot from the moment I saw you,' he said, running his tongue lightly over the stud. Then he explored her thoroughly, his tongue probing, licking and sucking, and she soared to a height and stayed there, on a delicious precipice of passion.

A primeval moan escaped her lips as she pulsed to meet his lapping tongue. When he pressed his lips over her clitoris and sucked the stud between his teeth she came with ferocity, crying out in passion. Head thrown back in ecstasy, the tightness in the pit of her sex exploded behind her eyes. She saw stars.

There was a ripping sound and she opened her eyes to see him tearing a condom from its packet, his open wallet discarded on the floor. He obviously came to work prepared. She watched as he quickly divested himself of his trousers and slid the condom over his hardened cock.

Spinning her around so that her breasts pressed against the hardness of the wall, he angled himself and slid into her. Angie arched herself slightly to assist him and was rewarded by the sensuous pressure of the head of his penis probing her moist entrance.

One arm circled her waist to hold her in position before he drove into her. She gasped in pleasure at his size, and the way he filled her completely. Fuelled by passion, her pussy stretched to accommodate every inch. At first he thrust slowly, steadily, as if learning the needs of her body. His cheek rested against hers, and she felt cocooned by his body as he pressed against her.

Time stood still and all she was aware of was him and her and his delicious plunging motion sending her back to the height of pleasure. She wanted to turn to face him, to watch him in his pleasure, but he manfully kept her pressed against the wall, thrusting rapidly into her until his motion became ragged and jerking.

'You love this, don't you?' he panted, never letting up his rhythm for a moment.

'Drive it into me,' she urged, her back arched for the deepest penetration he could deliver.

A low growling sounded in her ear as he bit her neck and tightened his grip on her waist, and the sheer animal excitement of the moment pushed her over the edge again. He joined her, matching her cries. She felt his cock pumping, releasing his seed, until at last he shuddered and his grip on her loosened.

Taking a few breaths to steady herself, she turned to face him. She adjusted the straps of her dress and looked at her watch. Her plane was flying in five minutes. 'Are you satisfied with your search?' she asked huskily.

'Very,' he nodded.

'And did you find what you were looking for?'

He laughed a deep throaty laugh and bent forward to kiss her gently on the lips. 'Uh-huh.' He nodded.

'Good. Then perhaps you can show me to my plane. It's leaving in a few minutes.'

'Don't worry. I'll make sure they hold it for you.' He adjusted his clothing and opened the door of the detention room for her before escorting her to the departure gate.

Sated and smiling, Angie waved goodbye. The security guard gave a soldier-like salute and she boarded the plane, relaxed, but wondering just what James had arranged for her when she arrived at the Island of Desire.

Chapter Three

'*H*otel Desire,' said Angie. 'I'm here at last.' She looked around. The place certainly lived up to her expectations. Set among lush palm trees, the hotel was *sangue di bue*, the colour of blood. Well-tended lawns surrounded the hotel, leading gently down to a crystal-blue lagoon and an expansive beach – the type of beach where a person could strip off naked, and walk for miles with no more company than the warm Queensland sun on her back. Sated by the surprise exploration at Sydney Airport, hunting could wait until tomorrow, but she still tingled at the thought of that long deserted beach and the wildlife she hoped to encounter.

To Angie, everything seemed more colourful here compared to the drabness of the city. She loved the vividness of the place and she was filled with a heady sense of excitement that a fresh hunting ground with unlimited opportunities was hers to discover. With regular planeloads of possible conquests being delivered during the week, she'd never be bored. 'Perfect.' Her nipples tightened in anticipation of her next hunt. 'This is exactly what I need,' she said, then she walked into the foyer.

'Angie Masters?' inquired a deep voice which Angie initially thought belonged to a man until she looked over to see a tall woman, nearly six foot, with raven-dark hair and liquid eyes enhanced by thick kohl pencil.

'Yes, that's me.'

The woman looked impatiently at her watch. 'Where's the other one?'

'Pardon?' asked Angie, confused.

'James told me he was sending me two students. I have staff down at the moment, and I need two staff on kitchen duty tonight.'

'Oh, you must mean Jacob. He wasn't on the plane from Brisbane. I'm not sure when he's –'

'Never mind,' the woman interjected. Angie noticed her ruby-coloured lips had tightened into thin lines of disapproval, and she turned sharply. 'Come with me, I'll show you around. I'm the hotel manager. My name is Tahillia Ash. You can address me as Ms Ash. I'll call you Angie. You and your work experience partner will be on kitchen duty initially, so you'll need to find your way from your room to the kitchen and that's all. Stay out of all guest areas – that includes the pool, saunas and spa.'

Angie followed her new boss but her eyes and ears were elsewhere. Hating rules, she switched off and instead took in her salubrious surroundings, then she held her breath in excitement. She had seen a rock star who was often in the tabloids checking in at reception. She was surprised she hadn't noticed him on the plane but she guessed he was in first class. 'That's Nick Holt from Animal Lair,' she said excitedly. The closest she'd ever got to him was when he'd pulled her from the audience to dance with him at his rock concert two years ago. He'd even slipped her his phone number but when Angie had called, his wife had answered and made it clear he was out of bounds.

Angie's mouth went dry, and that special tingle she'd

come to recognise switched on. This time Nick was checking in alone, and Angie had unfinished business. Man-hunting business.

'Don't even think about it.' Tahillia Ash caught her arm, pulling Angie in her direction. 'Guests are off limits to staff. You don't approach them. Don't speak unless spoken to and stay out of the guest bedrooms.' Her thin, high-arched eyebrows were drawn to a tight frown. But Angie didn't want to look at that stern, unforgiving expression. She wanted to see Nick again. He had a reputation as a terrific lover.

A man's laugh rang out through reception and Angie, despite her new boss's proximity, turned for one last look. Nick was tall and hunky with a shaved head. She knew from the time she'd danced with him he was strong and nuggety but that wasn't the thing that clicked Angie's switch. It was his red tongue with its gold tongue stud. He was waggling it at the girl at reception, who squealed in appreciation. Nick was known for his displays of exhibitionism.

She wanted to feel that tongue with its shiny attachment licking her most intimate places. She'd never seen a man with a tongue that long, and she clenched her secret muscles in anticipation. It was almost as long as a penis, and think of all the tricks it could do. She was heating up, and it wasn't just the tropical climate. The guard at the airport was just a memory. She needed a man. A man with a sensuous tongue like a snake who was willing to use it.

The hand on her arm clenched tighter, and reluctantly she turned to face her new boss. 'James told me you were disobedient,' she hissed. 'Break my rules and I'll have you on the first plane out of here. Don't think you can put anything over me. I've seen it all before. I'll be watching you closely. Nick Holt is not for you.'

'Don't worry,' said Angie, smiling, and with her

blonde hair like a halo, she looked momentarily like her angel namesake. 'You can trust me, Ms Ash.'

The woman looked her up and down suspiciously, then walked down a narrow corridor to the staff quarters.

To break every rule in the book, Angie thought mischievously, as she followed the manager to staff quarters at the back of the hotel.

'Your uniform is in your wardrobe. You'll be needed on kitchen duty at 5 p.m.'

Angie looked at her watch. She had two hours. She had sighted the man she wanted, and now it was time to begin hunting again. Nick Holt, lead singer of Animal Lair. She'd seen him howl on stage, and she wanted to feel that voice vibrate against her naked skin.

'Remember, 5 p.m. in the main kitchen. Don't be late,' barked the manager.

'I'll see you soon, Ms Ash,' said Angie pleasantly. 'Thanks for showing me around.'

The only problem was, she was about to see Tahillia Ash sooner than she thought, and in a very disturbing way.

Angie slipped the keycard she had taken from the housekeeping trolley into her pocket and carefully opened Nick Holt's bedroom door. She felt for her handcuffs, worried that, in her excitement of finding Nick's room, she'd left them behind. The suite had a large iron bed, en suite bathroom and a spacious lounge area overlooking the lagoon.

He was in the shower. She could hear him singing, his voice guttural and fierce as he hammered out a tune. The sound of his voice echoed through her body, sending vibrations of excitement throughout her. She had watched him leap around on stage for two hours solid and there was no doubt in her mind that the man had stamina. Desire built in her core as she placed her handcuffs in the middle of his bed. They would be a pleasant surprise for him, and she hoped he would agree to let her use them on him.

She ached to see him fighting his restraints, his muscular body tense with excitement. The urge to see him naked grew until she could no longer resist opening the bathroom door just a little.

Through the steam she could see him, his arms raised as he leant against the shower wall, letting the water gush over his head and back. He raised his head upward as he sang, his voice, deep and resonant, punching out a song that sent a thrill of pleasure throughout her. She wanted him to use that wonderful voice to talk dirty to her. The memory of his red tongue with its shiny metal stud was still vivid in her mind.

The thought of dominating this action-packed rock star was extremely arousing. Or perhaps they could play 'Tease', one of her favourite games, and whoever came first would have to wear the handcuffs. Though the way she was on the edge already, she'd lose and she didn't like the idea of losing. When it came to sex and men, she liked to stay on top.

Her gaze roved over Nick's naked form, taking in his highly tuned physique. His broad shoulders narrowed to a trim waist and firm, tanned bottom. He gyrated as he sang and Angie's lips parted in pleasure. His cock wasn't overly big but it was thick and aroused. She trembled with desire, thinking of what it would feel like having him inside her.

Her fingers rapidly pulled the straps of her dress from her shoulders. She hadn't seen Nick for two years but she'd never forgotten how it had felt holding him close. He was built for repeated fast, hot, against-the-wall, erotic sex. She unzipped her dress and it slipped over her erect nipples and fell to the floor. Then she froze.

Someone was knocking quietly on the door. 'Damn,' she said, standing naked in Nick's room, caught between surprising Nick and a possible visitor at the same time. This was a bad time for interruptions. Frantically, she looked around the bedroom wondering where to hide.

The person knocked again, more loudly this time. Snatching her dress, she climbed into it, only to be dismayed at the ripping sound it made as she managed to put her foot through the flimsy fabric. Quickly she raced to the bed and pushed aside the duvet, only to realise that the bed had a double mattress and there was no room to hide.

'Nick,' called a husky female voice.

Oh, no, Angie thought. He's definitely expecting someone. She heard the shower turn off, and though Nick was still singing, it wouldn't be long until he heard the knocking.

Anxiously, Angie looked around the room for some-where else to hide. Spying the built-in wardrobe, she raced across the room and pulled open the doors. Relief flooded every nerve ending when she saw there was enough room to crouch beneath the shelving. Urgently, she climbed in, closing the door behind her. Her heart was thumping so loudly that her chest hurt. The last thing she wanted to do was lose her scholarship; her ambition to manage her own hotel matched that of her sex drive. Unfortunately, the latter frequently meant trouble.

She heard the click of the bedroom door and the muffled footsteps of someone walking past the wardrobe.

'Well, this is a surprise,' Angie heard Nick say. 'It's been a while.'

'Too long,' a female voice purred. 'Welcome to Hotel Desire.'

He laughed. 'I like the new uniform. Though I can't say I've seen anyone wear it quite like you do.'

'I'm glad it pleases you.'

'It does,' said Nick, then his voice dropped an octave. 'It definitely does.'

'Mmm, I like that,' said the woman softly. 'I can't believe the size of your tongue. Do that again.'

Angie gritted her teeth in frustration as she crouched in the wardrobe listening to the soft sounds of pleasure emitted from the interloper. Did she want to try and open the wardrobe door a little, spy and see what she was missing out on? Of course she did.

Angie gently pushed open the door, just an inch, to be confronted by an elegant foot dressed in the highest black stiletto she had ever seen. She followed the line of one long slim leg and saw that the other leg was wrapped over Nick's shoulder as he knelt, growling with pleasure. Two feminine hands massaged Nick's shaved head, holding it between her legs while her foot flexed with every stroke of his tongue.

The little frilly maid's apron was pushed up to the woman's waist and Angie could see her pelvis pulsating in time to Nick's ministrations. His hands slipped under her skirt to hold her bottom. The woman let out a deep groan and Angie's throat went dry with desire. She wished she were there with her leg draped over Nick's shoulder.

'Oh, Nick, that feels so good. Run that stud over me again,' begged the woman. 'Yes, yes, just there.'

Angie watched transfixed as Nick held the woman firmly by her bottom, though she wiggled and trembled as he licked her vigorously.

Who was this woman? The shelving above her blocked her view. She wanted to push open the wardrobe door but with them making love so close to her, the risk of discovery was too high. Whoever the woman was, she had let herself in, so she had to be one of the staff. So much for Ms Ash's rules, thought Angie ruefully.

The woman moaned, her breath coming faster and

faster. Beads of perspiration grew on Angie's forehead as she watched transfixed as Nick alternatively sucked then licked, his strong hands binding the woman to his lips. The woman reached down, spreading herself apart as she arched herself into him.

Unconsciously Angie contracted her cunt muscles, desire building in her at the erotic sight of seeing Nick eagerly pleasing another woman. Angie held the wardrobe door open until her hand trembled but she couldn't afford to make the slightest noise. She stroked her nipple with her one free hand until it formed a tight little bud.

'Oh please, please,' moaned the woman as Nick shredded the uniform from her waist. Angie's throat went dry when Nick ripped what remained of the uniform and cupped the woman's luscious breast in his hands. His tongue never missed a beat, sensuously oscillating as the woman rocked to the rhythm of his tongue.

Angie bit her lip as her own hand left her breast and wove its way under her dress until she stroked herself in time to Nick and his partner's rhythm. She wanted to join them. What would they do if she suddenly emerged from the cupboard naked? Nick was taking his time but he was wonderfully erect and ready. Angie was certain he was man enough to satisfy two women. While she had never been with a woman herself, this arousing scene made her want to try.

'Oh, put your fingers inside me,' the woman groaned. 'Make me ready for you.'

'That's it, baby, sing to me,' said Nick, as he obliged.

The woman shuddered and cried out her release, her body writhing as Nick held the small of her back firmly so she couldn't escape, his snake-like tongue sliding in and out until the woman's fingers clawed into his shoulders, leaving red streaks.

Angie stroked herself, aroused to the point of orgasm. Seeing Nick in action was the sexiest thing she'd ever encountered. She wanted to trace her fingers over the scratch marks and let him satisfy her the way she'd seen him do the woman. The urge to join them became intense though she knew it would be madness to risk discovery.

Could she step out now, thought Angie, while the woman was sated and too weak to protest the presence of another? She wanted Nick, she wanted to feel his hard cock inside her, but she wanted to touch the woman too. She'd never felt another woman's breasts and the woman's large breasts with their dark nipples were so unlike her own. They seemed exotic and ready for exploration.

In one swift movement Nick picked up the woman and threw her over his shoulder. She was loose-limbed, relaxed from orgasm, but laughed softly as Nick placed her on the bed.

The movement surprised Angie and she quickly climbed to a kneeling position to see better but only succeeded in bumping her head on the shelving above. She bit her lip to muffle a cry and furiously rubbed the sore spot.

'What was that noise?' asked the woman.

'What noise?' asked Nick. 'I didn't hear anything.'

'You haven't got anyone hiding here spying on us, have you, Nick? You're not filming this, are you? I know how kinky you are.'

Angie stopped breathing, every muscle clenched in anticipation of discovery. Perspiration dribbled between her breasts. What would they do to her if they found her there spying on them? It wouldn't take them long to find her. There weren't many hiding places in the room. She should know, since she had found the only one.

Nick laughed, his deep voice rich with pleasure. 'No, it's just you and me, though I wish I'd thought of that idea. I've been waiting a long time for this. There aren't many women who like unusual sex the way you do.'

Unusual sex! Angie's ears pricked at the words that interested her most, cursing her position in the wardrobe. This she had to see, even if curiosity killed the cat. Gently she pushed open the wardrobe door a little further. She could see Nick standing by the bed, his cock fiery with excitement. The woman was lying with her legs open so that Angie could see her dark pubic hair and the crimson, satisfied slit between.

The woman pushed herself to a sitting position then bent level with Nick's cock and Angie nearly choked in shock. Tahillia Ash! No wonder she'd warned Angie off – she wanted Nick for herself.

Closing the wardrobe door in shock, Angie sat in the dark contemplating her short future in the hotel industry. There was no way she could risk discovery. Thank goodness she hadn't given in to her desire to join them. Perspiration dripped off her until her dress became clingy and uncomfortable. She could not see her watch, but she suspected she wouldn't be making kitchen duty on time.

But this she realised was the least of her worries when she heard a familiar clink. Someone had just discovered the handcuffs she had left on Nick's bed. When they realised they didn't belong to either of them, they'd come looking for the owner.

'Oh, Nick, use them on me!' cried Tahillia. 'You know how much I like it when you tie me down.'

'That's exactly what I had in mind. Though I have no intention of cuffing your hands.' He chuckled and Angie heard the handcuffs click into place.

This was not what she expected. Surely one of them would ask whom the handcuffs belonged to, but no, here they were happily having sex using her handcuffs, while she was stuck in a dark wardrobe listening to their pleasure.

'Oh, Nick, that's a wonderful idea,' Tahillia moaned in pleasure.

'You haven't lost your flexibility, Tahillia.' Angie could hear the desire in his deep voice and she nearly choked on her envy.

'Just let me get this condom on,' said Nick. 'There, I'm ready.'

'Slowly, Nick, slowly,' Tahillia sighed. 'That's exactly how I like it. Slide it in a little further. Oh, that feels so good.'

Angie gritted her teeth in frustration, listening to their pleasure. She couldn't bear it. Job or no job, she had to see what they were doing.

She pushed open the door and with the top of her head pressed against the shelving, she could see Nick entering Tahillia, who was lying on her back, her body quivering in pleasure. He'd handcuffed her ankles instead of her wrists to the bedhead, so that her bottom was raised and ready for him. Tahillia's hands gripped the bedhead as Nick slid into her. She could hear Tahillia panting as she built up to her next orgasm.

Angie knew just how good anal sex could feel if a woman was aroused by a skilled lover, and Nick was good. Very, very good. She wondered how long it would be until she hunted him down, and made him satisfy her the way he was doing to Tahillia. She would never get this erotic image from her mind unless she possessed Nick herself.

'You like it this way, don't you, Tahillia? This is the way you want it,' said Nick hoarsely.

Tahillia cried out in pleasure in response to his questioning. His rhythm grew faster and faster and she moaned and tossed her head. Her long, slender legs strained at the cuffs as Nick possessed her.

Angie watched, her tongue moistening her lips, now dry with desire. Every muscle in her body tensed, and though she was cramped, time stood still as she observed Nick and Tahillia with hungry anticipation.

Nick took hold of Tahillia's knees, spreading her further and growling with pleasure as he thrust deeply into her. She writhed under him, her eyes closed, her lips parted. Her sighs filled the room.

Angie ached for her own release, but she could barely move in case of discovery. Quietly she stroked herself, wanting Nick, wishing he were inside her.

A primeval groan filled the air as Nick shuddered. He then lay next to Tahillia, kissing her sensuously. One hand explored the long line of her legs from her ankles up to the thick black curls. His thumb trailed along her pink slit.

'No more,' she pleaded. 'At least not now. I have to go back to work.'

'I want you again, Tahillia.' He said her name like a caress. 'Meet me tonight?'

'Mmmm,' she sighed. 'Definitely tonight. But in the grotto after dark.'

'Not if I have my way,' Angie murmured through gritted teeth. 'You're not getting him all to yourself, you bitch.' She watched as Nick pushed himself to a sitting position, then ran his hands up Tahillia's long legs. She could see from his semi-arousal that soon he would be ready again.

'That was so clever of you to think of the handcuffs,' said Tahillia.

Angie saw Nick frown and look at Tahillia intensely. 'I thought they were your idea. They were on the bed after I had a shower.'

'Well, I didn't put them there,' said Tahillia.

'Oh, no,' groaned Angie, not even daring to close the wardrobe door in case the movement or noise caught their attention. Goodbye job, goodbye career, she thought. How long would it be before they pulled her from the wardrobe?

'Enough, Nick. Quit playing with me. I have work to do,' said Tahillia.

'I'm serious. I thought you put the handcuffs there.'

'Well, try and undo them or look around and find the key,' ordered Tahillia. 'I can't stay handcuffed like this much longer.'

Nick pulled at the cuffs, trying to prise them apart.

Despite her fear of discovery, Angie couldn't resist a smile as her fingers traced the key in her pocket. She'd had to seduce a policeman to get those handcuffs, and nothing short of bolt cutters would get them off.

'Damn you, Nick. Do something,' said Tahillia, her voice rising with concern.

Angie quietly pulled close the wardrobe door so that she could only see through a narrow slit. Tension built in her stomach as she tried to figure out an escape plan. If she wanted to keep her job, she had to get out of the room without being discovered.

'I'll look behind the bar,' said Nick. 'Maybe there's something there I can use to pick the lock.'

He walked to the bar and Angie lost sight of him. She knew the bar area faced on to the lagoon, and that for a few moments he'd have his back to her as he searched through the bar drawers for an implement.

Carefully, she slithered out from her hiding space, cursing to herself as her knee ripped through her already torn dress. Closing the wardrobe door, she crawled along the floor past the foot of Nick's bed.

She hoped Tahillia, in her unusual position, would not see her, but her heart was thumping so hard she was sure they could hear it. Nearing the door, she squatted concealed by a large decorative palm and caught her breath. Tahillia couldn't see her from this position but Nick could.

'Sorry, Tahillia, I don't think there is anything here that will do the job,' she heard Nick say. 'Do you want me to call someone?'

'Are you insane?' Tahillia's voice rose shrilly. 'Find something to get these damn things off me. Look in the bar drawers. I don't want my staff to see me like this.'

'OK, OK. I'll look again.'

Angie could hear him opening and closing drawers. She rose and crept along the short corridor to the bedroom door, hoping to slide out as quietly as possible.

'What was that noise?' screeched Tahillia.

Angie turned, her gaze locking with Nick's. She stared at him boldly, determined not to let him see she was rattled. His expression was stern and, as he walked towards her, Angie ceased breathing. She was on a one-way ticket to trouble, and from the frown on Nick's face he was going to enjoy giving it to her.

'Where are you going?' Tahillia screamed.

'To find some way to get you out of those cuffs,' said Nick.

Angie turned and made a grab for the door handle, pulling the door open. As an experienced hunter, she had learnt when to abort a mission. This was definitely the time to leave, except when Nick lunged, her escape option evaporated. Slamming the door shut, he pushed her against the wall, pinning her with his powerful chest. He was erect and she could feel him pressing against her.

'Nick,' called Tahillia. 'Come back. You can ring maintenance from the bedroom phone. Get them to pass in a pair of pliers. Nick, don't leave me here like this.'

Nick's expression changed to one of hungry desire as he looked into Angie's eyes.

'Let me go,' she hissed, her mouth inches from his. She struggled against him, trying to push him away, but he was too strong and she did not dare make a noise.

He wrapped one hand around her waist and the other behind her neck until she could feel the naked heat of his body pressed along the length of hers.

Desire for him seared through her, although she did not want to have sex now, with Tahillia only a few feet away, handcuffed to the bed. Nick bent to kiss her, forcing her lips apart with his tongue. She bit him, warning him to stop, her eyes narrowed in anger. But he continued to kiss her, the pain from her bite obviously doing nothing to quell his lust.

Constrained as she was, Tahillia could do nothing,

Angie realised mischievously, and her pent-up frustration from watching them ignited into a passion she couldn't contain. Nick was a sensational kisser, and she closed her eyes in pleasure, her tongue mating with his.

A remnant of common sense urged her to leave, and her hand snaked to the door handle, but when he pushed the straps of her dress aside and sucked on her nipples, her hand dropped away. She could feel the stud in his tongue rubbing over the sensitive tip of her nipple and she wanted to cry out in pleasure.

He reached down, scooping the hem of her dress to her waist, pushed her knees apart and plunged himself into her.

Angie gasped then instantly bit her lip, knowing silence was essential.

'Who is there?' demanded Tahillia. 'Nick, is that you?'

Nick smiled sensuously as he thrust into Angie and she responded, biting his throat in her effort to keep silent. Her hands traced the nail imprints left by Tahillia as the intensity of her excitement increased. Soon she left her own imprint, her nails digging into his back as she arched into him. With each thrust he almost lifted her off the ground and she wrapped her arms around his shoulders.

He lifted her by the waist and her thighs clenched his hips. Their passion was hot and urgent, and Angie fought to suppress a moan of pleasure. Nick held her so tightly their bodies interlinked. He cupped her mouth with his hand to keep her silent, but he was unable to keep quiet himself. His breath rasped in her ear as he came, followed by a deep moan of pleasure. Angie could feel the thump, thump, thump of his heart as he held her to him. She sagged against him, trying to regulate her breathing.

'Damn you! I can hear you!' screamed Tahillia. 'Whoever you are, uncuff me at once.'

Nick's eyes shone in pleasure. It was obvious that he

56

was enjoying this as much as she was. But would he let her go now he was sated? Or would he force her to stand before Tahillia?

Angie felt in her pocket for the key to the handcuffs. Tahillia bitch deserved to stay where she was. She frowned when she could not locate it. Pushing Nick from her, she spied the silver key glinting on the floor.

Nick, however, was faster than she was. He picked up the key and held it out of her reach.

'Give it back. Now,' she ordered, straining to keep her voice a whisper. She pulled on her tattered dress with difficulty and held out her hand.

'I want to see you again,' he whispered. He bent and traced the upper curve of her lip with his tongue. Angie shivered in pleasure, but she did not give in to his demand. It did not suit her to have Tahillia free just yet.

'The key,' she said, firmly. She had enjoyed the fast and furious sex. But if Nick wanted her again, he had to learn who was boss. She stared at him, her gaze unblinking. Obediently he placed the key in her hand.

'I'll find you when you least expect it,' she whispered.

'Who's there?' screamed Tahillia, but Angie just smiled naughtily.

'Soon,' she whispered, kissing him one last time. Her tongue brushed against his, exploring the stud. Once with Nick was not enough. She had not had time to explore all of him, but she was satisfied knowing he was hers in the future.

Nick nodded, then opened the bedroom door for her to leave. Quietly, she slipped from his room, realising that things had worked out better than she had planned.

Looking at her watch, she saw it was five o'clock, and she was going to be late for kitchen duty. But as she ran along the corridor to her room to change into her uniform, she realised with amusement that Tahillia Ash would not be checking up on her for a while.

Chapter Four

*A*ngie raced into the busy hotel kitchen, panting with
exertion. She had rapidly showered then changed
into her uniform consisting of a floral shirt and khaki
skirt. With her long blonde hair plaited neatly and her
fresh appearance she looked well suited for her new
role.

Jacob, her fellow work experience student, was busy
washing pots and pans at the sink.

'Hi,' he said, smiling with a boyish grin. 'Go introduce
yourself to the chef. He's freaking out because he's short
on staff and no-one can find the manager.'

'Fine,' said Angie, trying not to laugh. Instead she
managed a friendly smile. She had liked Jacob from the
moment she had met him at the training academy. He
was always pleasant and easy-going yet professional
about his work. Perfect for the hotel industry, thought
Angie, but not for me. With not a wild bone in his body,
Jacob did not raise her hunting instinct, but that was fine
by her.

Moments later, she stood beside Jacob armed with a
tea towel, wiping up as Jacob washed. 'Hope we don't
spend our whole work experience visit doing this. I've

already got a degree in catering,' she said quietly. 'I want to work in reception.' That way she could see who arrived and which room they were staying in. Keeping track of desirable quarry was easier in reception.

'I don't mind,' Jacob replied good-naturedly. 'You have to start from the bottom in this industry. Good food and service can make or break a hotel.'

'Well, we're not going to learn much staring at dirty pots and pans.'

'Patience, Angie. One day you'll be at the top, and you'll never have to wash a dish again.'

She stopped wiping and looked at him. 'How do you know that? It takes years to get a manager's job in this industry.' Though if Tahillia Ash ever discovered who the owner of the handcuffs was, she probably never would.

'I've worked in hotels since I was a kid. My parents still run a small hotel south of Sydney, plus another in the city. I've got five sisters, and we all ended up working in hospitality. I know potential when I see it,' he said, with quiet assurance.

She looked at him, not sure whether he was gently flirting or not. She liked him, although he was neither chillingly handsome like James Steele, nor an exciting exhibitionist like Nick Holt. Instead, he had a sort of innocence about him, which Angie had not encountered before. He was the type of man that girls liked to be friends with.

'Come on,' he said, 'these pots won't dry themselves. Chef says there's a full house tonight. He's a good bloke. He wants to put on welcome drinks tonight in his room, providing the manager is not around. Have you met her? Chef says she's tough on staff.'

Angie rolled her eyes. 'I've seen more of her than I'll ever want to.' She stacked the saucepans on their shelves, glad when she came to the end of the pile.

'Hi,' said a pair of voices, and Angie and Jacob turned to see a tanned young man and a busty woman.

'Hello,' Angie said.

'I'm Rick and this is my girlfriend Kate. Chef says you're both on work experience.'

'Yes,' said Jacob. 'We're here for a month.'

Angie noticed Rick slip his arm around Kate's shoulders. 'We're on night shift in the dining room this week. If you're both free tomorrow morning, we'll show you around. There are some great walking tracks and beaches past the lagoon, if you're feeling adventurous.' He raised his eyebrows and Kate giggled when he squeezed her shoulder.

'That will be great,' said Jacob. 'I love walking.'

Angie read the interest in Rick's eyes despite his obvious friendship with Kate. He was lean and athletic looking and she recognised a certain kinship.

'Sure,' replied Rick to Jacob, but his eyes were on Angie. 'We're in staff quarters, too, so we'll see you tomorrow.'

Angie nodded and her mouth twisted to a quirky grin. Instinct told her that Rick fell into her second category of man. A man ruled by his desire. Sexiness clung to him like a second skin, and she suspected that tomorrow would involve more than an innocent bush walk.

'They seem like a nice couple,' said Jacob.

Angie looked at him. Was he as naive as he seemed? Surely he wasn't a virgin? 'How old are you, Jacob?'

'Twenty. Why do you ask?'

'You seem young for the hospitality diploma course,' she ad-libbed, not wanting him to know what she was thinking. 'You have to have a degree and hospitality experience to get in. I just wondered how you fitted that all in by twenty.'

'I've just finished my degree and, as I told you, I've worked in my parents' hotel for years. Why? How old are you?' he asked.

'Twenty-four,' she replied.

'A spring chicken,' he joked.

Plenty of spring, thought Angie, but definitely not chicken. She thought of Rick and what she wanted to do to him. All she had to do was follow him to a secluded beach, and he was hers while his girlfriend watched. The chef interrupted her fantasy.

'Jacob and Angie, when you have finished washing up, bring me sixty dinner plates from the rack above your heads.'

She noticed how Jacob obediently did as he was told. He had the right temperament to work as a kitchen hand. No matter how reasonable the order, Angie hated being told what to do. The wildness in her character had rebelled against authority all her life, though she tried to curb it.

She helped Jacob, containing her impatience. Inside her, she was determined to reach the top and Jacob was right. Good food and service made a hotel. For now, she would try to follow orders and do her best because she knew she had to to achieve her long-term goal. Hunting men gave her the release she needed and after meeting Rick and Kate, tomorrow seemed promising.

Busy waiters started setting up the dining room, though, despite the frenetic atmosphere in the kitchen, Angie noticed that staff were friendly, stopping to introduce themselves as they went about their work.

There was a certain sexiness about the bronzed and vital permanent staff who worked at the hotel.

'OK, you two. I need all these potatoes peeled in half an hour,' said the chef, a short Englishman with a twinkle in his eye.

'Sure thing, boss,' said Jacob. He handed Angie a knife which he carefully held by the handle. 'Cut out the green bits.'

His hand grazed hers, and Angie was surprised that she enjoyed the warmth of his touch. He was handsome in a young sort of way but too easy a conquest. Angie loved a challenge and somehow seducing Jacob did not feel right.

'We're sharing a room,' he said. 'Hope you don't mind. The staff quarters are full. I think the manager thought James was sending her two women. I was sure he was going to send Isabella here.'

Angie thought of the dark beauty of Isabella. 'Glad he didn't. I can't stand the bitch, though men seem to like her.'

Jacob smiled. 'Actually, I think she is exquisite.'

Angie noticed his face became flushed at the mention of Isabella. 'Do you have a crush on her?'

'Gosh, no. She would never look at me. She's too sophisticated. I guess I prefer more down-to-earth women.'

There was warmth in his expression when he gazed at her, and Angie found herself enjoying his company. Perhaps a slow, easy seduction would be a change of pace from her recent exploits. Maybe kitchen duty would not be as arduous as she previously thought.

Guests streamed into the dining room, and the kitchen staff worked hard to fill the orders under the direction of the chef. The waiters carried plates laden with lobster, oysters and banana prawns as big as a human hand. Rick nudged Angie as she handed him a plate. 'Wear good walking shoes tomorrow, but don't bother bringing your swimmers. Kate and I know a great secluded beach.' Lean and hungry, he had an intensity about him that appealed to Angie's instincts. 'Find out what your start time is tomorrow from Tahillia.'

'She's bound to appear soon. She doesn't usually miss a chance to lord it over us in the dining room,' said Kate, who balanced plates laden with food up her arm.

'Speak of the devil,' said Rick, grimacing as he took several plates off the counter. 'The Black Witch has arrived.'

'There are guests on table five who want to order.' Tahillia clicked her fingers in Rick's face.

'Good evening, Ms Ash,' said Rick evenly as he walked past her.

'I cannot see what is good about it,' Tahillia answered sourly. She limped stiffly towards Angie. Despite the folly of allowing her eyes to be drawn to Tahillia's ankles, Angie could not stop herself from looking downward.

'You,' said Tahillia to Angie. 'I want to talk to you.'

'Great,' said Angie bravely. 'I would like to find out what my timetable is for this week.' She noticed the kitchen was suddenly quiet. Only the gentle hum of the dishwasher could be heard.

Tahillia held a clenched fist up to Angie's face. Opening her hand, she let drop a small piece of blue fabric that matched the discarded summer dress in Angie's room. 'I found this in Nick Holt's room. You had better be able to explain how it got there.' Anger exposed Tahillia's prominent teeth as her lips thinned. The imp in Angie's nature made her think of the manager as a furious rabbit.

Calm under pressure, Angie shrugged. 'I have no idea what you are talking about.' It would take more than a bit of her dress to make Angie confess. Obviously Nick had not told Tahillia anything. She promised herself to thank him when she saw him next.

'Hello, Ms Ash. I'm Jacob Hamilton.'

'Shut up. I did not speak to you.' Tahillia rounded on Jacob, and Angie watched in amazement as he foolishly turned Tahillia's attention on himself.

'I just thought you would like to know that that looks like a piece of Angie's dress.'

What was he doing? Angie glared at him, willing him to be quiet. How could he confirm Tahillia's suspicions? The last thing she needed was for him to turn a mere suspicion into fact. Angie tensed, and though she was not by nature a violent person, she wanted to hit Jacob.

'I know what it is,' said Tahillia. 'What I want is an explanation as to how it got into Nick Holt's room.'

'That's probably my fault,' replied Jacob easily. 'Nick's from the same home town as I am. We caught up in my room. Nick used Angie's dress to clean his guitar. It shredded in his hands and over his clothes. Sorry,' he apologised to Angie.

Tahillia snorted in disbelief. 'One wrong move from you,' she said, glaring at Angie, 'and your work experience report will read expulsion.' She turned and stormed from the kitchen.

'Are you crazy?' said Angie. 'That was the stupidest story I've ever heard.' What on earth was Jacob doing earning the wrath of Tahillia Ash? Angie did not need his protection. She could look after herself.

'It's true,' Jacob protested.

Angie looked at him in disbelief.

'Well, the bit about Nick being from my home town is true. We went to school together. He was a few grades above me,' he said with a grin. 'Don't worry. Nick will back up my story. The rest was the best I could come up with at short notice.'

'I do not need looking after,' said Angie, but she couldn't help warming to his boyish enthusiasm. 'How did you know that was a piece of my dress?'

'I saw you wear it at the Hotel Training Academy. It looked terrific on you.'

'Thanks,' she said, flattered.

'What did you do to set Tahillia off?' Jacob asked, his face gentle with concern.

For a moment she was tempted to tell him the truth just to watch the expression on his face. But she did not want to shock him. The less he knew the better. If she lost her scholarship, that was her problem, and she liked Jacob enough not to drag him into trouble.

64

'Never mind. Just do me a favour. Don't try to save me again. I do not need a hero. I can look after myself.'

He looked slightly crestfallen but Angie was determined to dissuade him from any further attempts to get involved in her life. She had never relied on a man, and she certainly did not want Jacob's help.

The chef walked over to Angie and Jacob, putting his arms around them. 'I am going to give you both a piece of friendly advice. Don't get on the wrong side of Tahillia Ash. Cleaning toilets for the rest of your stay could get kind of boring.'

'I think I'm already there,' said Angie, and curiously the thought did not perturb her. In fact, she rather enjoyed earning Tahillia's enmity so quickly. It would make life interesting in the future.

Angie stripped off her uniform, kicked off her shoes and sat on her bed. Her feet ached after ten hours of standing on them. Lifting one leg, she massaged her foot, glad to be finally off duty. The last hours had been a killer as Tahillia had exceeded her duties of hotel manager, and had stood over her and Jacob, making sure that every speck of dirt was removed from the kitchen and dining room.

'Gosh, I'm sorry.'

Angie looked up to see Jacob standing in the doorway, staring open-mouthed at her nakedness. He started to back out.

'Come in, Jacob,' she said impatiently. 'Unless you plan to spend the night in the hall.'

'But you're not wearing any clothes.'

She walked over to him, grabbed him by the hand and pulled him inside the bedroom. His gaze dropped to her shaven sex and his mouth opened in surprise.

'What is the matter with you? Haven't you seen a naked female before?'

'Um ... no,' said Jacob. 'Well, that is, if you don't

count my sisters when we were little.' Angie watched Jacob's face colour to the roots of his curly brown hair. He stared fixedly at her face, his chin averted so as not to explore her nudity.

'If you're going to share a room with me, get used to seeing me without clothes. I'm hot. I'm tired. I want to go to sleep, and I never wear anything to bed.'

'Sure Angie. I, um, am going to put on my pyjamas.'

He turned his back to her. Angie watched as he pulled his pyjamas from under his pillow and disappeared into the bathroom to change. Surely he could not be a virgin at twenty? The idea was too weird.

She sat on her bed, lifted the other foot and thought-fully started massaging under the arch of her foot. Jacob appeared from the bathroom clad respectably in his pyjamas.

Angie watched amused as he tried not to look at her. She spread one leg further apart and continued to massage her foot. Trying to restrain a grin, she enjoyed the mental battle he wore so vividly on his face. Morality won as he marched past her to turn off the light.

'Are you any good at massaging feet?' she asked, determined to get him to face her. 'Mine are aching terribly.'

Jacob switched off the light, but the room was lit by the cosy glow of the moon. 'No.' His voice had deepened and there was a slight tremor.

'Tell you what. How about you come over here. I'll massage your feet and you do mine.'

Keeping his back to her, he pulled the covers from his bed and climbed under the sheets. 'Some other time,' he said shortly.

Angie walked over to him and sat on his bed, near his pillow. 'Jacob, turn around.'

'Go away, Angie,' he said, his voice muffled by the sheet.

'I will, when you answer one question.'

'What is it?'

She pulled the sheet away from his face, so that he turned to face her, and leant over so that her breath blew across his cheek. 'Are you a virgin?'

'Go to bed,' he growled.

'Just thought I would ask,' she said pleasantly. 'After all, you were so ready to jump into my business before. I thought I'd better find out more about you.'

'Go away. Go to sleep.' He jerked the sheet from her hand and pulled it over his face.

She laughed and walked over to her bed. The question of Jacob's virginity was obviously a touchy subject. And Angie loved nothing more than to explore a touchy subject. She climbed into bed, but not before she had made a vow. By the time this work experience was over, she would find out if Jacob were a virgin. Then she would cure him of his affliction.

Rick carried a backpack as they trekked along the sandy track to Summer Beach. Kate walked beside him, dressed in a tight summer dress that barely covered her bottom. Occasionally she stretched and the dress rose up to expose her lack of underwear.

Angie, who walked beside Jacob, saw how little Kate was wearing, and wondered with amusement whether Jacob had noticed. How would he cope when they arrived at their destination if seeing her naked last night had embarrassed him?

The sun tickled Angie's shoulders, and she looked forward to a morning free of inhibitions.

Except for greenery surrounding Hotel Desire, the rest of the island was in its natural state. Covered with pockets of rainforest and gum trees, the island was a natural sanctuary. They had walked for an hour and had not encountered another person.

'We're nearly there,' said Rick. He stopped at a rock

ledge, which overlooked Summer Beach. 'Here we have it, folks. Nine miles of deserted beach.'

Angie glanced down at Rick's shorts and noticed that his excitement was not limited to his enthusiasm for the beach.

'Angie, come in front with me,' said Rick. 'There's a bit of a climb over some rocks. Jacob, could you go in front of Kate? She's afraid of heights. She might need some help climbing down.'

Kate giggled and moved aside to let Jacob pass. Shrewdly, Angie looked at Rick, recognising a set-up when she saw it.

Rick climbed over a large boulder, then turned, holding out his arms to Angie. 'Come here, babe. Let me help you down.' Reaching up, he caught Angie by the hand as she scrambled over the rocks. Lifting her down towards him, he pressed her hand against the front of his shorts.

She traced her fingers over his penis, which was large and rigid. Her desire for him grew and she realised she had not been wrong about him last night. But she was not sure where Kate fitted into the picture. 'What about Kate?' she asked.

'Kate's keen on Jacob. Don't worry, she isn't the jealous type,' he assured her.

Jacob bumped against Angie as he descended. 'Sorry.' He rubbed her arm. 'It's a bit slippery at the bottom.'

The place where he had touched her burnt, and she realised she enjoyed the sensation of his hands on her. If she let Rick take her, would Jacob join in as well? The image of both of them pleasuring her became vivid. Yet Jacob's response to her nudity last night left her in doubt. She could not understand how a cute-looking guy like Jacob could still be a virgin. Maybe he was gay.

'Come on, Kate,' called Rick. 'Climb down. The rest of the walk is easy.'

Kate peeled off her walking shoes, throwing them to

Rick. 'Take these. Jacob, can you climb up a bit in case I slip?'

'Sure,' said Jacob. He looked back at Rick who nodded. 'Go ahead, give her a hand.'

While Jacob climbed back up the rock, Rick put one hand over Angie's shoulder, then slid it under her top. 'Watch this,' he murmured, nuzzling her neck.

She leant against him, enjoying the feel of his penis nudging her back. His fingers lingered on her breast, teasing her nipples. Shivers of pleasure swept along her neck and breasts.

Kate smiled at them before brushing her auburn fringe from her eyes. She turned and slowly descended backwards down the rock with Jacob directly beneath, in case she slipped.

Angie saw his back stiffen as Kate's dress rode up, exposing her lack of underwear. She was a natural redhead and with her tanned rounded bottom seductively swaying towards Jacob, Angie could not see how he would refuse her obvious message.

'Do you think he's enjoying this?' asked Rick.

'I don't know,' Angie answered. 'I wish I could see his expression.' She pulled Rick's hand from her top and pressed it under her skirt. 'I'm enjoying every moment.'

He casually explored her, sliding his fingers back and forth. 'So I see,' he said, kissing the back of her neck.

Angie breathed in deeply when he deftly found the place where she needed him. She opened her legs, loving his exploration as she watched Jacob climb towards Kate. Rick was clearly experienced and knew exactly how to stroke her.

Kate looked over her shoulder. 'Jacob, do you think you can put your hands on my bottom, to stop me slipping?'

Awkwardly, Jacob pulled her dress over her exposed backside and placed his hands on the fabric.

'Not there,' she said throatily. 'Your hands will slip.'

'Kate's such an actress,' whispered Rick.

'Do you think Jacob is gay?' asked Angie, turning to Rick. She flicked open the Velcro tab on his shorts and slid her hand along his cock. He was as thick as her wrist, she thought with satisfaction. The end was moist and she began to wish Kate would hurry down.

'I don't know,' answered Rick. 'I thought he was with you.'

'No. We're only sharing a room.'

'Lucky Jacob,' said Rick appreciatively, as Angie stroked up and down his shaft. 'If these guys don't hurry, I'm going to have to take you here. Come on, Kate,' he called impatiently.

'No. I want to take my time to explore you with my tongue,' Angie said firmly.

Rick groaned and his penis jerked in her hand. 'Start talking dirty to me like that and we're not going to get to the beach.'

Jacob and Kate slowly made their way down the rock. Angie could see sweat dampening the back of Jacob's T-shirt. Kate turned to face him, so that his face was close to her pussy. Jacob seemed unable to move. Angie could see the rapid rise and fall of his breathing. Intrigued, she stopped stroking Rick, wanting to see what Jacob would do.

Kate flashed them a smile, her eyes alive with pleasure. She moved forward so that she was almost under Jacob. 'Oh, sorry, Jacob. The Island of Desire has slippery rocks,' she giggled, reaching between Jacob's legs.

Raising her hand to her lips, Angie licked her fingers, enjoying the taste and scent of Rick. The sight of Jacob poised above Kate was arousing and she wanted to see what he would do next. Angie had already noticed he had beautiful manners. Would he refuse Kate if she asked him to make love to her?

Jacob brushed Kate's hand away, turned and jumped,

landing at Angie's feet. When he rose, his breath was hot and he wiped the sweat from his face. He glared at Angie and pushed past her, following the track to the beach.

Rick, obviously impatient to get to their destination, strode over to Kate to help her down. Angie saw Kate hold Rick's ears and push him between her legs. It was obvious that Rick was going to be caught up for some time, so Angie ran ahead to join Jacob.

'I think Kate's got the hots for you,' said Angie, as she walked alongside him.

Jacob turned and grabbed her by the forearms, pulling her close. Excitement coursed through her blood at the unexpected anger in his movement. She had thought Jacob placid and easy-going. Though she liked his personality, his easy nature was not a challenge. But she sensed an internal struggle within him and she was savouring the change in his character.

'Let go of me,' she said, struggling. His grip tightened and Angie was enjoying every minute of the struggle. How far would he go? 'It's not my fault Kate wanted you. Why are you angry with me?'

His eyes narrowed and his lips parted. The tension emanating from him excited her. He wore baggy shorts, so she could not see if he was aroused, but she felt the familiar shiver of excitement. There were many ways to hunt a man. With Jacob, she would have to be subtle. Let him think she did not want him.

'I don't like women who flaunt themselves,' he said angrily.

'Perhaps you prefer men,' she said, determined to challenge him. 'Maybe Rick will oblige,' she taunted.

His face darkened with blood, and he bent inches from her face. 'That is not what I meant.'

'Oh, I suppose you mean me, then, do you? What's the matter? Can't you cope with an assertive woman?'

'No. I don't mean you at all. I'm just not interested in Kate.'

'You didn't have to climb up and help her. You could have refused.'

'I thought she really was afraid of heights.' He dropped Angie's wrists and looked up the hill. Angie followed the direction of his gaze, and saw Rick vigorously licking Kate as she writhed beneath him. The sound of her arousal was carried through the air.

Angie watched, spellbound. There was something about the very wildness of the island and the abandon of the couple before her that aroused her. She was wet with desire, and she needed to be satisfied.

'Can't you cope when a woman takes the initiative?' She watched Rick peel Kate's dress from her, freeing her rounded breasts. 'Kate has made it very clear what she wants Rick to do. There's nothing wrong with that.'

Kate massaged her large breasts as Rick continued to explore her with his tongue. Her nipples grew to tight peaks, her eyes closed as she squirmed. 'Oh, Rick, that's it, Rick,' she called. Rick pulled back to gaze at Kate, and Angie certainly saw the appeal. Kate had downy, russet-coloured pubes covering a plump aroused vagina. Her delicate pink inner lips were swollen and open. She was so sexy that Angie wished she had a cock and could plunge into Kate herself.

Running her fingers lightly over her nipples, Angie tightened and relaxed her inner muscles, wishing she were lying there in Kate's place. 'I do not understand you. How could you run from such a sexy woman?'

'I did not run.' Jacob's voice sounded angry. 'I like to do the chasing, that's all. I like to make the first move.'

'You should have been born in the last century,' said Angie, turning to look at him. 'Why should men do all the chasing? With that sort of attitude, you deserve to die a virgin.'

Kate screamed, thrusting wildly, and Angie turned

sharply, her attention riveted on Rick, who was rapidly divesting himself of his clothing. He was lean and muscular, his body finely tuned like an athlete. Within moments he thrust himself into Kate and Angie's throat went dry as Kate opened her eyes and smiled invitingly to her. Look what I am getting, she seemed to be saying. Angie knew Rick was large, and his cock was hard like his body. Kate was getting what she, Angie, needed.

Jacob was obviously going to be uncooperative, and she wondered with frustration how she managed to end up sharing a room with the only virgin on the island.

She knew if she looked at him now, Jacob would read her desire, and she had no intention of showing him she was interested. She would think of a way to bring him to his old-fashioned knees. 'You'll keep,' she murmured.

Suddenly she found herself being spun around. She cried out in surprise but Jacob's lips were on hers, kissing her with a passion she did not realise he possessed. His lips were hard and demanding. She fought against him because she liked the feeling of his possession, sensing that compliance might make him stop kissing her. She wished he would explore her like Rick had done earlier. Her nipples ached and she had a heavy liquid feeling in her abdomen.

'This is the way you want it, isn't it?' he asked.

'I'd rather have Rick,' she said, to annoy him. 'He's not afraid of women. See how he is satisfying Kate. When a woman screams like that, she is having real orgasms. Has a woman screamed like that for you? Do you know how to give a woman pleasure?' Frustration made her taunt him. 'Why don't you answer?'

Jacob glared at her. 'You're a teasing bitch.' He bent to kiss her again, but she refused to open her lips. He liked the thrill of the chase. Let him work for it, she thought.

She cried out in surprise when Jacob bit her lower lip. 'How dare you?' But he possessed her mouth, exploring

73

her with his tongue, and she forgot to be annoyed. Jacob could kiss. He was demanding yet sensuous, and she stopped struggling, enjoying the erotic sensation of his lips. His kiss spoke of experience. Manly and possessive. Maybe she was wrong about the virgin bit.

He broke the kiss the moment she complied, and Angie cursed to herself. 'That's what I meant,' he said.

'What are you talking about?'

'I like to make the first move.' He turned and walked down the track to the beach. Determined not to follow him like a besotted puppy, Angie went to join Rick and Kate. Jacob annoyed her with his games yet he had earned her respect. She had thought he would be an easy conquest. Well, she was wrong. Jacob was more complicated than she had first imagined. But at least that made him interesting. The familiar tingle ran up and down her spine as a hunting strategy formed in her mind. An easy conquest was ultimately boring.

Feeling hot, aroused and frustrated, she climbed up the rock. Rick's breathing was laboured as he possessed Kate, who turned and smiled invitingly to Angie. He pulled out of Kate before thrusting into her again. Urgent desire pulsed through Angie as she watched Kate being stretched to accommodate Rick's thick cock. Kate had one foot on Rick's thigh to stop him entering her fully.

That would not be my problem, thought Angie. I would welcome every inch of him. She pulled off her skirt and reached between her legs, stroking herself as she watched.

'Suck Kate's tits, Angie. Make her come,' said Rick.

Kate's large, firm breasts were certainly enticing. She leant over Kate, exploring her aureole with the tip of her tongue. Kate's nipples puckered in response. Angie took Kate's breast in her hand, exploring a woman for the first time. Her breasts felt soft and inviting, unlike the firm flat chest of a man.

Kate must have enjoyed the sensation because she closed her eyes and moaned. Thrusting vigorously to meet Rick, she cried out in pleasure. 'Oh, please,' she moaned, her mouth forming a soft 'O' of appreciation.

It was exciting to be this close. She could smell Kate's perfume mixed with the arousing scent of woman. Angie bent to kiss her. She was soft and sensuous, so unlike the erotic hardness of Jacob.

'Two women,' groaned Rick, the veins on his neck standing out with the strain. The sight of Angie kissing Kate was obviously too much for him and he gave one last thrust before collapsing over Kate.

'Do you know how long I have fantasised about having two women at the same time?' he said, panting with exertion. 'I have dreamt about this for years.'

The women looked at each other in understanding. What was the point of getting Rick excited if he could not look after them both, thought Angie. So like a man to think he could do more than he actually could.

'Well, you have hardly satisfied Angie,' Kate said, pushing him off her.

Rick rolled to a sitting position. 'Give me a moment to recover, you bossy woman.'

Kate laughed and began pulling on her dress. 'Poor Angie,' she crooned, stroking Angie's face. 'We'll make it up to you.' She wound Angie's hair around her fingers and leant over to kiss her again. 'I liked what you did for me,' Kate said. 'Rick and I both want you.'

'But not just yet,' said Rick, pulling on his clothes. 'I need some time to recover. Let's go down to the beach and find some shade.' He stood, helping Kate to her feet. 'Come on, Angie,' he said, extending his hand to her.

The sun was rising and Angie could feel it burning her skin. Picking up her skirt, she realised she needed to cool off. She had enjoyed Kate's kiss, but what she wanted was a hard pulsating cock. With Rick momentarily out of action and Jacob totally uncooperative, she might as well have stayed at the hotel with her vibrator.

Hunting in a pack never worked well – there were too many variables. She followed Kate and Rick to a shady patch of sand, but her thoughts were elsewhere. Where was Jacob? How dare he tease her with a kiss?

Stripping off, Kate and Rick ran into the surf, diving under the waves. 'Come on, Angie. Come and join us.'

Angie watched as Kate and Rick bodysurfed, catching the large rolling waves to the shore. She dropped her skirt on the sand and peeled off her top. No matter whether she cooled off in the water, she knew the dissatisfied ache that centred in the core of her would not leave until she began hunting again.

Walking into the surf, she enjoyed the sensation of the waves rushing between her legs, brushing her bare sex. Swimming naked felt different from wearing a costume. The sea had a way of invading every delicate crevice. The sensation was delicious as the frothy water tickled her bare skin.

Scanning the shoreline, she tried to find Jacob. 'I am not going to let you get away with teasing me,' she murmured, 'even if I have to tie you up.' But as she spoke, a more subtle way of seducing Jacob came to mind. They were, after all, sharing a room.

Rick caught a wave over to her and she smiled when he knelt at her feet. 'You are beautiful,' he said, kissing her snatch.

'You could look me in the eye when you say that,' laughed Angie.

'You are beautiful too,' laughed Rick.

Grabbing a handful of his hair, she pulled him to his feet. 'Prove it to me,' she ordered impatiently.

'Ouch,' he said, gingerly rubbing his head. 'I was just warming up. I thought women liked it when a guy starts down there.'

'Forget the foreplay. I've had enough of that watching you satisfy Kate.'

He put his arms around her, pressing her close. 'I'm sorry about that. But when Kate has me by the ears, it is kind of hard to escape.'

Angie could feel him hardening against her. His large penis brushed against her abdomen as he kissed her.

'Bite his nipples,' said Kate. 'It makes him hard.'

Angie turned and smiled at Kate, who pressed her body against Angie's back. The feeling of being sandwiched between two sexy people was sensational. The gentle waves rushed between their legs, cooling and teasing the heat of their loins.

Kate stroked Angie's back, kissing her neck, and Angie took Rick's nipple between her teeth, caressing it with her tongue.

'Two women, two women,' sighed Rick. 'Oh my God, my fantasy has come true.' The thought was obviously enough to make him hard because Angie could feel his cock pressing against her. Turning Angie so that she faced Kate, Rick took her from behind. 'Lean on Kate's shoulders,' he urged. 'I need to fuck you.'

Kate kissed Angie as Rick slid into her. She was swollen and wet from waiting and it was a tight squeeze. She could feel herself being stretched open inch by inch as he claimed her. Holding her hips, Rick ground into her, biting the back of her neck as he did so.

Kate sucked Angie's nipples, alternating between each breast. Her tongue felt slippery and hot.

Angie's head swam with desire as she was pleasured between them. Her knees almost buckled but Rick steadied her, holding her tightly as he thrust into her. Water boiled around their legs, occasionally spraying cool froth over their sun-hot shoulders. Rick thrust so hard that he almost lifted Angie off her feet. She was close to coming; the sensation of being between two urgent warm bodies was exhilarating. Then Kate stopped sucking her nipples and worked her way downward.

Rick wrapped his muscular arms under Angie's breasts, and she leant back on to him, letting him support her weight. He thrust into her and she could hear his raspy breathing as his rhythm became faster and faster. Her head was as frothy as the sea, and she could barely stand from the pleasure of what Rick and Kate were doing now.

Kate had peeled her open and found her piercing. 'I like your jewellery,' she said. Vigorously, she flicked over it with her tongue, and Angie decided she had found paradise on earth. Kate pressed her mouth against Angie's clitoris and sucked, rolling over the stud with her tongue.

Angie's breathing became short hard gasps as she shuddered from head to toe. Her legs were now rubbery and with her head thrown back on Rick's shoulder, all she could see was a sky full of intense never-ending blue. She pressed herself against Kate's skilful tongue, not wanting her to stop what she was doing. Tears of bliss seeped from her eyes and she closed them, concentrating on nothing but the ultimate pleasure of being satisfied by Rick and Kate.

Her whole body shuddered as another wave of pleasure swept through her.

With a roar that echoed across the waves, Rick finally came. Angie could feel his chest heaving and his hot breath in her ear.

Her limbs were liquid with satisfaction and she would have fallen but Rick kept hold of her waist. 'Steady, Angie,' he said, still breathing heavily.

'I'll help her,' said Kate, who put her arms around Angie's waist, and they walked from the sea and sat at the shoreline. Little waves tickled their feet and the sand was warm from the sun. Angie lay, propped on one elbow, watching Rick. He walked towards them, his penis red and semi-swollen, hanging like an elephant's trunk.

'I told you we would look after you,' cooed Kate.

Angie smiled lazily, her head still too fuzzy to talk. She was relaxed and satisfied, and she wanted to curl up on the sand and fall asleep.

'Let's go sit under the trees,' said Rick. 'We'll be burnt if we stay here. The sun gets hot in the middle of the day and you don't find out you are sunburnt until you have had a shower.'

'Good idea,' Angie croaked, her mouth dry.

Rick laughed. 'Come on.' He held out his hand to help her up. 'I brought some cold drinks and lunch in my backpack.'

'I could use a drink,' said Angie. She gulped down some mineral water that Rick handed to her, then passed the bottle to Kate.

'Isn't this beautiful?' said Rick. 'It's worth walking for an hour to have a whole beach to ourselves.'

Angie brushed her long blonde hair from her face and wound it into a knot at the base of her neck. 'Where's Jacob?'

'I don't know,' said Kate. 'I thought you two must have had some sort of a fight.'

'Angie thinks he's gay,' said Rick.

'That's a pity,' sighed Kate. 'He is very sexy in a reserved sort of way. I was looking forward to getting to know him better.'

'There's nothing wrong with him being gay,' said Rick. 'Makes less competition for me.'

Kate reached over and stroked Rick's penis, but Rick moved her hand away. 'Go easy, Kate. I'm not superman.'

Kate rolled her eyes. 'So much for less competition.' She rose and went to sit close to Angie. 'Are you worried about Jacob?'

'I don't know. I just think it's odd, the way he has disappeared. I wonder if he's walked back to the hotel?'

A shrill noise interrupted them and Rick groaned. Reaching into his backpack, he pulled out a mobile phone. 'This is one thing I should have left behind.'

'Hello. Oh, no. We're at Summer Beach. I'm with Kate and Angie. Fine. We have to walk back. I'll see you in an hour.'

'Who was that?' asked Kate, the tone of her voice annoyed.

Rick rolled his eyes. 'The Black Witch. Tahillia Ash.' He stood and started pulling on his clothes. 'She wants us back for the lunch shift. Two of the staff have just quit and she's furious.'

'That doesn't give us much time to walk back.' Kate quickly put on her dress. 'I'm not surprised staff have quit. Working for her is the only downside of this job.'

'I'm going to look for Jacob. I don't think we should leave him here,' said Angie. 'He mightn't be able to find the track back to the hotel.'

'That's probably a good idea.' Rick reached into the backpack and pulled out the bottle of water, handing it to Angie. 'You see the rock we climbed down? The track starts above it. If you stay on the track, you can't get lost. We'll see you back at the hotel.'

Angie waved goodbye, watching them disappear once they had climbed the rock. Untying her hair, she let it fall to her waist. She loved being alone. She could think clearly without interruption. It was time to hunt again for a rather elusive prey.

She scanned the water's edge. Nothing. If Jacob was not on the beach, then he had to be somewhere where the sand met the trees. That was where she would start looking for him, she decided.

It was easy to be silent, thought Angie, as she followed the line of trees, looking for solo footprints. Feet in sand made no noise. All she could hear was the call of seagulls and the crash of waves. Jacob was here. She could sense his closeness. Her skin prickled and she shivered, excited to be hunting again.

Kate and Rick had been incredibly satisfying and she looked forward to being with them again. But Jacob was different. Despite his friendliness, he drew the line at physical contact, and yet she did not think he was gay.

Angie stopped, bending to examine a trail of footprints that led from the water's edge to the trees. She followed the footsteps which stopped once she hit grass. Palms and scrubby bushes made it difficult to see. But she felt a thrill of excitement build in her stomach. Already her nipples were puckering and instinct told her she was close. 'Where are you, Jacob?' she murmured. 'I am going to make you want me.'

A sigh carrying her name made her freeze. There it was again. Careful not to make a noise, she stepped gingerly over the sticks and dried palm leaves. Jacob stood naked in a clearing of palms, stroking himself.

'Angie,' he said.

She stopped, thinking he had seen her.

She stepped closer and realised that his eyes were closed. Fascinated, she watched, enjoying the sight of his arousal. His skin was a creamy white across his buttocks. His cock was average in size but it had a thick knob, and Angie thought how nice it would be to have him in her mouth. She loved running her tongue over the head of a cock, exploring its ridges and tiny eye.

Her hand dropped to her sex, and she slid her fingers over herself as she watched Jacob. You want me, don't you? she thought.

Her eyes roved over Jacob, watching the way his muscular torso tensed as he stroked himself. He was not very tall but he made up for his lack of height in muscle power. His flat stomach was ridged with muscles, and his chest and arms were powerful. His face was flushed and with his soft, brown, curly hair and gentle, full mouth, he was ready to be plucked.

Angie walked silently until she was close enough to see the dewy end of his cock darken as his hand stroked up and down his shaft.

'You tormenter,' he said, his hand stroking faster. 'You and Kate together.'

Had he been watching them on the beach? she wondered. Well, she hoped he had enjoyed their little show because she was enjoying his.

He groaned and Angie could see the well-defined muscles stand out on the arm that was working his cock. 'You teasing, sexy woman,' he sighed.

What perfect timing, Angie thought. I have walked into his fantasy and I am the star.

'God, I want you,' he groaned.

And he would have her, she thought, but not until she had had the opportunity to explore him.

The veins on his neck bulged, and when his mouth pulled back in a grimace, she knew he was close.

Silently, like a cat, she picked her way over the uneven ground and knelt at Jacob's feet. His fist worked back and forward and the bulb of his cock was thick with blood. His body coiled for release.

Opening her mouth, she consumed him, sliding her finger into his anus as she did so. He yelled in shock but he was too far gone to pull away. Instead, his whole body went rigid with orgasm, and his yell turned to a deep groan as Angie sucked him until the base of his cock hit the back of her throat.

Finally spent, he pulled away, trying to catch his breath.

'Was I good for you?' she asked cheekily.

'Damn you, Angie. I didn't want to have sex with you.' He reached over and pulled her to her feet. His face was flushed with anger.

'Some men would say that wasn't sex,' she laughed.

'Anyway, I don't believe you. You were calling my name.'

She put her arms around his shoulders, pulling him to her, kissing him on the lips. She must have caught him at a weak moment because he did not fight her. Instead, he opened his lips and she poured the semen from her mouth into his.

He pulled back in surprise. 'That's disgusting.' He wiped his mouth. The flush staining his face deepened.

'I was just giving back what was yours. You should enjoy it. I did.'

'How long have you been watching me?' he demanded.

'Long enough to know you want me. Were you watching me on the beach with Kate and Rick?'

He nodded. 'How could I not?' he croaked.

'Did you like the way Kate licked me?' She took one of his hands and rubbed it over her sex. His hand felt smooth and hot on her silky skin. 'Kate was very good. She knew exactly how to please me,' she said seductively.

He swallowed and groaned, pulling his hand away.

'Stop it, Angie. I don't want you.' He looked around for his clothes. Finding his T-shirt, he quickly pulled it on.

While he was doing so, Angie walked over and scooped up his shorts, holding them behind her back.

'You know, you are a terrible liar. I know you want me.' She flicked her long blonde hair away from her face with her free hand. His denial excited her and she could not resist pushing him further. Most men would be begging by now. But Jacob was different. His mind was not totally ruled by his dick.

'Give me my shorts,' he demanded, holding out his hand for them.

'When you admit you want me. You know if we invited Kate to our room, she could suck you just like I did. While she is doing that, I could lick your balls right around to your anus, then push my tongue inside you.'

His head jerked upward and his eyes widened with surprise. 'Do girls really do that?' She watched as his hand reached down and took hold of his cock. He was soon fully erect and from the way his chest rose and fell, she knew she had got to him.

'Just think of both of us wanting you.'

'Oh God, Angie, why are you doing this to me?' The hand that was touching his cock began to move up and down. 'I told you already. I don't want to make love to you.' His voice sounded strained. 'Stop playing with me. I don't like your games.'

'I am not playing with you. You are doing that to yourself. I don't want to make love either. I want sex.' She walked over to him, so that she was only inches away. 'You know, I am different from other women,' she said seductively. 'I'm not frightened if another woman joins in. I love the way the skin puckers under a man's balls. I enjoy running my tongue up and down. Do you think you would last very long with me doing that while Kate sucked you?'

His hand dropped from his penis and formed a tight fist of restraint. 'I don't want to have sex with you and Kate,' he said through gritted teeth.

'Oh, I don't know about that.' Her gaze dropped lower to his penis. 'You know, there are some things a man can't lie about. His body won't let him.

'Did you see Rick take me?' she said softly, so that her breath blew on his face. 'He nearly split me apart with his thick cock. I would like you to do that to me. You know, there is nothing nicer for a woman than being fucked and sucked at the same time. So, do you think you could ask Kate to join us? She liked you. I am sure she would come to our room if you invited her.'

'I do not want to hear this,' he said, walking away from her, covering his ears. 'You are a manipulating b –'

He turned, his face strained, and Angie could see a muscle twitching in his jaw.

He wanted to swear at her and that meant he was losing control. She could see the sweat breaking out on his brow and she knew it would not be long before he was hers. This was his first time; she was sure of it.

Suddenly, he grabbed for his shorts, but as he did, she threw them high, so that they were caught in the nearest tree. 'Oh dear,' she said sadly. 'Looks like you will have to walk home semi-naked. Just think,' she teased, 'everyone will know you want me when they see your big hard-on following me home.'

'Damn you, Angie,' he shouted. 'This time you have gone too far.' He grabbed hold of her, carried her to a large boulder and put her over his knee. She struggled furiously, knowing she had won. She was going to enjoy this. He would not be able to resist her, now that their bodies had made contact.

'I will teach you to tease me,' he said, bringing his hand down hard on her bottom. She screamed as he spanked her. Wriggling over his knee, she could feel his erection pressing against her abdomen. The feel of his smooth skin against hers was erotic. He smacked her again and she writhed in response, but this time his hand lingered on her bottom. He kept a tight hold on her but his hand rubbed the tender skin where he had spanked her.

'I am sorry,' he said, loosening his grip. 'I shouldn't be doing this.'

He was sorry? The last thing she wanted was to hear remorse, especially when things were just starting to get exciting.

She bit into his arm, and he yelped with surprise, releasing her. Pushing herself to a sitting position, she straddled his knee, so that her sex was touching his. 'Is that the best you can do? Spanking me? Then apologising?' She rolled her eyes in disgust.

Reaching down, she took his cock in her hand. Then, moving her hips back and forward, she rubbed the thick knob of his cock over her clit. She was slippery and close to coming. Her whole body felt fresh and alive with excitement.

'You liked it, didn't you?' he panted, making no move to stop her. 'You weren't upset at all.'

'Yes,' she said. 'Very much.' Brushing her breasts over his smooth chest, her nipples peaked and she felt the first tremors of orgasm build inside her.

She rose slightly to mount him, past the stage where she could form words. All she could think about was him filling her.

He took hold of her hips just as his sex pressed against hers, then pushed her from him. 'I am not going to do this,' he said firmly. He rose and walked past her, his face flushed and angry. 'This isn't right.'

Angie stood there trembling. 'What are you talking about?' she shouted. 'We are here on a tropical island with no-one around. If this isn't right, what is?'

'You don't care about me. All you want is this,' he said, pointing to his erect penis. 'Well, I don't want to be used. I won't be your plaything.'

She watched him as he athletically climbed the tree where she had thrown his shorts. He reached for them, jumped down and pulled them on. Then without turning back to look at her, he walked away.

Chapter Five

'*I* have been looking for you.'

Angie groaned at the sound of Tahillia Ash's deep, husky voice that sounded like she smoked 60 cigarettes a day. It had been a long hot walk from Summer Beach in the middle of the day and she fancied a swim in the guest pool. There was an inviting drinks island in the middle of the pool, and she gazed longingly at the cocktails on the counter.

'Don't even think about it.'

'I was just looking,' replied Angie. Didn't the woman have a life?

'You are here to work. Go and get changed. I need you on reception immediately. We have a private jet landing in fifteen minutes, and I do not want to keep the guests waiting.'

'Who's coming?' Angie asked excitedly, pleased at her sudden elevation from kitchen hand to front desk.

'It seems that Nick Holt finds the Island of Desire too peaceful for his tastes. He has invited the rest of his band, including the roadies.' Tahillia sniffed with distaste. 'The wrong sort of people have too much money these days.'

Angie suppressed a smile. From the expression on Tahillia's face, she no longer enjoyed Nick's exuberant company. She gave the pool one last lingering look. Lined with palms and ferns, it was the largest pool, complete with grotto, she had ever seen.

She spotted Nick chatting to a sexy young woman. The woman, wearing a gold bikini, was stroking Nick's chest. He grinned and waved. 'Angie, come and join us,' he called.

'Sorry, the pool area is out of bounds for staff,' she called back. 'Anyway, you look like you don't need extra company,' she laughed.

With Tahillia Ash standing right beside her, she did not want to push her luck. Reception beat washing dishes. Nick Holt would have to wait until she was off duty.

'You seem to be on very friendly terms,' said Tahillia stiffly.

'A hotel worker should be pleasant to guests at all times. Page fifteen of our hospitality text from the Training Academy,' quoted Angie. And I *was* pleasant to Nick Holt, she thought, remembering the frenzied sex against the wall. Very pleasant indeed. She would not mind doing it all again with Nick, especially since Jacob had decided to retain his stuffy virginity.

'James Steele said you had a photographic memory, but do not think that impresses me. I need hard workers with practical ability, not a fancy memory.'

'Oh, I'm sure you will find I can be practical,' said Angie. Give me a few minutes in reception and I will memorise the room number of every interesting guest, she thought. Then I will put my practical skills to good use.

'The only reason I am putting you in reception is because I am short of staff.' Tahillia looked at her watch. 'You have ten minutes – and do something about your hair. You have got sand through it. I expect my staff to be properly groomed.'

Angie watched her as she walked away. Tahillia no longer limped, but there was a fine red mark on one of her ankles where the cuff had been. They must have had to saw it off, thought Angie.

A touch of remorse made her feel a little guilty.

Tahillia turned and though Angie quickly averted her gaze from her ankle, Tahillia's expression was deadly. 'Get a move on,' she snapped. Her eyes narrowed to thin slits. 'I have just got rid of two staff. Make sure you are not the next on my list.'

'I'll be right there,' Angie called. 'Bye-bye, guilty conscience,' she murmured, visualising exactly what she would like to do to Tahillia next. Who knows, maybe Nick would be able to persuade Tahillia to join him again.

She looked over at Nick, who slowly stuck out his tongue and ran it invitingly over his lips. The stud in his tongue glinted and the woman in gold laughed. 'You're missing out, Angie,' he called.

Tahillia's attitude annoyed her, and a little stress release with Nick Holt certainly seemed like a good idea. Nick was creative and fun. Still, with Tahillia dangerously on the loose, Nick would have to wait. But not too long. Truly kinky guys were hard to find, and Nick was certainly an original.

Angie blew him a kiss then hurried to her room. She wondered if there would be a spare staff bedroom, since Tahillia had fired personnel. It would be a shame if Jacob moved out, especially when seducing him was proving to be such an interesting challenge.

She stripped off her skirt and top. Looking in the mirror she saw that her normally pale skin now had a pink glow from the sun. In a couple of days, when her tan settled, she would look like she belonged on the island. Joy coursed through her. Despite the presence of the island's resident bitch, the Island of Desire was living up to its five-star rating.

Opening the bathroom door, she surprised Jacob in the shower. She noticed with amusement that he was sporting a semi-erect penis. Obviously, he had not been able to cure his problem by himself. She knew that he would remember the feel of her hot mouth on him. Virgins always remembered their first sexual encounter and by the time she had finished with him, she would be forever imprinted on his memory. Not that he would admit to his virginal status, but then, what man ever did?

'Don't you knock?' said Jacob, covering himself with his hand.

'No. Catching someone by surprise is always more exciting,' Angie laughed. 'What are you trying to hide? I've already seen what you have to offer.'

The presence of his hand on his cock made him harden. 'I'm not offering anything,' he said, looking down in dismay at the disobedient part of his body.

'Don't worry. You are safe for now,' she said. 'I have to be on front desk in ten minutes. That might be enough time to satisfy you but I would like more time. I would love to take you slowly, especially as it's your first time. I want to rub my naked body up against yours.' She stroked her hand over her sex. 'You know, the skin is so soft and inviting when a woman is shaven.'

'Don't start that filthy talk,' he said warningly.

She walked towards him and slid open the shower door. 'Have you ever showered with a woman? Just think of the hot steamy water washing over us. There's enough room for two. Would you like to stroke me? Just think, you could part me with your fingers, then slide that big cock into me while you are standing up. Think how good that would feel. I'm sure there is nothing better for a man than being inside a hot, willing woman.'

Jacob turned off the shower taps with a vicious twist.

Stepping out of the shower, he grabbed his towel and wrapped it around his waist.

'You know, Jacob, you really are going to have to teach a certain part of your anatomy to lie better. You can pretend you don't like me but –' with an exaggerated flourish of her hand, she pointed her index finger downward '– there is a certain part of you that doesn't agree.'

'Jesus, Angie, you push me,' said Jacob through gritted teeth. He walked out of the bathroom and slammed the door.

'Yes, I do,' she said quietly. 'Because you are different from other men and that makes me want you more.'

'No, I won't take another room,' the woman insisted. 'I'm Nick Holt's wife, so book me in with him.'

Angie looked at the peroxide blonde with dark roots standing belligerently in front of her at the reception desk. As soon as she saw Ellie Holt, Angie knew the woman was trouble. Angie had thought they were separated, but it was hard to keep up with the Holts' famed volatile marriage.

'Just a moment, Mrs Holt,' said Angie. 'I need to confirm this with Mr Holt. He hasn't left instructions with us that he is expecting you.'

'Of course he hasn't, you silly bitch,' insisted Ellie Holt in her irritatingly high voice. 'He doesn't know I'm coming. It's a surprise.'

And not a pleasant one, thought Angie, realising that Nick could well have his hands full with a certain woman wearing a gold bikini. 'If you could please take a seat in the lounge area, I will get Mr Holt.' And warn him that you are here, she thought.

Trust Tahillia Ash to direct the difficult client to me, thought Angie with a sigh. The hotel manager stood in the foyer greeting guests, issuing orders and seeing everything ran smoothly or, as in Angie's case, not so smoothly. Angie had the distinct feeling Tahillia Ash was just waiting for her to make a mistake.

Here comes a problem, thought Angie, when Tahillia Ash walked towards her. Angie had a fight or flight instinct for trouble, except this time, she was stuck.

'Book Mrs Holt in with her husband,' said Tahillia Ash smoothly. 'I am sure he will be delighted to see you,' she said to Ellie Holt. 'You can leave your bags at reception. The porter will take them to Mr Holt's room.'

After casting Angie a triumphant look, Ellie Holt smiled with pleasure, though Angie wondered whether Nick Holt would feel the same way.

'Angie, take Mrs Holt to the pool area,' ordered Tahillia Ash, and Angie did not miss the malicious sweetness in her tone. 'I think you will find Mr Holt there.'

'Come this way, Mrs Holt,' said Angie with a sinking feeling, thinking of the woman in the gold bikini. The fights between Ellie Holt and her husband had been magazine fodder for years. Hotel rooms often bore the brunt of Ellie's jealousy, but Nick Holt had been known to settle undisclosed amounts, if the odd person got in the way, when Ellie threw a tantrum.

She had to hand it to Tahillia Ash. Revenge came in different forms. If Nick's wife found him with another woman, there would be a scene, and Nick would think Angie had set him up.

She led Ellie Holt through the foyer and out to the pool. Anxiously scanning the pool area, her gaze darted over the couples enjoying the warm Queensland sunshine. Relief flooded through her and her breathing slowed when she realised Nick Holt was nowhere to be found. 'He doesn't seem to be here any more. Why don't you return to reception, and I will try and locate him.'

Showing persistence, Ellie Holt, former groupie, now celebrity wife, pushed past Angie and entered the pool area. 'We have hardly looked. This is exactly Nick's scene,' she said, walking past a couple of lovers enjoying the spa and each other. 'I can see why he likes it here.'

The sinking area in the pit of Angie's stomach sank lower as Ellie walked past a man-made waterfall then sighted the grotto adjoining the pool. She marched deliberately towards it and Angie hurried to catch her. 'I am sure he is not in there,' she said. 'Perhaps you would prefer a cocktail and a seat by the pool while I find Mr Holt.'

Her words did nothing to stop Ellie, who entered the grotto with Angie just behind her.

Peering into the darkness of the small cave, Angie could see the water boil and froth from the jets. When her eyes adjusted, she let out a sigh of relief. The blonde in the gold bikini was enjoying the coolness of the grotto. Fortunately she was alone. Her eyes were closed, her head resting against the rocks, her body submerged.

Sorry to disappoint you, Tahillia Ash, thought Angie with a small satisfied smile. You are not going to get a scene at my expense after all. 'Looks like Mr Holt is not here,' said Angie. 'He may have returned to his room.' She turned to leave.

Then Ellie Holt let out a piercing scream that bounced off the grotto walls, and Angie stiffened in horror as Nick Holt's recognisably bald head emerged from under the water, his tongue still licking between the blonde's legs.

He turned mid-lick, his eyes wide with dismay. 'Ellie?' he said. 'It's not what you think.'

'You filthy slut!' screamed Ellie, focusing on the blonde in the gold bikini rather than Nick, much to Angie's chagrin. Her pink fingernails resembling talons extended towards the blonde. 'You think you can have my husband?' she shrieked.

The blonde scrambled out of the water but not before Ellie had managed to grab hold of her hair.

Angie sprang into action, realising that the blonde

embedded with pink talons would not be a good look. She grabbed on to Ellie Holt's arm to pull her away. 'Help me, Nick,' she implored.

The blonde knew when to run and run she did, minus a fistful of hair and her bikini bottom. There goes one dissatisfied guest looking to check out early, thought Angie grimly, keeping a tight hold on Ellie Holt's arm.

'Please calm down, Mrs Holt,' said Angie, trying to maintain a vestige of professionalism.

'You knew my Nicky was here all along, didn't you, you stupid bitch?' Ellie Holt turned on Angie, her eyes narrowed with rage. 'You're already calling him by his first name. Has he fucked you too?'

Before Angie had time to answer, she was rewarded with a savage push that sent her flying head first into the grotto. Her head hit something that left her gasping, and she swallowed a mouthful of warm, salty pool water.

Nick grabbed her and she clung to him, trying to catch her breath. But when she tried to stand, her legs wobbled underneath her.

'You hit one of the rocks. Are you all right, Angie?' asked Nick.

'I think so,' gasped Angie. Her head throbbed and she clung to Nick for support. Ellie Holt stood by the side of the grotto, her hands on her hips.

'How do you know her first name, you bastard? Have you fucked her, too? Have you gone through the whole place?' she screamed.

Her fists clenched, Ellie Holt advanced to the edge of the grotto pool, and Angie watched, horrified, wondering whether Ellie was about to jump in and attack her too. The woman is crazy, she thought. The blonde had been right to run, and she would have too, if her legs had cooperated.

'Of course I haven't, love.' Nick's tone was conciliatory. 'You know I am not that interested in sex. The blonde reminded me of you, except you are more beautiful.' Nick flicked off Angie and waded over to his wife.

Still seeing stars, Angie fought to retain her balance, but her legs were still wobbly and she just managed to grab Nick's shoulder for support. Not interested in sex, indeed! Of all the lies she had heard in her life, Nick's was the feeblest. His future alimony payment had just increased, she thought.

'What is going on here?' said an unmistakably deep voice. Angie groaned. Trust Tahillia Ash to turn up when she was least wanted.

Angie turned to see Tahillia Ash surveying the scene with a distinctive look that combined a small measure of disapproval and a large dose of malice.

'That bitch is after my man. Look at the way she's all over him.' Despite her wobbly legs, Angie quickly removed her hand from Nick's shoulder.

'Stop it, Ellie,' said Nick. 'You know she doesn't mean anything to me. I love you.'

Nick is learning to crawl faster than he can walk, thought Angie, staggering to the side of the grotto. She pulled herself out of the water, then gingerly touched the quickly forming lump on her head. She watched as Nick climbed out, took his wife in his arms and hugged her close.

'Come on, love, don't be angry,' he crooned, and it dawned on Angie that divorce for wealthy pop stars was expensive these days.

'Please excuse my new member of staff, Mrs Holt,' said Tahillia Ash. 'I can see she has obviously upset you. I will make sure that this doesn't happen again. Now, I have a beautiful honeymoon suite available. Naturally, it will be free of charge, if you would overlook this disturbance.'

'That would be nice, wouldn't it, Nicky?' Ellie's face became animated and she giggled. 'I expect you to prove you have been missing me.'

95

'Sure, love, anything you say.' Angie saw Nick's shoulders slump. Looks like Nick is in for an evening of satisfying the wife, thought Angie with amusement.

Not seeming to notice her husband's despair, Ellie Holt took hold of his hand and pulled him out of the grotto area.

'Well, I can see you are not suited to reception,' said Tahillia Ash with a victorious sneer. 'Get yourself cleaned up and report to the chef. From the moment I saw you, I knew you were trouble. It seems to me that kitchen duty was the right place for you. You won't be able to cause any trouble with your face in the sink.'

Angie's head throbbed. She could feel the lump, now the size of an egg, forming on her temple. Despite feeling woozy, she wasn't going to let Tahillia get away with this. 'You knew Nick was here with another woman,' she said, challenging Tahillia Ash. 'You deliberately set me up.'

Tahillia smiled. 'Yes, I did. You see, Angie, I don't like it when staff disobey me. I believe in teaching recalcitrant staff a lesson.' Her fine arched eyebrows raised. 'I doubt you will be entering Nick Holt's bedroom now that bulldog of a wife is there.'

She was right there, thought Angie, rubbing her temple. Ellie Holt definitely deserved to live on a leash, though she suspected that the only one on a leash this visit would be Nick.

'Oh, and another thing. I believe this belongs to you.' Tahillia Holt held up a small handcuff key. 'I found it when I searched your bedroom. Remember that you are on my island. I thought about getting rid of you, but I have changed my mind. I have realised that it would be more satisfying to watch you washing dishes and scrubbing floors for the rest of your stay.'

She threw the key in Angie's face. 'Oh, and one more thing. I was the one who invited Ellie Holt to the island. I told her what a wonderful surprise it would be for her husband.' Tahillia's mouth rose to a slight smirk, then she walked off. The sound of her high heels clicking on the paving echoed through the grotto.

Revenge took many forms, thought Angie. Of one thing she was certain; Tahillia Ash intended to make her pay. But a plan formed in her mind which fuelled her spirit with excitement. It was time to hunt again.

Angie washed saucepans and rinsed and stacked plates until she thought she would never be able to look at a piece of crockery again.

'I don't know what you have done, girl, but the boss specifically said to leave you on clean-up duty,' said the chef. 'I don't like to misuse staff,' he added kindly, 'so when you have finished this pile, make sure you take a fifteen minute break and grab something to eat.'

It was close to midnight and the dining room was quiet. Rick gave Angie an encouraging smile when he came through the door from the dining room, his arms full of dirty crockery. 'This is nearly the last lot,' he said. 'There is just that pop star with his wife left in the dining room. The wife has ordered dessert, but they shouldn't be too long. Are you interested in joining me in the grotto after work? Kate is already there.'

'Not tonight, thanks, Rick,' she said. The grotto held no attraction after this afternoon's fiasco. Not when Nick Holt sat so glumly with his wife in the dining room.

Angie had a score to settle with Ellie Holt, and the familiar shiver worked its way up her spine. It was time to hunt.

'One serving of the mango ice-cream,' Rick called to the chef.

Angie walked to the kitchen door and held it open, watching Nick and Ellie Holt arguing at their table. Ellie Holt jabbed her finger in her husband's face. Whatever was happening, it was clear from Nick's expression that he was not having a good time of it.

'I think it's time to cheer you up, Nick Holt,' murmured Angie. 'Let me see whether the man who was "not that interested in sex" changes his mind.'

'Rick?' Angie asked. 'Do you think you could distract Ellie Holt for me?'

'What do you mean?' Rick quizzed.

'See if you can get her away from the table for a few minutes.'

Rick picked up the mango dessert. 'I heard about what happened to you this afternoon. Ellie Holt is a total bitch, attacking a member of staff, and Tahillia Ash shouldn't have let her get away with it.'

'Yes, the wife is a tough nut,' agreed Angie. 'But I haven't planned to let her get away with it.'

Rick grinned and gave her a quick hug. 'This place has certainly livened up since you came. I will see what I can do.'

She held the door to the dining room open for him, and he passed through, making his way to the Holts' table. Angie knew Rick had a great manner with guests. He shook Ellie Holt's hand and chatted to her. Pulling out her chair, Rick led Ellie Holt to the large antique drink cabinet and began showing her the different after-dinner drinks.

'I've nearly finished up here,' called Angie to the chef. 'I'm not hungry, but I could use a quick break.'

'Right you are,' said the chef, giving her a wave.

Angie walked purposely towards Nick Holt, stopping at his table. 'Hello, Nick,' she said softly.

'Jesus, Angie, what are you doing here?' Nick looked at her in horror. 'Don't let Ellie see you. She is wild enough already.'

'So I noticed this afternoon,' she said.

'I am sorry about what happened,' said Nick, 'but you have to go. I don't want Ellie to see us together.'

'Don't worry about that,' she said, looking across the dining room at Ellie, who was laughing as Rick flirted with her. 'Rick is keeping her amused. I have just come to see if you are still not interested in sex,' she said, with a small mischievous smile.

'Of course I am,' he said. 'But not with that bitch of a wife who is threatening to take me to the cleaners. I am going to lose everything. Go, Angie. Please,' he urged.

Angie, not wanting to be disagreeable, did as she was asked.

Crouching low, she climbed under the table and in between Nick Holt's legs.

'No, Angie,' hissed Nick when she reached for his fly. He locked his knees together, keeping a tight hold on the top of his pants.

'Who are you talking to?' asked Ellie Holt in her high voice.

'No-one,' said Nick, still keeping a firm hold on his pants, much to Angie's amusement.

Rick pulled out Ellie Holt's chair for her. 'I will leave you to enjoy your dessert and the complimentary port, Mrs Holt,' said Rick. 'Thank you for your autograph. I loved your documentary on the wives of rock stars.'

'Such nice staff here,' said Ellie, crossing her legs.

Angie pushed forward, parting Nick's legs to avoid Ellie Holt's foot.

'Except that stupid bitch who tried to stop me from seeing you,' added Ellie Holt.

'Yes, love,' agreed Nick, the tone of his voice flat.

How dare Nick Holt agree with his wife? thought Angie indignantly. She would have to see what she could do to change his opinion. Angie knew she had faults, but one of them was not stupidity. She leant forward and took hold of one of Nick Holt's hands, the hand that was not busy protecting his fly, and took a deep bite.

'Fuck,' shouted Nick, withdrawing both hands to safety above the table.

Angie quickly unbuttoned his jeans and unzipped him

before Nick had time to stop her. Now she was in business. Nick would not be agreeing to her stupidity soon. She would make sure he sang her praises.

'Whatever is the matter with you?' asked Ellie Holt.

'Nothing, love,' said Nick.

'Well, what are you screaming "fuck" for? If you could do it as much as you say it, our marriage would be better.'

Angie extracted Nick's penis, marvelling at its thickness despite its flaccid nature. She gave it one long lick from base to top, tickling it with her tongue just under the head. Nick's cock jerked in response. The thought of getting caught with it in her mouth was extremely exciting. She wanted him and wished there were some way she could ride him without his demented wife taking her pound of flesh. She could see from the episode at the grotto how Ellie Holt had earned her jealous reputation.

'There is nothing wrong with our marriage. I told you that already,' said Nick, reaching under the table and grabbing hold of Angie's hair.

Warningly, Angie bit down gently on Nick's sex, and he quickly withdrew his hand. It was always wise to let a man know who was boss, she thought. She took him further into her mouth, sucking gently, and already she could feel Nick hardening to the touch of her skilful tongue and lips. Her arousal made her legs shaky so she leant on Nick's thighs for support.

Despite his fear of his wife, Nick was obviously enjoying this as much as she was because he began stroking her hair in rhythm with her tongue.

'Nothing wrong?' said Ellie Holt. 'We have the best suite on the island, and you can't get an erection. I tried to get you interested all afternoon. First you say you are tired, then you say you are not interested. There is something wrong with you!'

Well, there was certainly nothing wrong with him

now, thought Angie, as she gently stroked Nick's cock at the base with her hand while she explored the top with her inquisitive tongue. Nick was thick and hard, a sure sign he was enjoying her manipulations.

'Sorry, love, I just don't feel like sex right now. I'm a bit preoccupied at the moment,' said Nick.

'Whatever with? You have a number one hit in five countries. You are earning millions. What could possibly be bothering you now?' screeched Ellie Holt.

'Something unexpected has come up,' said Nick, the tone of his voice breathy.

Angie moved her hand and swallowed Nick's cock until it touched the back of her throat. Withdrawing so that her mouth surrounded the huge bulbous end, she flicked her pointy tongue over the end. Back and forward, back and forward, then teased him under the delicate head. Nick's cock jerked and became rigid. He was hers, thought Angie, now that he was thinking with a different part of his anatomy.

She was careful to keep her mouth wet as possible by not swallowing any saliva. Men had told her that her wet mouth and lively tongue were sensational. When she swallowed him again so that his cock nudged the back of her throat, Nick let out a groan of pleasure. The sound of his enjoyment coursed through her. Her arousal pooled in her loins, and she desperately wanted to feel him enter her with his big thick cock.

'Whatever is wrong with you?' asked his wife. 'What has come up? You are not making sense.'

'I . . . um . . . I . . . oh God, I don't want to talk. Eat your dessert and shut up.'

That's the spirit, Nick. You are finally standing up for yourself, she thought with a giggle. She tasted the sweet pre-come on the head of his cock. It was sensational and Angie could feel her nipples tightening in appreciation. She wished Nick could reach under the table and caress

101

her. Or better still, climb under the table and plunge his thick cock into her.

The danger of being caught and the enjoyment of sucking Nick brought her to the edge. She began to rhythmically take him deep into her mouth. She heard a sigh of appreciation and Nick's hands firmly held her head as she maintained a sensuous rhythm.

'How dare you tell me to shut up!' said Ellie Holt. 'I fly all the way from Sydney to see you and you can barely talk to me. You obviously do not want to continue this marriage.' Ellie shifted her chair back and Angie stopped sucking Nick. Ellie stood and walked over to Nick. 'I expect to have sex with my husband, and unless you can do something better than that pathetic performance you put on this afternoon, I am going to divorce you.'

Angie pulled back to brush her hair from her face. Hastily she wound it into a knot at the base of her neck. She smiled at the sight of Nick's angry red penis. Despite his reticence at the beginning, he certainly was enjoying himself now.

'Oh, please,' groaned Nick. 'Don't go.'

Angie wondered whether he meant Ellie or her. His hands searched under the table for her face. Well, that certainly decides who he wants to stay, she thought, taking him in her mouth again. His hips rotated enough to drive himself into her wet mouth but not enough to cause suspicion.

Ellie walked back and sat in her chair. 'So you will make it up to me?'

Angie curled her lips around her teeth and tightened her hold on Nick's cock. Knowing that he was near the edge, she drove down on him, moving her tongue like a swivelling snake under the base of his penis.

'Yes,' groaned Nick. 'Yes, yes, yes.'

'It's about time you came to your senses,' said Ellie Holt sharply.

'Is everything all right here?' asked Tahillia Ash, who was doing her last round in the dining room, checking that the guests were satisfied.

Angie stopped sucking Nick momentarily. She recognised the deep voice and the black crocodile shoes. Trust Tahillia Ash to appear when she was not wanted. But come to think of it, the less Angie saw of Tahillia Ash the better.

'I trust the food was to your taste,' said Tahillia.

Angie slid her tongue up and down Nick's cock, which looked as if it was about to burst. Delicious, she thought, better than anything she had seen on the menu. Taking him in her hand, she concentrated on pleasuring the top of his penis with her lips and tongue while she kept a firm but gentle hold of the base.

'Yes,' sighed Nick, and Angie realised that despite sitting facing his wife, Nick was in heaven.

'Everything is wonderful now, thank you,' said Ellie Holt. 'I'm very pleased with the honeymoon suite.' She let out a high-pitched giggle. 'Nick and I plan to make good use of it tonight.'

'I am glad you are enjoying Hotel Desire, Mrs Holt, despite the bad start. I have punished the silly girl who upset you by keeping her in the kitchen. No doubt she is washing your dishes as we speak,' said Tahillia Ash.

Angie took a look at Nick's penis. As far as she could see, it didn't look like a dish to her.

'Really, Tahillia, I don't know why you keep that stupid girl. You should get rid of her. Don't you agree, Nick?' said Ellie Holt.

This was getting rather personal, thought Angie, and since she couldn't, given her present position, voice her opinion, it was time Nick Holt did. She removed her lips from covering her teeth and gently bit Nick's rigid penis.

'Angie! No!' shouted Nick.

She continued to suck and pleasure him, pleased with his vociferous response. Quite obviously Nick wanted her to stay right where she was. She stroked his balls, which were tight with arousal, running her finger underneath his testicles to his anus.

'It seems your husband doesn't agree with you,' said Tahillia Ash. 'Never mind, you let me know if Angie bothers you or your husband again.'

'Huh!' said Ellie Holt. 'I don't intend to let that bitch near my husband.'

'That's the way,' laughed Tahillia Ash. 'Enjoy your evening.'

'Well, that serves that bitch right,' said Ellie Holt. 'She's washing dishes. Ha, ha, ha. Looks like I got the last laugh, after all.'

Angie took Nick fully in her mouth, and sucked him hard down to the base of his cock as he finally let go. His cock throbbed repeatedly and she heard him groan in pleasure.

'Oh God, oh God, that's good,' Nick cried.

'Yes,' agreed his wife. 'It is good, isn't it? Hold my hand, darling. Nick, be gentle! You are squeezing my fingers off. You know, darling, I haven't seen you look at me like that for ages. I can't wait to have you. Let's go to bed.' Ellie Holt stood up so quickly that her chair tipped over.

Angie stopped breathing. She knew what she had been doing was risky. If Ellie Holt stooped to pick up the chair, she and Nick were going to have a lot of explaining to do. That was if Ellie Holt gave them the chance to talk at all.

She watched as Ellie Holt's high heels tottered over to her husband, and Angie started breathing again. She was obviously so keen to have her husband that she was not going to bother to pick up the chair.

Quickly, she reached over, tucked his penis away and zipped up his pants. From the way he was slumped in his seat, she doubted he had the energy to do it himself.

A small satisfied smile spread across Angie's lips. She

was wet with arousal from wanting Nick. He tasted wonderful, like slightly salty almonds, but for now he was spent. Somehow, she doubted Ellie Holt was going to get what she was expecting tonight.

Chapter Six

*A*ngie sensed a feeling of *déjà vu* when she entered her bedroom that night. Her feet ached and the man she wanted to massage them was already in bed.

The bedroom light was off and through the moonlit room, Angie could see Jacob spread out on his bed, the sheet barely covering his hips. She walked over and stood at the end of his bed. When he did not greet her as she came in, she suspected he was either asleep or pretending to be. So, she reasoned, it was time to wake him up with plan A.

Jacob was quite beautiful, she thought, studying him. The moonlight gave his body a milky glow. With his soft curls, straight nose and generous mouth he reminded Angie of a Greek statue. His broad chest softly rose and fell with each breath. She wanted to trace her fingers over his chest and feel the ridge of each well-toned muscle. He had a body made for sensuous exploration.

She remembered the feeling of being taken in his arms and put over his knee. His skin had a young, silky texture but underneath he was firm and muscular. There was no doubt in her mind that Jacob had an eroticism just waiting to be explored. She would certainly like to be his teacher if she could just crack his irritating do-good virginity.

Yet she was not exactly in his good books since their encounter on the beach. Jacob had barely spoken to her when they were on kitchen duty together. Instead, he had busied himself with his work with a genuine enthusiasm no matter how menial the task.

Tahillia Ash had ordered him to finish up early, ensuring that Angie was kept occupied with the worst chores with as little backup as possible. But just the thought of her entertaining time with Nick Holt made Angie smile. The evening had certainly been eventful and her spirits remained buoyant. Tomorrow would be another brilliant sunny day and she had the day off to hunt. But right now the prey she had in mind lay sexily naked and unsuspecting. It was time to turn Jacob's dreams into a waking fantasy.

Standing at the end of his bed, Angie slowly peeled off her uniform, undoing the buttons one by one. Slipping the shirt from her shoulders, she let it drop to the floor. It made a clicking sound as the buttons made contact with floorboards.

'I want you,' she murmured. 'I always get what I want,' she said, her voice a little louder.

She smiled, biting her inside lip to restrain a giggle when she saw Jacob lying there so innocently. 'Even you, Mr Virgin, will be surprised at what I make you do.' Jacob stirred, his face turned from facing the wall to the other side.

Angie walked over to him so that she was in his direct view. His eyes remained closed but the rhythm of his breathing had changed. She slowly pulled down the straps of her bra so that the lacy fabric just covered the firm swell of her breasts. The graze of the fabric caused her nipples to tighten so that the tips became sensitive and aching to be sucked.

Reaching around to her back, she unclipped the bra. Scrunching the flimsy bra in one hand, she raised the bra to her nose and smelt the fabric. There was a hint of her perfume combined with her own scent. The side of her mouth twitched into a cheeky grin. If Jacob really were asleep, she would find a way to enter his dreams.

Quietly, she knelt at the side of his bed and placed the bra near enough to his face so that he would breathe in her scent, but she was careful not to touch him.

'Jacob,' she whispered, sotto voce. 'I'm undressing just for you. I have taken off my lacy bra. My breasts are firm and silky to touch. You want to reach out and fondle them, don't you?' She saw his eyelids flicker then still. A moan almost as soft as a breath of air left his lips. She hoped he was on the edge of consciousness, so that her voice would drift in and out of his dreams.

Unzipping her skirt, she let it slip over her hips on to the floor, so that she was wearing nothing but skimpy underwear that matched the elegant bra. She slipped her underwear over her slim hips, noticing her pants were damp, then placed them near her bra. She bent to his ear so that her words could barely be heard. 'I'm real. You can smell me. You like me so much you want to taste me. Think of me writhing under you as you explore me with your tongue. Imagine asking me to do anything you like. Anything at all.'

Jacob's nose twitched, he took in a deep breath and a moan, more audible this time, escaped his lips. One of his hands moved downward and slipped under the sheet. Angie bit back a laugh, determined not to wake him just yet. There was something distinctly thrilling about getting her way when the prey was unsuspecting. She could see from the rubbing motion under the sheet that the quality of Jacob's dreams had changed for the better. Kneeling by his bed, she leant close to his face.

'Think how much you want me,' she whispered, her words so quiet they could have passed as a sigh.

A frown creased Jacob's forehead.

'Don't fight how you feel, Jacob,' she whispered. 'This is just a dream. Remember how you had me over your knee? Did you like it when I struggled? Did my skin feel hot against your cock? You can have me in your dreams. You know you want me. Dream about how good it would feel to part me with your big cock. Imagine sliding inside me. I'm hot and wet and I want you. Think about driving that big cock into me again and again until I wiggle so much you have to hold me down.'

She saw his lips part. 'Angie,' he groaned, but his eyes remained closed.

The sheet slipped from his hips and she could see he was swollen, his hand rubbing over the head of his penis. She was determined to wear down his resistance and Jacob was proving to be extremely difficult, but then she had never encountered a stubborn virgin before. Still, she realised he was not wearing his stitched-up pyjamas to bed. That in itself was definitely progress.

Angie raised her eyebrows and smiled. Things were going very well. Slowly she leant over and kissed him fleetingly on the lips. His lips were soft and silky. Reaching down, she parted herself and slid her fingers over her piercing. Her muscles contracted and her nipples tightened until they ached.

She slid her fingers further into herself, until they were wet and slippery. Withdrawing her fingers, she brushed them over Jacob's lips. 'You would like to taste me, wouldn't you? Imagine what it would be like if I spread my legs and wanted you to push your tongue into me like a slippery, darting cock. What would you do if I cried out your name and begged you to satisfy me?'

She brushed her fingers lightly over the tip of his penis and it pulsed to her touch. 'You like it when I touch you there,' she said quietly. 'Have you ever let a

109

woman suck you? I don't think you have, but I bet you have thought about it.'

Very gently, she brushed her fingers again over his cock, noticing how hard he was. Jacob frowned, turning his head from side to side. 'Remember this is just a dream,' she cooed reassuringly. 'You can do anything you like in dreams.' Patiently, Angie waited until he relaxed back into sleep.

'You know, I would love to lick you from the base of your cock to the tip. I see you looking at me sometimes. Why are you waiting? Are you scared you might like it too much? Do you think you could get addicted to wanting me? You know now how good it feels to have me suck your cock. You didn't want me to do it before, but I know you loved it.'

She ran her hands over her breasts and down to her shaven sex. Gently, she stroked herself while she talked. She was swollen yet silky, and she looked hungrily at Jacob. Her mind flooded with her fantasy of what she wanted Jacob to do to her. But by the time she finished with him, Jacob, being a man, would think it was all his own idea.

'Think about how nice it would be if I licked you with my hot tongue. You are dreaming of me now. My wet tongue is sliding up and down your cock.'

Unable to resist, Angie leant over and ran her tongue lightly up and down Jacob's cock. It jerked to her touch and he thrust his hips forward.

Whether he liked it or not, he wanted her, thought Angie with satisfaction. She returned to stroking herself and little warning waves of approaching orgasm spread throughout her sex. Engrossed in her fantasy, she leant close to Jacob's softly parted lips, needing to connect with him.

'You take me by the hair,' she whispered hoarsely, her need of him urgent. 'You push my mouth down on you until I'm forced to swallow all of you. Your cock brushes the back of my throat and I pull away. I look at you with frightened eyes and beg you to be gentle.' She stroked herself faster, up and down the little stem of her sex until she was on fire. 'But I have teased you so much, you decide you want to punish me.' Her breath came faster at the thought of Jacob being man enough to dominate her and she didn't know how long she could last.

'No,' groaned Jacob, and he stopped stroking himself.

Angie rolled her eyes in disgust. Even his subconscious was respectable. He deserved to lie there with a hard-on all night and wake up with blue balls. 'Don't worry,' she forced herself to say sweetly. 'Remember this is just a dream. Anything is allowed in dreams.'

Carefully, she leant over and licked again from the base of Jacob's penis to the tip, running her tongue over and around the head. It stuck straight up, the thick head swollen with blood. He groaned and took his cock in his hand, stroking it back and forward.

'That's better, isn't it?' she said soothingly. Now where was she? thought Angie with a frown. Trust Jacob to be contrary in his sleep. She started stroking herself again, and the sheer pleasure of touching herself made her relax back into her fantasy. 'I tell you I don't want to suck you any more. I tell you I don't like you, but you don't care. You are aching to have me and you are going to make me do what you want. I have made you angry, so you pick me up again, like you did on the beach. I try and fight you but I am not strong enough. You can feel me struggling against you. Your lust for me makes you want to dominate me.'

Angie noticed Jacob's muscles in his arms flex and his whole body tensed. He was with her in this fantasy and her sex tightened in anticipation. Carefully, she stroked her hand down his chest, over his washboard stomach, before descending to his tight, curly pubic hair. 'You tell me to stop struggling and that you won't hurt me. But I

111

have to do what you want.' Jacob groaned and his breathing quickened.

'You tell me to kneel before you and I don't know what is going on. You get dressed in your work clothes but your prick is so thick and stiff you have trouble putting it away. You like it that you are wearing clothes and I am not. It makes you feel powerful. You lean over and kiss me and tell me you will be gentle but you are still going to punish me. You tell me it is time I learnt to be dominated by a man.' Angie kissed Jacob and his lips matched her faint pressure. She smiled, knowing he was still with her.

'You grab your tie and tell me to turn around. I'm angry because I hate to be bested. I glare at you and tell you to get stuffed.' Her breath came hard and fast as the fantasy anger mingled with lust built up inside her. Angie pinched and twisted her nipples until she balanced precariously on the edge of orgasm. Not yet, not yet, she thought urgently. She bit hard on her lower lip, letting the pain stop her from going over the edge. She didn't want to come. This was going far better than she expected.

'You grab me by the wrist and pull me to my feet. Then you spin me around so that my wrists are pinned behind my back and force me to walk in front of you. I scream at you. I tell you that I don't want to leave the bedroom, but you bind my wrists with your tie when I won't cooperate. Your cock is straining at the edge of your pants. You are so horny you want to fuck me against the wall. You want to feel what it is like to be inside me.'

Angie watched with satisfaction as his cock pulsed all of its own accord. He was dreaming her fantasy; she was sure of it. 'You march me into the foyer and Tahillia Ash is there. The foyer is busy but all the noise stops and everyone turns to watch. You tie me to the luggage trolley and you can see respect in the eyes of the other men. The women look at you in awe.'

Angie closed her eyes, imagining the scene as her fingers slipped up and down. The throbbing sensation in her clitoris made her throat dry as she deftly massaged the little stem over and over. She was acutely aware that she would not be able to last much longer.

'Tahillia comes over and demands to know what is going on. You tell her you are going to punish me because I am disobedient. She says that it is about time I was punished and she comes back with a small riding crop. You let her use it on me. You watch, rubbing your cock, keeping it hard and ready as you enjoy Tahillia punishing me.'

Jacob frowned. 'No,' he moaned.

'Just softly,' Angie amended, not wanting to let her fantasy go. She resisted an urge to slap some sense into Jacob, but only because she did not want to wake him. 'Just enough to make my bottom pink and tender. You push Tahillia away, telling her that is enough. You are ready for me. You tilt me forward and take me, forcing my pussy lips apart. You drive your cock into me, all the while knowing that everyone is watching. You like it when you have an audience.'

Jacob stroked himself faster and faster. 'I manage to free one of my hands, and I dig my fingernails into you. I scream at you and beg you to stop fucking me in front of everyone.' Angie took hold of his forearm, digging her nails in, not hard enough to wake him but enough to keep him in her fantasy.

'You thrust into me, over and over again until you can feel your balls tighten. I tell you I hate you and I will never forgive you, but you don't care. You love the heat of my sex and being inside me. It is better than you have ever imagined.' Angie looked longingly at Jacob's rigid cock. His balls were tight, and she wanted him inside her.

113

'You tell me you are going to make me come. You reach around to the front of me and delve your fingers between my legs. She increased the pressure on her clitoris, knowing it would send her over the edge. She pulsed up and down and groaned deeply as all the muscles in her back tightened.

'I cry out and beg you not to make me come in front of all the people in the foyer. I squirm and twist, trying to make you take the pressure off my clit, but Tahillia Ash peels me apart and exposes me to everyone. I take a handful of Tahillia Ash's hair with my one free hand. You love it. You see two women struggling as you are inside me. You bind me with your arms, loving the feel of my body struggling against yours. You find me again with your fingers as you fuck me and I can't bear it any more. I'm lost to you.' Angie gasped as the first wave of orgasm hit her, then another and another.

She stroked herself firmly, imagining Jacob filling her with his thick cock. Her orgasm was so exquisite that she had to bite back a scream. She still wanted Jacob, and she was determined to have him. Her whole body trembled, and she arched as pleasure coming in waves hit her again and again. Finally spent, she sat on her haunches gasping, trying to recover her breath.

'You liked that fantasy, didn't you?' she whispered, noticing Jacob's cock was suffused with blood. 'But you are still in the dream and you haven't come yet. You still want me. You can't get enough of me. You want to come but, before you do, Tahillia unties me and pulls me away from you.'

Angie reached down and stroked herself, sliding the wetness from herself over Jacob's cock. His sex felt thick and throbbed in her hand. She moved her hand up and down in a steady rhythm. 'You know how good it feels inside me when I am hot and wet. You are determined to have me.' She released him, stood and stepped away.

'You can't forget the feeling of being inside me. You hate not having your cock inside me.'

She ached to climb on top of him but she fought the idea. She was determined to hypnotise him, so that she could have him over and over again. That was the advantage of having a younger man with energy.

A sigh left his lips and Angie saw Jacob's eyelids flicker. Satisfied to leave him for a moment, she decided not to wake him. He was more receptive in a deep slumber. She hoped his dreams erotically frustrated him enough to compel him to slide into her bed and become her slave.

She nodded as she watched him. 'You will be mine soon,' she said with determination. She walked into the bathroom and switched on the light. Leaving the bathroom door open, she turned on the shower. If Jacob awoke in his aroused state, he would be able to see her. Let him think his erotic thoughts about her were his own entire, guilty dream. The thought of his continued reluctance made her smile as the warm water gushed over her.

She slid the soap over her nipples, noticing how sensitive they were. She was definitely more than ready for him, she thought, as she slipped the soap back and forth over her vulva. It was impossible to see if Jacob was awake, so she sighed loudly, hoping he would hear her.

She stepped out of the shower and dried herself. Standing under the light in the bathroom, she massaged moisturiser into her skin, paying special attention to her breasts. Turning her back to Jacob, she bent to rub the moisturiser into her legs, allowing him a view of her long, tanned legs, bottom and pink slit. She set the moisturiser bottle on the vanity with a clatter, and stepped out of the bathroom.

She deliberately left the bathroom light on so she could see Jacob better. To her acute disappointment, she

115

noticed he had shifted his position since she had entered the bathroom. Both hands were tucked close to his face and not on his erect cock, where they should be. She watched in frustration as it slowly subsided like the Titanic.

She pursed her lips in annoyance. His expression was relaxed and Angie felt like shaking him. What was wrong with this man? How had her brainwash technique failed? There was no use waking him, she thought grumpily, he would only get angry. Plan A had just failed.

She pulled back her bedcovers and lay on the cool sheets. Gently, she stroked herself, thinking of Jacob and his annoyingly virtuous cock. She could easily imagine him entering her. She pushed one finger into herself but that spoilt the fantasy because her fingers were too slim. Then she thought of plan B and cheered up immediately.

She walked over to her wardrobe, trying to remember where she had put Valiant-The-Vibrator. She was glad she had invested a fortune and bought the large size with the rotating end and the clitoral tickler. The vibrator was perfect for her, and sometimes she thought God had got it wrong when he made man, by forgetting to attach a tickler.

She returned to her bed and, lying down, switched on her vibrator. With the bathroom light on, Jacob would be able to see everything should he ever wake up from boring snore zone.

With the end of the vibrator nudging at the entrance of her plump slit, she slowly pushed it into herself, enjoying the stretching sensation. Closing her eyes, she moved her hips until her body undulated with pleasure.

'Angie,' said Jacob groggily, 'do you have to make so much noise?'

'Sorry, did I wake you?' she asked, delighted that he had finally surfaced from the land of sleep. She took out the vibrator but left the end just inside herself, enjoying the rotating sensation.

'Go to bed. It's late,' he muttered. 'Tahillia wants me on the breakfast shift tomorrow.'

Well, I want you on the slave shift now, she thought. 'I am in bed,' she said cheerfully, spreading her legs further, inserting the vibrator again, and turning up the speed dial so that it hummed.

The sensation was scintillating and now she had an audience. She closed her eyes, fantasising that she had Jacob's erect cock inside her and his fingers skilfully flicking over her clitoris.

'What are you doing?' Jacob asked. She heard the bed creak as he sat up.

'Masturbating. Would you like to watch?'

'What! No way!' Angie looked over and noticed Jacob had lain down again, his face to the ceiling, his hands clasped over his eyes.

Oh well, plan B had just failed, but she was enjoying herself so much that she no longer cared. Jacob could die a stuffy virgin and it would serve him right. She slid the vibrator in and out, in and out. The first tremor of excitement spread throughout her. Clenching her vaginal muscles, she arched her back, moaning softly.

'Angie,' said Jacob.

'Mmm?' was the best she could manage.

'Do girls really do that? I mean, um . . . I thought just guys, you know.'

What a time to ask her such a stupid question, she thought. Still, he was showing interest, and he well and truly deserved to be tortured after what he had put her through tonight. She lowered the speed dial.

'Come over and watch,' she said huskily. 'See what girls like to do.'

She heard a ripping sound, and when she looked over, she noticed he had draped himself in his bedsheet. He walked over and sat at the end of her bed, looking like an unfinished sculpture. By the time she had him tonight, she would have chiselled that sheet away.

'I think it's only fair that you watch me, seeing as I enjoyed watching you on the beach.'

'Watched! You jumped me when I wasn't looking.'

'Well, I will allow you to return the favour. I wouldn't like you to think I am unfair.'

'You know that wasn't what I meant,' he protested.

'Oh, shut up. I'm busy here.' She spread her legs, knowing the light from the bathroom highlighted her vulva. 'See this here,' she said, removing her vibrator. She stroked the little ridge of her clitoris. 'This is my most sensitive part, and I would love you to lick up and down it with your tongue. But even better is if you roll the stud with your tongue. That just about pushes me over the edge.' She looked him in the eye. 'You would like to see that, wouldn't you? Have you ever made a woman come?'

'No,' he croaked.

'Rubbing that erect knob of your penis that you are hiding under the sheet would be wonderful. Sliding it over and over where I'm putting my fingers would make me cry out for you. Imagine me crying out your name, wanting you inside me.'

She noticed Jacob pulled the sheet tighter around himself, but that did not bother her as she stroked herself. Jacob could not take his eyes from what she was doing. It was about time he attended the Angie-School-For-Reluctant-Hard-ons. She was determined to break his will power and this was the way to do it. It had not taken much to convince him to come over. Perhaps she had been able to affect his dreams, after all.

She rocked her hips back and forward, pinching her breasts. Arching her back, she stretched her feet out until they were touching Jacob. 'Move a little closer,' she murmured. 'You don't have to touch me. I like you watching. In my fantasies I think about you entering me just as I come.'

'I had a dream about you too,' he said softly. 'I did so many things to you.'

She patted the bed. 'Sit between my legs and tell me.'

'I can't tell you. The things I did . . .' He brushed his hand through his curls.

'Well, if you don't want to tell me, at least come closer and be useful,' she said, determined to make him tell her later when she was in the mood to enjoy his embarrassment. But right now she needed him for another purpose. Talking could wait. He did as she asked without further protest, and Angie knew she was getting somewhere. His eyes were fixed on her sex as she moaned softly and increased her rhythm. She reached down and parted her lips so that the crimson inside beckoned invitingly to him.

'Suck my nipples,' she ordered.

'You said I didn't have to do anything,' he protested.

'I said you don't have to touch me and I didn't ask you to use your hands. Just flick your tongue over them. I bet you would like to know how a woman's breasts feel. Mine are quite firm.' She turned up the speed dial of the tickler on her vibrator then began pushing the vibrator in and out, in and out, while she stroked her breasts with her free hand. Jacob's mouth dropped open as he gazed upon her writhing body.

'Oh God, Angie, you keep pushing me,' he moaned, his voice hoarse. He fumbled under the sheet, but when his hand got caught in the folds, he ripped the sheet away. His cock was engorged, and Angie couldn't understand how he had the will power to resist her.

'In my fantasy, I think about you entering me, like this vibrator is doing,' she said softly so that he had to bend over to hear what she was saying. 'I dream about you stretching me apart,' she said, pulling the whole length of the vibrator out then plunging it in again. 'You want to be inside me.'

'Oh God, Angie, you are a teasing bitch.' He stroked himself, seeking release, but Angie was not going to let him get off that easily. He seemed so excited that it would be all over in a few minutes and that would never do. It was time to occupy him so that he couldn't satisfy himself.

'You know instinctively what I like. You know I like my nipples licked over the sensitive peaks. Come closer, Jacob, and lick my nipples,' she said again. Mesmerised, he sat between her legs, stroking the length of his shaft, seeming not to hear her.

'Jacob, if you don't do what I say, then you will have to go back to your bed and spend a lonely night with your erection.'

His head jerked up in response to her sharp tone. She could see him deliberating between his urgent desire to watch her and please himself, or to lick her nipples.

'Now,' she ordered. 'Come here and kneel by the bed and take your hand off yourself.'

'You are so damned bossy,' he growled, and Angie tingled with anticipation. It was so difficult to make him angry. He walked round and knelt by the side of the bed. Tentatively he licked one nipple and then the other. 'Yes Jacob, yes. Don't stop doing that. Now suck them,' she ordered. 'Take the whole nipple in your mouth and tickle it with your tongue.'

Jacob stopped sucking and looked up at her face. 'Was I doing it right?'

'Just shut up and keep sucking.' The first tremors built up inside her and she arched her back. It was a wonderful feeling having him do her bidding at last. He had a constant erection just biding its time before he filled her.

'Jacob, push the vibrator in and out of me,' she gasped, so close to coming that she could barely speak.

He stopped sucking her nipples and gingerly held the vibrator. He lifted it up and examined it, watching the rotating head and furious vibrating tickler. 'This is awesome,' he said.

'And men think diamonds are a girl's best friend,' said Angie, coming down slightly from her orgasmic plateau. 'Huh!' she grunted. 'What do men know?' She reached over and grabbed Jacob's hand. 'Do you know why I like my vibrator so much?' she asked, her voice soft and teasing.

'No.' He shook his head, his eyes wide. 'I mean yes. I . . . um . . . I have never touched one before.'

She reached down and took his penis in her hand, stroking it up and down. 'Mmm, you are very hard.' She ran her fingers up and down over his penis, noticing for the first time that he did not stop her. 'The vibrator never runs out until the batteries are drained. Do you think you could keep going like that? Would you like to satisfy me? I would be very patient with you.'

He nodded, and from his husky cough she suspected his throat had gone dry. A thrill of excitement filled her. He was finally hers.

'Good, but I want you to use the vibrator first,' she ordered. 'It is time you learnt how to please a woman.'

He pushed the vibrator into her so gently that Angie, driven by lust, wanted to grab him by his soft curls and force him to fuck her. Only the thought of the erotic torment he must be feeling at this point stopped her. Let him and his rock-hard erection suffer. He deserved it for being so disgustingly innocent. She had never met another man like him.

'Slide it in harder,' she ordered. 'You won't hurt me. Watch my rhythm and match it.'

'Like this?' he asked.

But his question went unanswered because he was doing it right. Angie lay back on the bed, her eyes closed, as she let the rhythm build within her. She had held back her orgasm, but it had been worth it to teach Jacob what to do. She pinched her own nipples as her body undulated like a wave, returning again and again to the shoreline.

With her eyes closed, she could feel Jacob caressing her thighs. His hands were like velvet on her delicate skin. Small tremors started again inside her and just the thought that Jacob was waiting his turn to claim her, his penis hard and willing, sent her over the edge.

Soon she was groaning, her back arched, her hips rising, offering her sex to Jacob. High after high hit her until she lay gasping and helpless.

As if sensing it was now his turn, Jacob withdrew the vibrator and tossed it aside. He lay beside Angie, kissing her and taking her in his arms.

Angie relaxed. All of her aches and pains from being on her feet had vanished. All she could feel was the woozy sleepy feeling of the truly satisfied. Already she could feel herself drifting. Vaguely, through her sleep, she could hear Jacob calling her name.

'Angie,' Jacob said softly, stroking her hair from her face. 'Angie, I want you. I dreamt about you tonight. I can't get you out of my mind. Angie, please wake up. I have to have you.'

She could hear the urgency in his voice, and she smiled a sleepy satisfied smile. She turned her back and pulled the sheet over her. 'Get some sleep, Jacob,' she murmured. 'I wouldn't want you to think I used you.'

Jacob lay alongside her, his penis pressed into her back, hard and ready. Gently, he stroked her breasts before cautiously moving down to her sex. 'Please, Angie. Wake up.'

But she was tired after a hard day, and the vibrator had done its job. Besides, Jacob had tormented her enough this evening. Fancy hiding such a wonderful erection under a sheet. 'Good night, Jacob,' she murmured.

In the distance she could hear Valiant-The-Vibrator humming a moonlight melody, and she drifted into a satisfied sleep.

Angie woke. The sun streamed into her bedroom and she stretched, enjoying the thought of a new day on the island. She felt beside her but Jacob was no longer there, which was a pity. She certainly could have used his erection now. She liked morning sex. Fast and frenzied was what she felt like at the moment. Oh well, Jacob would have to keep his virginity one more day. Anyway, there was always Valiant-The-Vibrator.

She sat up and looked around the bedroom. Jacob's bed was perfectly made without a wrinkle in place. Angie wrinkled her nose at Jacob's anal-retentive tidiness. The clothes that she had dropped around his bed the night before were no longer there. Usually when she stripped off, she kicked her clothes into a pile on the floor and only gathered them up when she needed to wash them, but the floor was bare.

Jacob had obviously gone into a state of virginal frustrated neatness before he started his morning shift. She walked over to her wardrobe and pulled open the door. The pile of clothes she had thrown in there was arranged beautifully. Hers on one side and Jacob's on the other. Angie began to worry.

Prickles of suspicion crept up her back. Something was wrong. It wasn't that she minded Jacob being a slave and cleaning up the bedroom – though she would have preferred to be wearing a black corset and sharp high heels while he tidied up in front of her.

Her stomach turned over as she flicked through the clothes, turning them over and over in her search. In a frenzy, she pulled all of Jacob's clothes from the cupboard. She searched under the beds. Nothing!

Flicking her hair from her face, she marched into the bathroom and pulled open the vanity cabinet. Empty! The worst had happened. Jacob had finally got the guts up to revenge her treatment of him. Valiant-The-Vibrator was missing!

Chapter Seven

'*D*on't you realise that a girl without a vibrator is like a man without hands?' said Angie furiously.

Jacob grinned at her. 'Shark boat,' he said enigmatically. Dressed in the island uniform of floral shirt and smart khaki cargo pants, he looked fresh, young and disgustingly neat. He stood at the entrance of the hotel veranda greeting guests and showing them to their tables for breakfast.

'What are you talking about?' hissed Angie.

'Just a moment,' said Jacob to Angie as Nick and Ellie Holt approached. 'Good morning, Mr and Mrs Holt. Would you like a table for two?'

'I want a table overlooking the lagoon,' said Ellie Holt abruptly, stopping momentarily to glare at Angie. 'A good view is about all I'm going to get this holiday.'

Angie murmured good morning to the Holts and watched impatiently as Jacob showed them to a table. Nick Holt turned and winked and Angie smiled.

Jacob returned, his eyes alight with amusement.

'What are you talking about? What is a shark boat?' she asked, irritated that Jacob had got the better of her.

'You would know if you bothered to get up early and

124

find out how this hotel runs.' Jacob looked at his watch. 'The shark boat goes out past the reef every morning. It gets rid of the kitchen scraps and other useless items.' He waggled ten fingers in her face and chuckled. 'The boat will be leaving in about ten minutes from the jetty,' he said, looking at his watch. 'I think you will find what you are looking for in the garbage skip.'

'Oh no! You couldn't have.' Anxiously, Angie bit her fingernail.

Jacob raised his eyebrows. 'I think I got about two hours' sleep last night, lying next to you.' There was a look of hunger in his eyes that made her think of last night. He was ripe, just for the picking. She recalled the way his muscles had definition even in his sleep, and how she had enjoyed stroking him. A warm feeling stirred in her loins.

Maybe she should have had sex with him last night, to get him out of her system. He was incredibly attractive, and she wondered why she had not noticed him earlier in class. She made a silent vow to seduce him and forget him, but right now she was on a mission to save Valiant-The-Vibrator from the sharks.

'I can't believe you took my vibrator. It cost me a fortune. I had to save for three months on my student's allowance.'

Jacob laughed and folded his arms in a distinctly masculine way. 'Next time you'll invest in the real thing,' he said pleasantly.

'You wish,' said Angie crossly. 'It had better be there.'

'Good luck.' Jacob grinned. 'The men that run the boat might help you search. They're great guys.'

Jacob was so pleasant she wanted to torture him then and there by stripping off in front of him and dancing naked on the breakfast tables. That would throw a spanner in his mild-mannered breakfast supervision. But she saw Tahillia Ash approaching and decided to make a hasty exit. Tahillia could well put her on an extra shift, and Angie had other more exciting plans for her day off.

Wearing nothing but a strategically tied sarong, Angie made her way along the lagoon and walked up the jetty. A barge was moored, its engine running. Angie sniffed, the smell of diesel fuel and over-ripe food greeted her nostrils. One fit, tanned man was unravelling the port rope that docked the barge.

'Hi,' called Angie. 'Mind if I come aboard?'

The man looked up at her, his muscles straining as he pulled on the rope that held the barge in place. His body was finely tuned like an athlete, and although it was still early he was slick with sweat. Angie quivered with pleasure, realising that she might find more than Valiant-The-Vibrator on the barge.

'Hey, Cole,' called the man, 'there's a babe that wants to come aboard. That OK with you?'

An enormous, blond-haired man stepped out of the cabin. 'Do you get sea sick?' he called. 'We are going out past the reef.'

'No,' replied Angie looking at both men, who wore nothing but rough shorts, workman's boots and traces of dirt. A delicious tingle raced up her spine.

How right Jacob was, she thought enthusiastically. Getting up early to explore how the hotel worked was a good idea, after all. A most thorough search of the barge and its occupants was necessary, she decided, to solve the problem of Valiant-The-Vibrator's abduction.

'Come on, then,' Cole nodded. 'Give her a hand, Rod. We don't want guests in the water.'

The dark-haired man named Rod frowned, then reached over to help her on board. His hand was rough with calluses, and there was an oil smear across his broad chest. Angie stepped off the jetty and on to the boat, savouring the well-developed muscles of Rod's tanned body.

The boat bumped against the jetty and she raised her

126

hand to Rod's chest to steady herself. His mulberry-coloured nipple tightened under her palm, but the heat of his skin did not match the expression in his eyes. Instead, when she looked at his face she saw an ambivalence that confused her. He glared at her with piercing green eyes, and removed her hand without saying a word.

Still, his silent rebuff did nothing to subdue Angie's spirit. Here she was with two men, and the freedom of the open sea. Things were looking up. The dawning of a new day had definitely brought possibilities.

She watched Rod cast off, and the engine roared as they left the jetty. He had black hair cropped to a number one, and his green eyes were fringed with thick dark lashes. His face was fine-boned, almost feminine, but there was nothing remotely feminine about his body. She leant against the cabin gazing at him, enjoying the movement of his hard workman's physique. She could see sweat dripping off him as he worked coiling the ropes.

He walked over to her, his eyes narrowed, and Angie smiled, but Rod did not return her smile. 'So, what brings you out here?' He had a broad Australian accent, barely moving his top lip when he spoke. 'Tourists don't usually do the shark run.'

'I'm not a tourist. I'm doing work experience.' Angie studied him. He was a good-looking guy but his manner was reserved. She could not tell whether he was uncomfortable in a woman's presence, like other Australian men she had met, or gay.

'A trainee.' He nodded, looking her up and down. 'I met the other one. Jacob's a good bloke.' There was warmth in Rod's eyes at the mention of Jacob that gave Angie a sinking feeling. She was filled with a sense of foreboding that she had just entered a male-only zone. 'You haven't answered my question,' said Rod. 'Why are you here?'

'I have lost something. I was told it was on the boat.'

'There ain't nothing here but the garbage from the kitchen.' He motioned past the cabin to the end of the barge at an open skip full of food scraps. He shrugged. 'Help yourself. What you don't want, the sharks will have.'

Gay, thought Angie, her spirits sinking. He has to be gay. Trust Jacob to think they were friendly. She made her way to the back of the boat and leant over the garbage skip, hoping to locate her vibrator. Her heart sank when she realised she had no chance of locating Valiant among the multitude of dinner scraps. She did not think Rod would oblige if she asked him to search the garbage for her. She pressed her lips together in a grimace. 'Bye-bye, Valiant,' said Angie sadly. No wonder Jacob had looked smug. Maybe he knew he was sending her out on a boat with two gay guys and a lost vibrator.

'Hey, Angie,' called the blond-haired man. 'Come up. Have a chat.'

Angie made her way to the cabin, grabbed hold of the handrail and pulled herself up the narrow steps. The acrid tinge of male sweat and sea salt made her wrinkle her nose appreciatively. She liked a man to smell like a man. Flowery and sweet colognes did nothing for her.

'G'day,' the man said. 'The name's Cole.'

Cole's hair was bleached white from the hot Queensland sun. He could not be more than 30, guessed Angie, but crowsfeet already lined his sun-weathered face. His gold-tanned skin was speckled with freckles across his shoulders.

'My mate tells me you lost something.'

His gaze was inquisitive but not lewd, and Angie felt a glow start in the core of her and work its way throughout her body. The cabin was cramped and Cole was a giant of a man. Angie assessed him carefully for potential. He was friendlier than his mate, but chameleon that she was, Angie realised a more subtle approach was needed to snare her fish on this voyage. Brazen women put off some men.

She hoped her initial impression that the men were gay was wrong. If she played her cards carefully this adventure could be fun. She brushed her hair slowly from her face, studying Cole. There was one way of finding out if this was going to be a boring trip out past the reef. Angie hated boredom. 'Jacob hid my vibrator,' she said, looking him straight in the eye.

Cole laughed and slapped his thigh. He was not traditionally handsome, but she liked the way his blue eyes lit up when he was amused. 'So that's what he threw in the skip. Came and introduced himself to us at the crack of dawn. The office types don't usually bother. Wants to go scuba diving with Rod. Got the hots for you, has he?'

Her gaze roved over his huge, tanned chest and down to his shorts. In his sitting position, Angie could clearly see the enormity of him. Her breath caught in her throat. His sex outlined by his shorts snaked horizontally past his hip and around. A thrill of excitement set her body alight. Tingling with pleasure, she wondered whether something like that would fit in her mouth or anywhere else.

'I'm sharing a room with Jacob,' Angie explained. 'He thinks deprivation will make me interested in him. Personally, I hope Jacob gets speared,' said Angie, looking out of the cockpit at Rod. 'And not with a spear gun,' she murmured thoughtfully. Maybe she should arrange an interesting surprise for Jacob if Rod would oblige. Hiding a girl's vibrator was a serious offence, and she was not going to let Jacob get away with it.

'Annoyed you that much, did he? Call me a simple bloke,' said Cole, 'but I don't think a man should resort to tricks to win a woman.' He shook his head. 'Funny, that Jacob didn't come across as a dishonest bloke, but you can never tell.'

Angie sighed and looked at him under her lashes. 'He just never leaves me alone, but what can you expect when a man is only twenty. I was glad to come out here to get away from him. It's not that I don't like the opposite sex, mind you.' She smiled prettily at Cole. 'I like a man who knows how to look after a woman. Jacob is too young for me.'

Cole reached out and put his enormous hand on her shoulder, and her nipples tightened appreciatively at the warmth in his touch. She could easily imagine those large hands playing with her breasts while Rod looked on. Would Rod be jealous, she wondered? Would he want to join in?

'Never mind,' said Cole. 'Doesn't surprise me that men would go after a gorgeous bird like you. Some blokes don't know when they are not wanted. Want me to have a word with Jacob for you?'

'Oh no,' said Angie quickly. 'I'm a modern woman. I can look after myself.'

Cole laughed again. 'Don't get too modern on me. I like to look after a woman.'

Angie returned his smile. 'That sounds nice.' She leant against the side of the cabin, enjoying the vibrations of the engine while she thought about seducing Cole. He seemed a slow, taciturn type of man, and she knew she had to play the game carefully.

Cole steered the boat through the lagoon, and out into the deeper water. He made an average-sized man look like a pygmy by comparison. His thighs had the thickness of tree trunks, and her fingers itched to uncover what lay between.

Years of hunting had taught her that the size of a man's penis could not be reliably assumed from the size of his nose or fingers. But height was reliable, and Cole was the largest man she had ever seen.

130

The colour of the sea had turned to deep blue but in places she could still see large heads of coral just beneath the surface. Cole slowed the boat and turned to her. 'You're lucky the sea's flat today. You like watching sharks?'

'I have only seen them in the aquarium,' said Angie. 'They are very efficient hunters,' she said with admiration. 'They take what they want and have no fear. I like that about them.'

Cole nodded. He cut the engine. 'Come and watch. You'll enjoy this.' He stooped to leave the cabin and walked to the back of the boat.

Angie followed him. Already she could feel her sex swelling with desire. She was nearly six foot but Cole was a good head taller, and more than double the thickness of her body.

'Only man is a better hunter,' he said, before he went to help Rod tip the skip into the ocean.

'You forgot about woman,' Angie murmured, raising an eyebrow as she watched the two men. 'Women are good hunters, too. Better than men, because what they lack in strength, they make up in cunning.'

Her body tingled as she watched them work. The men angled themselves like weight lifters, in order to tip the food scraps from the skip into the ocean. Rod glanced at her, his look unfriendly, but that did not stop Angie admiring the sculpted muscles of his torso and legs. She wanted to tease him by making him watch as she seduced his partner. Would he be able to remain aloof while he watched?

'Come on mate, lift,' said Cole, levering the skip so that the food waste tipped into the sea.

Soon the water was churning with sharks, rolling and fighting over the food scraps. Small colourful fish darted and leapt into the air in their effort to gain a share of the food. In what seemed like seconds there was little waste left, but something caught her attention. Valiant-The-Vibrator lay floating on the surface.

'Quick, Cole,' said Angie. 'Have you got a net?' But before the words had left her mouth a great grey shark, its mouth full of jagged teeth, swallowed Valiant-The-Vibrator, and vanished below the surface of the sea.

'Sorry, Angie,' said Cole, holding a small scoop-net. 'I was too slow.'

He may be, thought Angie, but she certainly wasn't. 'Oh dear, I'm going to miss my vibrator,' she said sadly. She let her gaze drop from his face, to his shoulders, then below to his shorts and stay there momentarily. Angie had never seen anything like it before, and she had to drag her gaze away as its owner approached.

Cole walked over to her. He was breathing heavily from his exertion. 'I don't know much about women, but I don't hold with those electrical gadgets.'

'Well, I shall certainly miss it,' Angie said despondently. She looked at his shorts again before forcing herself to meet his gaze. The man was thick, and she was not just talking about his brain.

'I would like to make it up to you.' He gazed at her. 'You are a beautiful woman.' He shook his head sadly. 'I'm a big man,' he said with some embarrassment.

His reluctant description of himself got Angie's attention immediately, and though her whole body tingled with anticipation she knew instinctively that she had to slow her pace with this man. 'What do you mean?' she asked, with mock innocence.

Cole breathed a great sigh. 'It has been a long time since I have had a woman. Most women can't cope with me. I am larger than the average bloke.' His face fell, his expression filled with remorse. 'I don't mean to, but I scare women.'

A shiver spread throughout Angie's body, but not of fear. She could not stop looking at his shorts. His hardening sex strained at the fabric. 'So I see,' she said with awe.

'I'm sorry, Angie. I don't want to hurt you.' Cole lumbered past her and back to the cabin. Angie caught Rod's hard gaze, but he said nothing. Normally she might have tackled him on his attitude, but she raced after Cole, unable to think of anything else but joining the twelve-inch club. Her blood thumped through her body with the excitement of her discovery. She certainly enjoyed a big cock, but she had never seen one longer than a ruler.

She followed Cole into the cabin. He started the engine and turned the barge in the direction of the lagoon.

'You know, Cole,' Angie said, not wanting to miss out on a once-in-a-lifetime opportunity, 'I'm sure you wouldn't scare me. I mean, that is if you would like to ... you know ...'

She let the offer hang in the air, sensing Cole's reticence about the magnificent size of his sex.

Cole glanced at Angie and tightened his lips. 'You think you would like me. Other women have thought that too. But I end up putting them off. I'm a monster.'

The blood swirled through Angie's head, and she almost fainted at Cole's extraordinary description of himself. She took in a deep breath to steady herself. The man was reluctant and she needed to think clearly. She had met reluctance in her life. After all, Jacob was a walking model of virginal reluctance, but this was different, and she was momentarily confused about how to handle the situation. She had never met a man who apologised for his large size. Once she had hunted a gym instructor who apologised when she finally discovered he had a three-inch weenie, but she had bolted immediately in horror.

It was time for gentle persuasion. 'You know, maybe you should let me decide on whether I can cope with you.' She moved closer, massaging Cole's shoulders while he sat steering the barge.

Cole groaned as she touched him. 'That's so good,' he said. 'My shoulders are stiff.'

Who cares about your shoulders, thought Angie. Peering over him at his shorts, she had to stop herself from digging her fingernails into his back. When it came to men, Angie knew her statistics. There were only a thousand men in the world that had a cock bigger than twelve inches. Why did she have to find the modest one?

Her brow knitted in a frown as she concentrated on massaging away his reluctance.

'That feels great,' said Cole as he stretched.

Encouraged, Angie worked her way down, her fingers trembling with excitement. Her hands seemed tiny against the firm expanse of his back. She moved around to his side and ran her fingers gently over his chest. His chest was hairless and his nipples stiffened when she teased them with her fingers. Angie longed to climb on to his knee and lick them, but she had to remind herself to keep a slow pace. 'Does that feel good too?' she purred.

Glancing at her, he nodded before shifting in his seat. He seemed to be concentrating on the sea in front of him, but his eyes were glazed. When Angie looked at his shorts, she wondered how many litres of blood it took to fuel his sex. Slowly, she traced the palm of her hand over the ripple of each of his well-defined stomach muscles. He made no move to stop her exploration.

She hoped she did not seem too eager to have him, unable to bear the disappointment if he stopped her sensuous exploration. Her nipples were swollen and rubbing against the gauzy fabric of her sarong. What would he do if she undid the top and let the fabric drop to her waist? Well, it was time to find out, she decided. Holding back was not in her true nature, and she had been restrained for long enough. She reached around to her back and untied the knotted fabric. 'I thought you might like to touch me too,' she said seductively.

'Oh God,' he said, when he saw Angie tease her nipples with her index finger and thumb. 'You are the sexiest woman I have ever seen. The problem is –' He shifted uncomfortably again in his seat '– it just won't fit!'

He pulled the throttle and the barge increased in speed. To her dismay, Angie could see the lagoon in the distance and she realised she would have to get him to cut the engine to allow her the time she needed to seduce him.

'Why don't you let me be the judge of whether or not you will fit?' She shrugged her shoulders. 'I mean, if you are too big, there are other things we can do for our mutual satisfaction.' She looked him straight in the eye and undid the second knot on her sarong. The fabric floated to the floor and she stood before him, totally naked.

'Oh my God,' he croaked, 'it's been so long.' His gaze dropped to her shaven sex and the barge started turning in circles.

She reached out and boldly stroked him over the fabric of his shorts. He was thick and a wave of dizziness overcame her when she realised she was having trouble finding the end. She looked at him, her mouth open in amazement.

Cole put his hand over hers. 'I'll steer us into a reef if you keep doing that.'

So what? thought Angie. At this particular point in time, she could not have cared less. She wanted him. 'Then stop the boat,' she ordered. Her excitement overwhelmed her and she could no longer slow her pace. She was determined to have every inch of him.

Cole shook his head. 'It's pointless,' he said.

The hunter reared in Angie. This big game was not

135

going to escape. It was time to take control. With determination, she reached over and turned the ignition key to off, then pulled it out.

'Hey,' said Cole, 'what are you doing?'

'If you want this back, you will have to come and get it.' She walked out of the cabin and around to the front of the barge. Pulling herself up to a sitting position on the railing, she opened her legs.

Through the cabin window that separated her from Cole, she could see him lean forward to stare at her, his sea-blue eyes wide with surprise. She held up the key and rubbed it over her sex. 'Come and get the key,' she called.

Cole climbed down from the cabin and walked towards her.

'OK,' she said, 'stop there.'

Cole's eyes bulged. 'What's going on?'

'Take off your shorts.'

He started to walk over to her, closing the gap between them, but she held the key over the water. 'Come any closer and I will drop the key. I'm tired of your modesty. Take the shorts off now.'

'Are you crazy? If the barge hits coral, we will sink. There are coral heads all over this area.'

'Then you had better do as I tell you. You have teased me enough. I am not prepared to wait any longer.'

'I've told you. I won't fit,' he said stubbornly. He stared at her. 'Maybe you'll believe me when you see for yourself.' Slowly his thumbs hooked over the elastic of his shorts. Angie stopped breathing.

Cole peeled off his shorts, kicking them away with his foot. Angie gasped and nearly toppled backward over the railing. The man had a cock like an elephant's trunk. It was not quite erect, but stood out thickly from his nest of pubic hair, then arced downward. The thick head of his penis bulged at the end.

'You are amazing,' she said, unable to take her eyes

off him. For the first time, she believed him. Perhaps he would not fit – but nothing would stop her trying.

There was a sound of footsteps, and Rod came to the front of the boat. 'Why have we stopped?'

Cole turned to Rod. 'She's threatening to throw the key in the water unless I do what she says.'

Rod barely glanced in Angie's direction, but she noticed he also was unable to take his eyes off Cole's magnificent sex. So she was right about Rod, she thought. He was gay.

'Rod, I want you to stroke Cole's cock.'

'What?' exclaimed Cole.

'Do as I say or you can both swim to shore. I hope no sharks have followed the boat.'

'Jeez, mate,' said Cole, turning to Rod, 'I don't know what to do.'

Angie noticed that despite Cole's confusion, his cock was still growing. Her nipples tingled with pleasure, and she loved the feel of the breeze on her bare sex. She wanted Cole to take her against the railings.

'I think we should do what she says. It's a long swim,' said Rod, not taking his eyes off Cole for a moment. His tone was eager. Angie observed him, suspecting Rod had waited a long time for this day to arrive.

'I'm no poofter,' said Cole stubbornly to Angie. 'If I had known what you were about, I would never have let you on this boat.'

'But I am here now.' She stared at him boldly, then reached down and began to stroke herself. 'I am going to have you.' Her fingers were slippery with her juices, and she could not stop thinking about how it would feel to have such a big man sliding inside her. 'I want to watch Rod caress you. I want to watch your cock grow. Then I am going to let you fill me.'

Cole shook his head from side to side but Angie was only interested in the opinion of the part of his anatomy that agreed with her.

She caught Rod's eye, and the expression on his face had changed from dour to one of delight. There was no doubt in her mind that she had found the key that sparked Rod's engine. Now it was time to break Cole's resistance.

She imagined fitting the bulbous head of Cole's sex inside herself, inch by pleasurable inch. The thrill of seeing him naked before her made her head swim with desire.

She spread her legs further, giving Cole full view of her. 'You can watch me while Rod pleasures you. You can pretend it is me stroking you,' she said seductively. 'I know you like the idea. You can't hide anything from me.'

She watched as Cole's heavy sex continued to swell, but it was still unable to defy gravity. He was enough for two people to enjoy, and she knew from the gleam in Rod's eye that Rod thought so too.

In the corner of her vision several small fish leapt in the air, near the stern of the boat. She looked over into the water to see what has caused the commotion. 'There's a shark circling the barge. It must have followed us in.' It was time for Cole to choose between the hunter above or the hunter below. 'The shark or me. Which is it going to be?'

Cole was breathing heavily. Frowning, he placed his hands on his hips.

Angie knew it was not a difficult decision to make, but she decided to give Cole a little more time. She wet her lips with the tip of her tongue waiting for his answer. She turned to Rod. 'While we are waiting for Cole to make up his mind, I want you to drop anchor. We are going to be here for some time.'

Rod obeyed her immediately. She could see from the bulge in his pants that he was finding this as exciting as she was. There was only Cole to conquer.

'You told me it has been a long time since you have

had a woman.' She raised her eyebrows. 'Imagine how good it would feel if you let both of us enjoy you,' she said seductively. 'I'd like to have you while Rod licks your balls. You would like that, wouldn't you? Imagine both of us giving you pleasure.'

Cole began to stroke his massive cock. 'I have never let a bloke touch me. But if you want sex, then go ahead.'

'It would be more exciting having both of us. I would never tell. Is that all you are afraid of?'

He nodded. 'Rod's a great bloke but I wouldn't want my mates to find out.'

'No-one would know, except you, Rod and me. It would be our secret. I'd like to see Rod pleasuring you.'

Cole shook his head stubbornly. 'I don't want to turn into a poof.'

'Oh, you wouldn't be,' she said smoothly. 'Being with a man once doesn't make you gay. You would just be enjoying both of us.'

She watched as he nodded, clearly thinking about what she had said to him. The idea must have had some appeal because he continued stroking his cock. The heavy end was swollen and starting to tilt upward.

'Anyway,' she said, dangling the ignition key in front of him, 'you could always blame me. I am making you do this.'

The expression on his face lightened. 'Yes.' He nodded in agreement. 'I could blame it on you.'

Angie restrained a grin, glad that Cole was as thick as his sex.

'I've got bad news,' said Rod, returning from the bow of the boat. 'Angie is right about the shark. I've dropped anchor, but we are floating above a coral head. When the tide drops, we will hit it. Best do what Angie says.' Rod gave her a wink, and she bit her lip to stop herself laughing at his change in demeanour.

'Rod, I want you to lick along Cole's shaft while I

139

watch. Then when he is excited enough I am going to join in.' She did not want to miss the thrill of watching Cole grow erect. It was important to get him to the point of no return, and then both she and Rod could enjoy him.

Cole still looked uncertain, but his sex was larger than ever. Angie gazed at his cock in amazement. She could understand why he scared women off but she was not afraid. At this moment, she cared for nothing but the frenzy of the hunt.

'Remember, this is all my fault,' she said to Cole, her voice smooth and hypnotic. 'I am going to make you a happy man.'

She turned to Rod. 'Take off your shorts. It isn't fair that we're both naked and you're not.'

Angie watched as Rod rapidly stripped, flinging away his shorts. Standing next to Cole, his cock seemed tiny, and reminded her of the tickler on Valiant-The-Vibrator. But she was not remotely worried about his size because together, she knew, they would make a wonderful replacement for her vibrator.

'Drop to your knees,' she ordered, nodding at Rod. 'Lick along Cole's shaft.'

Cole looked at Rod and he nodded. 'Best do as she says, mate. I don't fancy being shark food.'

'Look into my eyes while he licks you,' she ordered Cole. 'Imagine it is my tongue stroking you up and down your shaft.'

A soft moan left his lips when Rod eagerly circled the enormous knob of Cole's penis with his tongue. Holding Cole's sex with two hands, Rod ran his tongue up and down the most sensitive skin under Cole's shaft.

Cole closed his eyes, rocking on his feet, his face a picture of pleasure.

Hungrily, Rod attempted to stuff the thick end of Cole's sex into his mouth.

'Look into my eyes,' said Angie. 'Keep your eyes open.

He is making you ready for me. I want to see what you feel. I want to see you enjoying every movement of Rod's mouth.'

Cole obeyed her but he moaned softly as he struggled not to break her stare. He cupped his balls in his big hand, watching as Angie stroked herself. Rod sucked him with the enthusiasm of a starved man. Just managing to fit the end into his mouth, Rod took hold of Cole's shaft with both hands and stroked him until he was hard.

When Cole started to rock on his feet, Angie wondered if the blood had totally drained from his brain. She gazed at Cole's sex. He was longer than her forearm, and as thick as where her forearm joined her elbow. She stroked herself in a fever and when the first waves of pleasure erupted, she knew she could wait no longer.

'I want you,' she said excitedly. 'I want you to shove your big cock inside me.'

Rod pulled back and Cole's cock left Rod's mouth with a soft plopping sound. When Cole walked towards her, Angie noticed that even fully erect, his cock rose no further than the horizon. It was so damn big.

'You won't like it. You won't be able to take me.'

'Shut up. Do as I say,' she ordered. She took hold of his cock, which was wet and hot from Rod's mouth and placed it at the entrance of her sex. She could feel it nudging her, threatening to stretch her wide.

'Hold me around the waist,' she said, realising that she was balanced precariously on the barge's rails. She needed to use her hands to guide him into her. Her sex muscles tensed with excitement. She needed him to split her, to fill her completely.

'Lift me on to you,' she ordered. Cole picked her up as if she were a light toy, and held her over his swollen cock. Slowly he lowered her on to himself. Heated with desire, she let the large knob stretch her until she thought she could take no more. But she was wet and slippery, and when she looked down she could see her plump bare lips surround him. 'Yes, yes,' she cried in pleasure.

She was vaguely conscious of the roughness of his hands as he held her bottom. Her fingernails dug into his shoulders. She looked him in the eye. 'Fill me,' she ordered. 'I want as much of you as I can take.'

Inflamed with lust, she gripped her legs around his hips, rocking her pelvis and savouring the sensation of his sex entering her. She moaned in pleasure, closing her eyes. With every movement of her hips, she allowed a little more of him to enter her until her love muscles resisted no longer.

Intoxicated with the opiate of pre-orgasm tremors, she ground down on him. She opened her eyes and looked down. Only the head of his penis and a third of the shaft could fit. She soon saw that she was not the only one enjoying Cole. Rod knelt underneath her, licking Cole's balls.

Angie's face contorted in pleasure. Knowing Rod was nibbling at Cole's large sac while she rode him was sending her over the edge.

'Am I hurting you?' asked Cole, his face concerned.

'No.' She shook her head. 'This is fantastic. I'll remember this moment for the rest of my life,' she gasped. 'I never thought I'd live this dream.'

'Good,' he said. He gripped her tightly and began to thrust into her. 'That feels so good. Rod, you and me. Oh God.'

Tears of pleasure trickled down Angie's cheeks. She couldn't quite believe she had found heaven on earth. 'Let Rod fuck you too,' she panted. 'Balance me against the rails. I want him to take you while you take me.'

Cole nodded, clearly too excited to disagree. He sat her bottom on the top of the barge's rail. Holding her tightly around her waist, he increased his rhythm, edging more and more of himself into her. Rod hurried from his kneeling position and stood behind Cole.

Cole's eyes widened and he stopped thrusting. Angie could see Rod gripping Cole's hips as he worked his way into the large man. Cole's hips jerked forward as Rod entered him. 'That feels good,' Cole sighed. His blue eyes bulged, and he took a great breath. 'I had no idea.' He started thrusting into Angie again. 'No idea at all.'

'You like it, don't you?' said Angie, panting. 'You like having Rod's cock up your arse.'

'Yes, yes,' he groaned, pulling her closer as he thrust into her with abandon. Cole closed his eyes, his breath ragged on Angie's face. Angie's sex throbbed as she writhed in ecstasy. Cole bent and kissed her, filling her mouth with his tongue, and it seemed to Angie as she hovered on the edge that she was full everywhere. Intoxicated with pleasure, she cried out.

'Oh, fill me.'

Cole rammed into her, sparing her nothing, and Angie thought she would die with excitement. She fought for air, but Cole followed her mouth with his lips, claiming her as he thrust still deeper inside. Angie was on fire, every nerve ending screamed as she writhed under Cole, meeting him thrust for thrust. She could hear Rod cry out. He slumped against Cole's pulsating body.

Rod moved over to Angie and stood looking at her. His little tickler may be finished, thought Angie, but she still had use for him. She reached over and grabbed him by the ear, pulling him to her breast so that he sucked her nipples, his tongue darting like a snake. The peaks of her nipples were sensitive. The pleasure from his tongue spread through her like the ripples on the sea.

'Use your fingers on me,' she ordered.

Slowly he worked one finger into her arse, then two, then three, until she thought she would surely split apart. She could not believe that there would be room for Cole's fat cock and Rod's intense fingers. The muscles

143

of her arse tightened around him. Angie came, crying out in pleasure, sure that she would shatter into a thousand fragments. Her voice echoed over the sea, matched by Cole who shuddered and cried out as his enjoyment overtook him.

Angie held tightly on to his shoulders, her sex quivering as he slowly withdrew from her. Cole helped her down from the railing. 'Are you all right?'

'Yes,' she croaked, barely able to speak.

Gently he sat her down on the warm deck. 'I didn't hurt you, did I?'

'No,' she said, though in truth she felt she had just ridden a wild stallion, and her legs refused to close.

'Well . . . um . . . I had better get back to work,' said Cole, and he went to start the barge. 'Come on, mate.' Cole gave Rod a slap on the back. 'Time to pull up the anchor.'

Angie lay on the deck, her legs apart, looking at the blue sky. The barge roared to life underneath her and she lay there, enjoying the sensation of her prolonged ecstasy. Finally, she pushed herself to a sitting position, glad that her head had stopped spinning.

Rod walked over to her, her sarong in his hands. 'Thanks,' she said, reaching up to take it.

'No. I should thank you. You weren't the only one who got what they wanted today.'

Angie nodded. 'I know. I think you and Cole are going to have a great sea-going relationship.'

Rod laughed and nodded. 'You work experience students are something else.'

Angie's mouth twitched mischievously when she thought of Jacob, remembering her former vow. 'Yes,' she said. 'I am adventurous. So is Jacob,' she added. She let his name hang in the air between them. 'Are you giving Jacob a scuba-diving lesson this evening?'

'Sure. The sun doesn't set until eight. We should get a couple of hours.'

'That's nice. Jacob told me he rather fancied you.'

Rod frowned, his eyes narrowed. 'That's funny. I could have sworn Jacob's straight.'

'Oh no,' said Angie. 'He told me he is bisexual. He says it doubles his chances at parties. Though he said he likes to play hard to get. The boys get a bit rough. Jacob likes that.'

Rod's eyes gleamed, and Angie could see from his expression that Jacob was going to have a very interesting scuba-diving lesson.

'Well,' said Rod, 'I'd better get the ropes ready to dock the barge.'

'Yes,' she agreed. 'We're nearly there.'

She stood and retied her sarong. She was glad Jacob had thought to arrange such an interesting morning for her, and she was determined to repay the favour. She shook her hair from her face, delighted she had kindly found someone to fill Jacob's lonely evening.

It was a pity she was on kitchen duty, she thought. She would have loved to see Rod seduce Jacob. She could imagine Jacob's reaction when Rod attempted to kiss him, and the thought was extremely arousing. She certainly had enjoyed Rod's questing fingers. Perhaps Jacob would too. Angie's wicked grin widened to a smile. Revenge came in many forms, she thought. 'That, Mr Jacob Virgin, will teach you for getting rid of my precious Valiant,' she murmured.

When the boat docked, Rod climbed on to the jetty and held out his hand to help Angie off. She turned and gave Cole a wave. She was now a proud member of the twelve-inch club, she thought with satisfaction. Except membership did have one major drawback. Her legs stubbornly refused to close. So instead of her normal sexy stroll, she hobbled along the jetty and up the steps of Hotel Desire, her hunting antennae turned firmly off for the rest of the day.

Chapter Eight

'Wake up,' commanded a male voice.

'Hey!' yelled Angie, suddenly shaken from a wonderful erotic dream. It was too dark to see, but the man gripped her hard by the shoulders. Instinctively, she dug her fingernails into the man's arms then lashed out with her feet.

'Damn you!' shouted the man, releasing her.

Angie had no idea of the identity of her attacker, but she fought fiercely, determined to get the better of this stranger. She did not feel fear. Angie did not know the meaning of the word. But heaven help the man who dared to wake her out of an erotic dream-filled sleep.

'There's nothing you wouldn't stoop to, is there?' growled the man before he pushed her back on to the mattress, pinning her with his hard body. His hands sought hers and Angie struggled, but he caught her by the wrists until she could move no more. 'You have gone too far this time.' His hot breath fanned her face.

'Jacob? Is that you?' she questioned, now awake enough to recognise his voice. This behaviour was so out of character for Jacob, it had never occurred to her that it could be him.

'You told Rod I was gay, didn't you?'

There was steel to his voice that Angie had never heard before. Mr Placid Virgin was steaming mad, and Angie fought to restrain a giggle. The tenseness of his body spelt out danger. She could feel the hardness of his chest against hers. Her nipples tightened in pleasure as she rubbed them against him.

'Of course I didn't.' She continued to squirm, pretending to throw him off by raising her hips, savouring the sensation as he fought to keep her pinned. She knew he did not believe her, but his anger excited her; made her determined to annoy him further. Who would have thought Mr Virgin would jump her in her sleep?

'Damn you, Angie. I know you're lying to me.' His grip on her wrist tightened. Her eyes adjusted to the darkness. She could make out his face just inches from hers.

So, she had got to him at last by working out his secret fear. Young guys, she knew, whether they were gay or not, questioned their sexuality at some point. She could just imagine Jacob pushing his hard cock into her; intent on proving he was not gay. The thought was immensely satisfying because Jacob was turning out to be the most difficult of all her prey to catch. She fought him, rotating her hips, enjoying the feeling of his growing erection. That familiar tingle of excitement spread throughout her. It was definitely hunting time.

'I want some answers,' Jacob insisted. 'Did you tell Rod I was gay?'

'No,' she said. Well, bisexual was not the same as gay, she reasoned, though she would have been quite happy to lie. She had pierced his pleasant virginal core, she thought with delight. Soon he would be hers. She just knew it.

Pinning both of her hands with one of his, he reached over and turned on the bedside light. He stared down at her. 'I know you are lying to me. I can see it in your eyes.'

She stared right back at him, her tongue lingering on her top lip. Since when had Mr Placid Virgin ever been able to work out what she thought? 'Now why do you say that?' she queried. Thrilled and tingling, she waited to see what he would do next.

'He came on to me.' There was fury in his voice, the depths of which she had never encountered from him before. His body burned hot on hers. He smelt of a delicious combination of salty combined with sexy, angry male; so it wouldn't do to change his mood.

'Did you enjoy it?' she asked huskily. She remembered Rod's well-built physique, and his handsome yet feminine face, intense with pleasure as he drove his cock into Cole.

'No!' shouted Jacob. 'I hated it.'

Agitation made his skin slick and his cock just the way she wanted it – hard! Angie bit back a smile. What had Rod done with Jacob? Had he parted him and pushed his little penis determinedly into him? The thought was extremely arousing.

'What did you hate?' She wanted to know every detail. Oh, how she wished she had been there. She would have sucked Jacob's cock while Rod plundered him.

'Did he suck you? Did he explore you with his tongue? You know gay guys like to lick everywhere. They even like to lick inside you,' she said, feeling her breasts swell at the thought.

She could feel Jacob's whole body tense above her. There was something about the feel and smell of him that aroused her. An unsatisfied ache grew in the pit of her abdomen. God, how she wanted him.

'I would love to see you lying there with your legs spread while Rod tongued you. That's how guys get each other wet and ready. You'd like that, wouldn't you?' she purred. The thought turned her on; made her want him to take her. She knew some men loved having their sensitive, hidden places licked.

'That's never going to happen, you . . . you . . .'

She watched amused as Jacob struggled for self-control. His face was crimson with fury.

'Come on,' she taunted, delighted that Mr Placid Virgin could barely contain himself. 'Why don't you call me something dirty?' She rubbed her breasts against him, savouring the erotic sensation. 'Why don't you say what you really think? Call me a filthy slut. Tell me all the depraved things you'd like to do to me.' She raised her eyebrows expectantly. 'I'm waiting.'

'I am not some toy for you to manipulate with your disgusting sex games. And I am *not* interested in men,' he added fiercely.

She remembered Rod's red, pointy tongue working its way over Cole. 'Oh, I don't know,' she continued, the level of her arousal building. She wanted to keep him holding her down so that she could press her mound into him. 'Men always say that, but you wouldn't be the first guy Rod has converted. I've seen him in action. He can be extremely persuasive.'

Just the thought of Jacob and Rod together made her want to open her legs. So she did. She was swollen and moist with wanting Jacob. He would be a sensational fuck if she could turn his anger to passion. 'Imagine Rod licking your balls, taking them into his mouth and sucking on them. He's got the reddest tongue I have ever seen. Did he want to stick it up you?'

'Don't say that revolting stuff to me,' said Jacob, his voice trembling with fury. 'I know you are behind this. You set me up. Rod told me you said I was gay.'

'Maybe you are. You don't seem interested in women.' But even as she spoke the words, Angie knew differently. Jacob was swollen with anger. She could feel him pressing against her.

She rocked her pelvis slowly against him. What a pity he had come to her bed clothed. Unable to contain herself, she positioned herself so that his cock, constrained in his shorts, pressed against her sensitive clitoris. Already, she could feel the first tremors shooting like tiny sparks. She pushed her head back, thrusting her breasts forward as she rubbed herself against him.

'You know I like women, you manipulative witch. I have never been into men.'

Jacob, she thought with amusement, was oblivious to her approaching orgasm. He was too busy defending himself against her ludicrous charges. All she had to do was keep him talking. His voice excited her.

'Rod thought you were,' she lied, her words sailing on short, hot breaths of air. 'He told me he thought you were beautiful. Gay guys know these things. They know when other men want it,' she added, just to drive the objectionable point home.

His fingers tightened on her wrists. 'That's a damn lie. He came on to me because of you.'

She struggled again underneath him, wanting him to kiss her, willing him to unleash himself and fill her. She wriggled until she positioned the firm head of his penis exactly where she wanted it. The heat of him lying on her, covering her, his angry deep voice, built her orgasm until the tension became almost unbearable.

'He came on to you,' she panted with excitement, 'because he liked you. Don't blame me. I can't make other people do things. Why are you angry?'

Erotic images flooded her mind. She tilted her pelvis forward. She wanted to keep him talking as she rubbed herself against him. But more than anything, she wanted to hear every filthy detail. 'Did he ask you to suck him?' she asked, her voice hoarse with desire. 'Or did he start slowly and kiss you with that pretty mouth of his? Did he try and undress you? Did he take you in his hands and slowly rub you?'

'He kissed me,' Jacob said, the disgust evident in his tone. 'I was so shocked I just stood there. He put his tongue in my mouth.' He tightened his grip on her hands until his fingers dug into her wrist. 'And it's all your fault.'

'Yes,' she panted. 'Yes, yes.' She arched against him as another wave of pleasure hit her, building up to a crescendo. Her nipples ached. She wished he'd suck them, but she wanted to keep him talking too. She was so hot she couldn't decide which would give her more pleasure. Images of Rod and Jacob swirled in her mind. Light-headed with desire, she knew she was about to tip off the edge into a land of hedonistic pleasure.

Aroused and ready for his cock, she was certain Mr Virgin was going to finally prove himself to her. She could barely wait. Oh, how she wished she could have seen Rod seducing Jacob. She wanted to hear more; she now desperately needed the release.

'Tell me everything. I have to know. Rod's a very sexy man. Did you like it when he stuck his tongue in your mouth? He does wonderful things with that tongue of his. I saw him licking Cole's balls.' She stopped, trying to catch her breath. 'Maybe we should ask him back to our room and he can do that to you,' she said, her head spinning at the thought.

'That's disgusting.'

'Yes. Yes,' she panted. 'Just think, he could lick you. I could take you in my mouth. Imagine how good that would feel.' She held her breath as heat flooded her pelvis. Arching against him again, she cried out, balancing precariously on a razor's edge of pleasure.

Jacob groaned. 'No. No! Oh God, he licked Cole's balls, then kissed me. Where's the mouthwash?' He rolled off her and rushed to the bathroom.

Damn, thought Angie, sitting up so quickly she had to steady herself. Why did she have to say the wrong thing just when she was about to come? Rapidly, she followed Jacob to the bathroom and turned on the light, watching as he swallowed the mouthwash neat. Then he reached for his toothbrush, doused it in mouthwash and began scrubbing his teeth.

He looked genuinely distressed, and if Angie were the sympathetic kind, she would have felt sorry for him. She wasn't.

'So you admit you set me up. I knew you were behind this.' Jacob glared at her, slamming down the bottle.

She leant against the cool bathroom wall, enjoying the sensation on her bare skin. 'And what would you do to me if I were?' she challenged. Casually, she pirouetted, then bent, waggling her bottom at him. She knew her slit was swollen and pink. 'Would you put me over your knee? Would you spank me again?' She would like that, she thought. She would like him to make her bottom pink with pleasure.

Jacob stood frozen, his breathing heavy and fast, then he moved with lightning speed. Grabbing hold of her shoulders, he spun her around to face him. 'The trouble with you, Angie, is you don't believe the word no. When someone says no to you, that is like a challenge. It makes you want to do whatever it is they don't want.' Jacob glared at her. 'I'm not gay and I'm not stupid. Don't think I didn't know what you were doing in bed. Upsetting me turns you on, doesn't it?'

Angie raised her eyebrows. 'So what if it does?'

Jacob's fingers dug into her shoulders. 'If you ever try and set me up with a man again I'll –'

'What will you do, Jacob?' She raised her chin in challenge. 'Why don't you prove to me that you are not gay? Why don't you take that frustrated cock out of your pants and show me what you can do with it? Come on. Prove to me you don't like men,' she taunted.

'I don't use people for sex. I need to care about the person I'm with.'

Angie rolled her eyes in disgust. The guy was a

romantic. Next he would be appearing with roses and violins. It was time to snap him into the real world.

'Where does that do-good attitude get you? By the time you finally find someone you care about, you'll burst. It will be all over in a second.' She put one hand down, rubbing him, teasing him. 'You're hard with frustration,' she said, her voice deep with desire.

'I'm not frustrated.' He pushed her hand away and marched into their bedroom.

She followed him. 'You know, Jacob, guys like Rod can smell your frustration a mile off.'

'Don't be ridiculous,' Jacob snapped, turning on her. 'Do you want to know what it's like to be used?' he said furiously. 'Do you want sex where the guy doesn't care about you?'

Yes, thought Angie. That's exactly what I want. Hard, fast, uncomplicated sex. Now!

'Do you have any idea how hard it is to resist you? The way you walk around naked, I can't get you out of my mind. You're in my dreams, night and day.' His gaze dropped from her face, lingered on her breasts and travelled downward. 'You're beautiful.' His voice was thick with wanting her. 'But you only like sex when you pull the strings. You want to be in control. You don't even care about the man you are with. Well, I won't let you manipulate me like you do all the others.'

So that was his problem, thought Angie. She had finally figured him out. Jacob needed romance. He wanted to feel special; wanted some sort of caring, perhaps a commitment from her. Next he'd be asking her to be his girlfriend, and taking her home for roast dinners with his family. She sighed, trying to keep the horrible images from her mind. She shrugged. Well, a girl had to do what a girl had to do. There was nothing worse for a girl than to be left mid-orgasm.

Angie put her arms around him, pulling him close.

'You know that's not the way I feel about you,' she lied. 'You're special to me. We have a friendship, don't we?'

Jacob studied her carefully. 'I've always liked you. You know that.'

Angie smiled, then, putting her arms around his neck, pressed her lips to his. His lips were soft but he did not open his mouth to welcome her. She pulled back slightly and looked him in the eyes. 'You know I've always liked you too,' she said. Liked to torment you, tease you and have you as my slave, she thought. Well, even slaves needed a bit of maintenance sometimes.

'Oh God, Angie,' he said, pulling her close. 'I just can't take this teasing. I can't stop thinking about you.'

'It's time to stop thinking,' she whispered. Gently, she pulled his face to hers, kissing him, sliding her tongue into his mouth. He did not reject her kiss. She was conscious of the hardness of him pressing against her. Even angry, he still wanted her, she thought with satisfaction.

Jacob was a gentle guy, she realised, so he needed a gentle touch. 'Let's not stop what we feel for each other.'

Slowly, she unbuttoned his shirt, careful not to rush him. She did not want his boring do-good conscience to get started all over again. A shiver of pleasure spread through her. His skin felt smooth and warm against hers.

'I have been trying to give us time to get to know each other,' he sighed. He held her firmly to him, one hand exploring her sensitive breast. There seemed to be an imaginary bow that joined her nipple to her clit. He stroked one and the other responded. 'You are different from any girl I have met before.'

Oh, shut up and just get on with it, she thought impatiently, barely resisting an urge to bite his nipples. She wanted him to slide his fingers in between her pussy lips, but she forced herself to be patient.

He kissed her passionately this time, his tongue

searching for hers. Taking his tongue between her lips, she sucked him as she moved her hand downward. Careful not to break the rhythm of her kiss, she pulled open his shorts, pleasantly surprised to find he wore no underwear. Perhaps she was influencing him, after all.

He moaned softly, breaking the kiss. 'Touch me.'

She wanted to do more than touch him. She wanted to take him in her mouth and suck him, take him to the edge. Again, she reminded herself to be patient. With difficult prey, a hunter had to be cautious.

Softly, she stroked him, enjoying the feel of his silky skin stretched tight over his penis. She was savouring the heady feeling of success. Jacob was so hard to get; having sex with him seemed more exciting.

Carefully, she nibbled at his throat, moving lower, past his tight stomach muscles until she knelt at his feet. Looking up at him, she licked the head of his penis, circling it with the tip of her tongue. Then she teased the little eye open, pushing the tip of her tongue inside. Jacob's cock jerked upward in response to her tongue. 'Do you like this?'

His gaze met hers, though his eyes seemed somewhat glazed. 'No-one except you has ever done that to me,' he said, his voice hoarse.

No-one has done anything to you, she thought. It was difficult to contain her enthusiasm. There was something special about being the initiator, the first ever. She opened her lips to take in the head of his penis, licking the pre-come, enjoying its sweet taste.

She watched as his hands moved to his nipples, pinching them, matching her rhythm. He was no longer looking at her. Instead, his gaze had moved to a distant place. Angie swallowed him until his cock touched the back of her throat.

A deep moan left his lips and he cupped her head in his hands. Moving rhythmically, he thrust himself into her, but she held him by the hips, digging her nails into his buttocks. She was not going to let him come. That would be a waste. Anyway, she needed him to fill her. Tormenting him had brought her close to the edge, but she wanted to feel him opening her, thrusting inside her. She loved the sensation of that first moment when a man was about to enter her.

Holding his sac with one hand, she teased along the delicate ridge of skin underneath his testicles with her fingers. Deliberately, she slowed her pace as she sucked him. She could feel a pumping sensation and she realised that he was about to come.

Suddenly, he grabbed hold of her hair and pulled out of her mouth. Holding her hair so that she could not move, he stared hard at her. With one hand he jerked rapidly until he came, releasing her only when he was finished.

Angie looked at him with shock. She knew he was close, but she had no idea he would have the guts to come other than when she chose. 'What the hell did you do that for?' she asked angrily.

'I'm not stupid enough to think you could fall in love with me. I know you don't care about me. I'm just another man for you to use.' His eyes narrowed and he pulled her to her feet, holding her so that she could not get away. 'I want you to know how it feels to be used. Did you like it, Angie?'

'You know damn well I didn't.'

'Don't ever set me up with a man again. You went too far this time.' He straightened his clothes, then walked past her as if she no longer existed. Pulling his travelling bag from under the bed, he proceeded to pack his belongings.

'What are you doing?'

'Packing.'

'I can see that.'

He looked at her over his shoulder. 'A room has come free. I'm moving out. It's not hotel policy to have men sharing with women unless they are in a relationship.' He walked past her and pulled all his belongings out of the wardrobe, then stuffed them into his suitcase.

'Well, we're not,' she stated strongly. The last thing she wanted was a boyfriend trying to bind her with rings and rules. That had never been her style.

'You always misunderstood what I wanted from you. I wanted a friendship first,' Jacob said. 'You're not made for a love relationship. I've learnt that.' He turned, shut his bag and walked to the door.

'Good. I'm glad you're going. You would have to be the most boring room-mate I have ever shared with.'

'Well, I think you will find your next one more interesting. Your new room-mate has just arrived.'

'What are you talking about? No-one has told me about a new room-mate.'

'The beautiful Isabella di Bellini is here. I saw her in the foyer.' Jacob raised his eyebrows.

'That bitch! I'm not sharing a room with that stuck-up, stupid, crawl-up-James's-arse –'

'Enjoy,' said Jacob simply. 'Goodnight, Angie.'

Angie paced the bedroom. What was she going to do? She still had the smell and taste of Jacob on her lips. She could kiss sleep away tonight. Just the thought of sharing a room with that stuck-up princess Isabella made her sick. So Jacob found her beautiful. The thought made her angry if not a little jealous. Men liked Isabella because of the way she sucked up to them. Angie could not stand her.

She would have to come up with a plan to get rid of her, but for the moment nothing came to mind. She needed to relax and Jacob, she thought with irritation, had made that impossible.

Searching her wardrobe for her bikini, she decided to go to the grotto. Though the area was banned to staff, she doubted Tahillia Ash would be checking on staff so late at night.

As she walked along the staff corridor, she wondered where Jacob had secured a room. He deserved to be tormented in his sleep again. Fancy him leading her on like that. Her opinion of him changed to one of admiration. Who would have thought Mr Virgin had it in him?

She stopped near Kate and Rick's room. There was nothing but silence. She was not sure whether they would appreciate being woken in the middle of the night for some frenzied sex. No. The place to go was definitely the grotto. On a hot night like this, one never knew who might be taking a swim. If she were in luck maybe Nick Holt would be there without his disgusting wife.

She stepped into the warm night air and made her way from the staff quarters to the pool area. The paths were lit with low lights but that didn't stop her from nearly stepping on a cane toad. A small shriek left her lips, and she clamped her hands over her mouth. Kangaroos hopping around the island, she could deal with, but the cane toads were gross. 'They never put you lot on the travel brochures,' she said, skipping over the toad and its multitude of revolting friends.

She opened the pool gate, giving the area a once-over, but the pool seemed to be empty. All the prey were disappointingly asleep.

Walking into the grotto, it too was quiet. One low light allowed her to see that the grotto was empty. Disappointment fuelled her frustration, sharpening her desire to hunt, but she would have to resume hunting tomorrow when the natives were awake.

Her eyes adjusted to the low lighting, then she realised all was not lost. An immensely pleasing idea filled her thoughts. Slipping off her bikini, she stepped into the warm water and waded over to the edge of the grotto.

She could just make out the silver button which started the jets. She pushed it and a thrill of delight swept through her. It was time for a special private party.

Soon the water was bubbling like a cauldron. Her nipples tingled with appreciation as the frothy water danced around her breasts. There was nothing worse than being left on the edge of orgasm. Jacob was incredibly selfish to chuck out her vibrator then leave her unsatisfied. She missed Valiant-The-Vibrator, but Angie was never short of an idea when it came to pleasure; especially her own.

She positioned herself close to one of the jets at the side of the grotto pool. Already, she could feel the erotic vibrations of the water pulsing against her vulva. Placing her hands on the edge to steady herself, she rocked her pelvis, directing the throbbing water on to her sensitive clitoris. It was rare to get this wonderful sensation while standing. She imagined what it would feel like to be a man. The current from the jet reminded her of a long penis.

It had always been a secret fantasy of Angie's to have a penis. Not that she wanted to be a man because she was of the mind that women had a distinct advantage over men where sex was concerned. But the idea intrigued her. She fantasised that the jet of water was her penis, attached right where her clitoris lay. Her sensitive bud protruded, her full outer lips pushed apart by the current of the water.

She stood there, thrusting like a man, savouring the heat of the water jet. Bubbles of frothing water tickled her nipples until a tight feeling centred in the small of her back. Already she was arching, moving closer to the jet. The only thing she would have liked was a cock to fill her at the same time as she came. Her orgasm erupted suddenly with an intensity that overcame her. A razor of heat scorched her clitoris. Her fingers gripped the edge of the grotto as she arched her back. A moan that started somewhere in the pit of her stomach echoed around the grotto walls.

Just as the wonderful sensation ebbed, another exploded, and she threw her head back, screaming in pleasure, her breath subsiding to short, hot pants of indulgence.

'You always put on a good show, Angie. I could hear you from the pool.'

She did not turn, needing to stay on her high. She knew that deep voice. It reminded her of rich, dark chocolate. It had been a long time since she had heard him speak.

'Fill me,' she gasped. 'Put your cock in me now.'

The man entered the water, moving behind her. It gave her a thrill not to look at him. He put his hands on her hips to steady her. She could feel the tip of his cock nudging at her entrance. Shivers of excitement raced through her because she had no idea how big he was. She smiled with satisfaction. She was about to find out.

Wet from repeated orgasms, she knew he would have no difficulties entering her, yet she gasped as he plunged into her with one clean movement, filling her completely.

'Ah, you little tease. I've been waiting for this day. Did you really think you would get away with your little private show? You're ruthless when it comes to getting what you want, but I intend to make you pay the price.'

Angie wondered what he meant. She knew he did not mean money. No, this man was kinky and demanding. He would want something unusual. A certain thrill rushed up her spine.

The man began thrusting rhythmically, pushing her sensitive vulva closer to the pulsating jet. His fingers teased her nipples, pinching then stroking the sensitive tips. All her concerns vanished. The man was divine. He definitely knew what he was doing. If there were going to be a price, she would be ready to pay it.

Angie cried out in happiness as another wave of pleasure hit her. She threw her head back, arching into the jet. The man pinched her nipples hard enough for her to register pain, but the sensation only increased her excitement. He pushed deeply into her. It was exactly what she needed. Angie decided she had found heaven.

'This is what you wanted all along,' he growled in her ear.

'Yes. Yes,' she gasped, almost unable to talk. A searing sensation flooded her inside. Her moans filled the grotto. Barely conscious of anything else except her own fulfilment, she slowly became aware of the man talking to her. She did not want him to talk. She loved the sensation of his hard chest against her back. She just wanted him to keep thrusting into her so she could stay on her sensational high.

'This is what you need, isn't it?'

'Yes. Yes.' This man was the perfect fit. The way he filled her, the way he plunged into her, left her delirious.

He tightened his grip on her, making her listen. 'From the moment I saw you I knew what you were. Sybarite. I will own you. Soon you will bend to my will.'

His voice was hypnotic. She tried to shut out his sinister words. Each thrust took her again to the edge of unspeakable ecstasy. He held her closely, his hands caressing her breasts as he whispered into her ear. 'You are mine to do with as I please.'

'Shut up,' she said, but already another wave of orgasm was building. The throb, throb, throb of the water jet vibrated against her. Her pussy muscles crunched down on him, the thrilling sensation almost too much to bear. Her mind screamed warning signals to break away from the man's hypnotic suggestions, but she wanted the pleasure he gave her. She dug her fingernails deep into his arms to try and shut him up.

161

'Don't try and stop me. You are a creature of indulgence,' he said. 'That is how I will trap you.' He bit then sucked the soft skin of her neck, just enough so that the sensation of pain mingled with rapture. His fingers stroked her nipples, strumming the tight peaks, and all Angie's thoughts of fighting him subsided.

Their bodies undulated together. He was impossible to resist. He seemed to have the ability to stimulate every part of her. Angie's skin tingled until her neck, her breasts, her mound and every sensual part of her longed for his touch.

The man reached over and turned off the grotto button. Suddenly the water was still, yet Angie could barely move. Though her limbs were sluggish, every erogenous part of her remained aroused, awaiting his touch.

Still inside her, the man sat on the underwater seat of the grotto with Angie on his knee. He reached over and parted her legs so that she was widely exposed to his touch. He stroked her breasts, moving his hands slowly downward until his fingers reached her sensitised sex. Then his fingers strummed her clitoris, his fingertip just grazing over the tip until Angie strained forward for his caress. 'You are mine now. No man will ever satisfy you once I have had you.'

Angie rested her head back against him. Weak from the intensity of her multiple orgasms and the heat of the grotto, she could not resist him. Somewhere in her conscious thoughts, she wished he would come so that she would be free from his hypnotic voice.

'I own you,' he murmured, his teeth nipping her ear, tugging on her sensitive earlobe.

'No.' She shook her head from side to side, trying to block out his words. All she wanted was to concentrate on the wonderful sensations he was giving her. The light pressure of his fingers on her clitoris tormented her. She had to come again. Her whole body was trembling for its final release.

'Do not try to shut me out. You want what I can give you.' He wrapped one arm around her hips, holding her in place as he thrust into her. Angie matched each thrust by tightening her pelvic muscles. The effect was sensational. She ground down on to him, wanting every inch to fill her.

Opening her knees wide, she wrapped her ankles around the back of his calves. He had staying power that she had never encountered before. Experience, she thought, had taught him to play a woman's body like an expert. She arched again, straining to meet his fingers, but though he continued to stroke her, he moved his fingers away so she could not quite get the pressure right.

'You want release, don't you?'

'Yes, yes,' she moaned.

'Then beg for it.'

'No.' Shut out his voice. Shut out his voice, she repeated to herself. Just concentrate on the pleasure he gives you.

'You cannot fight me. I will make you addicted to my touch. No man will ever please you. You will long for me.'

He continued to stroke her until the effect was maddening. She tried to concentrate on the wonderful sensation of his cock moving inside her. Tried to shift into a position so that she could come internally. But the man seemed to read her thoughts, shifting her slightly, keeping her on the edge of release.

'Beg me,' his voice growled. One of his hands continued to strum her while the other slid up and down her body, caressing her nipples before moving lower to her mound. Gently, he parted her so that her clitoris popped from its hood, allowing his finger intimate access. Tears of pleasure tracked her face. He stroked from the base of her clitoris up over her sensitive bud, gently pulling her piercing.

'I see you have changed your decorations. I have always liked a woman to wear jewellery.' Then his inquisitive fingers explored further, pushing back her delicate clitoral hood, teasing the sensitive fold until she could not bear it any longer.

'Beg me. I want to hear you say the words.'

She needed him to satisfy her. Urgently, she crunched down on his cock again and again but he slowed his thrusting, keeping her ultimate goal just out of reach. 'Please,' she whispered.

'That's it, Angie. I want to hear you beg.'

He continued to play with her until she squirmed urgently. Every nerve ending screamed for release.

She bit hard on her lower lip, straining forward for him.

'Beg me, damn you. I want you to beg.'

She could not block out his voice. Only release from his addictive touch would free her. 'Please. Please. I beg you. I have to come.'

'Ah, Angie,' he said. 'I knew I would break you.'

He increased his pace, thrusting deeply into her. His fingers stroked her rhythmically, no longer teasing, no longer moving away every time she strained against them. This time he kept the pressure right. His fingers moved to the place where his cock drove inside her, then slid up over her marble-like bud, tracing over and over the little hill until she could stand it no more. She climaxed; her whole body shuddered.

A moan starting deep inside her rose to a crescendo. The inky darkness of the grotto filled with tiny stars. For a moment time stopped. Pleasure consumed her until finally she could bear it no more. She cried out and her voice echoed off the walls of the grotto, filling the chasm. Ecstasy spread like molten lava throughout her until there was no part of her free from the exquisite torture of his possession.

Finally, she slumped against him, barely able to raise her head. In the distance she could hear someone calling her name, but she was too weak to answer. Her captor's voice blocked out the other. His words resonated through the grotto. 'You are mine now. My creature, to do with as I please.'

She closed her eyes tightly, tried not to listen though his hateful words seeped like poison into her soul. Yet, somewhere deep inside, her courage soared to the surface. 'Never!' Her voice, detached and weak, seemed barely like her own.

She shuddered, wanting to get away from him. She no longer wanted him to touch her, but she seemed to have no strength in her limbs. The man stroked one hand over her mound. Her whole body quivered in response. He laughed. 'We both know that is not true. You are mine for ever now.'

He lifted her off him, leaving her lying languid on the grotto seat, and stepped out of the pool. Then James, the man that she wanted and loathed in equal measure, was gone.

Chapter Nine

'Angie. Angie. Wake up.' Jacob touched her shoulder. For a moment she could not recall where she was. She seemed to remember Jacob calling her before. She opened her eyes; she was not in her bedroom. She was wet and hot. Too hot. Moving her hands, she became aware of the water. It took her a few moments to realise that she lay submerged in the water, her head resting against the edge of the grotto.

'Jacob.' Her throat felt raw and dry. 'Help me out of here.' Hot and sluggish, she could barely move. 'I need fresh air.' Fumes smelling of chlorine seemed to cling in the sticky heat of the grotto. Angie sniffed, her nose wrinkling. She was sure she could smell James's scent. Strong and dominating, his erotic tang lingered in the air.

Jacob bent over, hooked his hands under her arms and pulled her from the water. She slumped against him, her legs wobbly.

'What are you doing, falling asleep in the grotto pool? You know that's dangerous. Even the sign outside says no more than twenty minutes.'

Good old never-break-a-rule Jacob was back, lecturing her, telling her what to do. Only this time she was glad.

'I wasn't asleep.' It was more like a post-orgasm-induced coma, she thought. Not that Jacob would understand. 'I ... I was too tired to move. Let me sit. I feel dizzy.' She sat at the edge of the grotto cave, welcoming the fresh breeze that blew in from the entrance.

Jacob dipped his hand in the water. 'This water's way too hot. No wonder you can't move. How long have you been in here?'

'I don't know. What time is it?' Already shafts of sunlight lit the entrance of the grotto, signalling that morning was fast approaching.

'It's early morning. I've been looking for you everywhere. You can't stay here. I need to cool you down.'

He picked her up and carried her in his arms to the pool. 'Wait there. I'll get some towels.' Lying her on a deckchair, he walked over to the cabana and returned moments later with several pool towels. He dunked them into the cool water from the swimming pool, then pulled another deckchair close, and proceeded to sponge her.

Angie watched him, her eyelids heavy with fatigue, her lips slightly apart. His face was serious as he placed the wet towel on her heated face and torso. Cool water dribbled between her breasts, pooling in her navel. She would like Jacob to follow the pathway of water with his tongue. Angie sighed, glad that despite her lack of energy, she was still interested in Jacob. James and his stupid hypnotic suggestions worried her. This was exactly what she needed to still her troubled mind.

She had sensed right from the beginning that James was dangerous. Now she knew why. He was determined to dominate her both mentally and physically. Sex did not seem a game or even a pleasure to James. He used sex as a powerful tool to trap an unwitting victim, the way a spider did a fly. There was no way she was going to let him manipulate her again.

'Are you feeling better?' asked Jacob.

'Mmm,' she answered. 'Just keep doing that.' She stretched, savouring the sensuous sensation as he squeezed out a towel, the cool water trickling over her sensitive nipples.

Jacob had the most beautiful blue eyes, she thought. The colour of topaz, they were clear with honesty. In fact, he was exactly the type of man that did not normally attract her. Yet he was light to James's dark nature. Just at the moment, while she was languid with exhaustion, she was glad Jacob was there, caring for her.

Jacob pressed his palm to her forehead and cheeks. 'You don't feel so hot now.'

The cool air and Jacob's gentle ministrations revived her. 'Don't stop. I like what you are doing.' Already she could feel her strength returning. Opening her legs, she enjoyed the trickling sensation of the water running over her swollen labia.

Angie let out another deep sigh. She definitely would need some pampering after James's treatment of her. Jacob was just the person to do it. She took his hand in hers and pressed it to her breast. For once, he did not argue or snatch his hand away. 'I'm still hot from here down,' she said, looking at him sideways from under her long eyelashes.

He smiled and shook his head with amusement. 'You never give up.' He teased her nipple with his thumb, rubbing it from side to side. Angie was relieved he had finally stopped fighting her. She enjoyed his touch. After James's spooky brainwashing, she wanted to be sure that nothing had changed. It hadn't. She still wanted to seduce Jacob.

'Do you ever stop thinking about sex?' he asked.

'No. Well, maybe sometimes. Like when I'm totally satisfied. That isn't often.' She thought of Cole and his magnificent cock. That adventure had satisfied her for a few hours. Angie looked at Jacob, her gaze uncompromising. 'I'm not going to pretend I don't like sex just because I am a woman. I don't intend to take a back seat waiting for some man to fancy me. I go for the man I want.' She pursed her lips, her gaze drawing him closer. 'When I'm interested in a man,' she said huskily, 'I tell him what I like him to do.'

'I noticed.' Jacob frowned thoughtfully, his fingers stroking her breasts, catching stray drops of water that lingered on her nipples. 'What do you like the most?'

Angie's ears pricked up. So Mr Virgin was changing his tune. He wanted to know what turned her on. 'I like stroking, licking and kissing. I'm not fussy about the order.' So long as you become my slave and do all three, she thought.

'I like it when a man isn't afraid to experiment.' Angie raised her eyebrows, warming to her subject. There were so many possibilities. 'Quickies are fun, if I'm really turned on, or sex in different locations. For instance –' she paused, leaning closer to Jacob so that her shoulder was touching his '– imagine if someone were watching us now. Think about someone standing hidden, watching you trickle water down my breasts.'

It was just a hunch but she had a feeling that they were not alone. She had learnt not to dismiss her gut feelings. A hunter had to rely on instinct. What if someone were watching them? An early riser chasing the sunrise. 'You know something? The thought that we might be discovered turns me on.'

'Well, it scares me,' Jacob said, looking around. He stood and carried the towels over to the towel collection bin. She noticed the way he pulled his shorts away from his crotch. Good, she thought. He was hard. He had resisted her long enough already. 'I don't think there's someone here,' he called. 'I can't see anyone.'

'No,' she said quietly. 'You might not be able to see

anyone, but I know we are not alone.' The hairs on her arms stood up. She scanned the shrubbery surrounding the pool. Nothing. Not a movement. But Angie was intensely aware that every minute she and Jacob stayed by the pool they risked discovery.

She decided to give Jacob a little job to get his mind off their possible exposure. It was time for poolside hunting games. 'Could you get me a glass of water?' she asked him. 'Put plenty of ice in it.'

'Sure.' She watched him vault the bar, admiring his lithe physique. He was deliciously innocent. She loved observing the way he moved. He was tall and slim, still sinewy with youth. Everything that James was not.

Some movement in the bushes caught her attention, breaking her train of thought. So, they were not alone. Her hunch had been right. She strained to see, but whoever was hiding just beyond the pool enclosure was keeping still. Little tingles started all over her. If she could just keep Jacob oblivious to their intruder, she could put on an entertaining show.

'Here you are.' Jacob handed her the glass.

She drained half the glass, the cool water bringing relief to her dry throat. 'Why did you come looking for me?'

'I felt guilty.' Jacob sat at her side. 'What I did to you in the room.' He shook his head, his blue eyes soulful. 'I'm sorry. I had no right to treat you like that. I was brought up to respect women.' He frowned, then pushed his hand through his hair. 'What I did was not respectful. I shouldn't have taken advantage of you like that.'

She bit the inside of her cheeks, forcing herself not to laugh. So Jacob's do-good conscience got the better of him after all. Well, if it was time to play the heart-broken martyr, she would have to rise to the occasion. 'You wounded me. I thought you were different from other men.'

'I'm sorry. I never intended to hurt you. I was just so mad with you.' Remorse filled his handsome face.

Believe me, Angie thought, you are going to make it up to me. I intend to take full advantage of you.

'I went back to apologise, but you weren't in your room. Then I tried to get back to sleep. The trouble was I knew I had hurt your feelings. You are so wild sometimes, Angie, I wasn't sure what you would do next. I couldn't sleep, so I decided to search the hotel, then I went for a walk, looking for you. When I heard you moaning from the grotto, I thought you were injured.'

Trust Jacob not to recognise the sound of a woman in full-flight orgasm. 'No, I am not hurt. You left me in such a state I decided to go and experiment with the water jets in the grotto.'

Surprise crossed his features, followed hotly by confusion. 'What did you . . . um . . . No, don't tell me.'

Angie laughed, the sound throaty and deep. She decided not to tell him about James. No man liked to hear about the exploits of another. It would not surprise her if Jacob considered James competition. 'I'm glad you came looking for me.' She reached out and held his hand. 'I like the way you watch out for me. It's kind of cute.'

The bushes moved again. This time she could see someone standing partially hidden. Her nipples peaked with excitement. She had plans for Jacob. Plans that would not only soothe his guilty conscience but bring her intense pleasure.

'Someone has to watch out for you. You seem to get yourself into all types of trouble.'

Exactly, thought Angie with satisfaction. Watch being precisely the right word.

She drank some more of the water then balanced the glass on her abdomen, watching her magnified vulva through the glass. 'I'm still so hot,' she sighed. Beads of

171

perspiration formed on her skin. Already the early-morning sun was warm.

'Why don't you have a swim? The pool water is cool. Then we should get going. The gardeners start work soon.'

All the more reason to stay, thought Angie. It was time Mr Guilty Conscience paid his dues. 'I don't feel like a swim. I think I've had enough of water for now. I'd prefer to stay dry.' Purposely, she flexed the muscles in her abdomen, watching the glass tip. The water ran over her mound, trickling inside her, cooling her pink, sensitive inner lips. Cubes of ice slithered over her, landing on the deckchair. 'Oh dear. Look what I have done.'

Jacob automatically reached for a towel, handing it to her.

'No,' she said, holding her hand out to stop him. 'I have a better idea.' She picked up the glass and put it aside. 'Why don't you lick all the drops of water away? I don't want a rough old towel touching me where I'm so sensitive.'

Jacob's face flamed from the neck upward until he was the colour of the sunrise. 'Angie. It's five in the morning. Some of the guests get up early. We will get into all sorts of trouble.'

'I know,' she answered simply, glad he was feeling the heat of her suggestion. 'You said you felt guilty. That's why you came looking for me.'

'I did. I said sorry and I meant it.'

'This isn't primary school, Jacob. You used me. I looked after you. I sucked you until you were satisfied, then what did you do? You walked away. You owe me. Prove to me that you are sorry.' She moved her hand downward and stroked the top of her mound. It was tender in places from James's prying fingers. Only Jacob's tongue would soothe her.

172

'Angie, stop. Put on a pool robe. I'll do anything you like. Let's go back to your room.'

'No. I don't feel like it,' she said, noticing the way his gaze moved from her face to her breasts then down to her pink mound. She pulled her knees up, arching her back to get rid of the ache from James's intense possession, then rested her legs either side of the deckchair. 'What's the matter? Wouldn't you like to lick me? That's how to get me ready for your cock.'

Jacob groaned. 'Don't start teasing me. I'm burning already. Come on. Let's go.'

She noticed the pace of Jacob's breathing increase. Served him right for leaving her in the night. She knew he would be back for more. 'Do you like my new jewellery?' she said to distract him. She opened her legs further to show him. 'I've changed from a stud to a ring,' she teased. 'Look, I can hang decorations off the ring.' She raised the ring, showing him the small gold bauble that hung off it.

'Oh God, Angie. You don't need anything to make you beautiful,' he croaked. She opened her legs wider still then looked at Jacob. His mouth was slightly open; his gaze riveted on her shaven mound and its decorative jewellery.

'You know, I'm sure it would feel nice if you put the tip of your tongue through the ring and pulled gently. I'd like you to do that to me.'

Tentatively, he reached out and stroked her. 'You are so soft. So silky.' He closed his hand into a fist as if trying to stop himself exploring her.

'You haven't seen a shaven woman before, have you?'

'No.' He shook his head. 'No-one except you.'

'I love it when a man licks me when I am bare. That's why I shave. It intensifies the sensation.' She reached down and put her index finger inside herself. Her inner lips parted to her touch. She took his hand and placed it on her.

173

'Oh Angie. Don't start doing this to me here. It's too dangerous.' She could see perspiration forming on his brow.

'Don't move your hand. Touch me. I'm silken on the inside too.' He explored her softly with his fingers. Little tingles of pleasure spread from her mound to her nipples. She was aroused by his touch; wanted more of it. 'You know, Jacob, I like it when you do that to me. Your fingers feel terrific.'

'I've never met a woman like you. You are so bold. You don't care if someone sees us.'

Angie laughed, but the sound came out as a purr of pleasure, like a cat being stroked. That was exactly what she wanted. The idea of Jacob licking her while the man stood watch, partially hidden from view, fuelled her fantasy. She could imagine him there in the bushes, hard with wanting her. It was exciting to know that if Jacob could not satisfy her, the man in the bushes would be waiting to take his turn. At least that was what she hoped. The familiar pooling of tension started just above her mound. She could barely wait for his hot tongue to find all her secret places.

'Don't keep me waiting, Jacob. It's my turn to be pleased.'

Jacob stood, looked around him, then knelt at her feet. Angie slid down the deckchair, positioning herself under him. 'Start with sliding your tongue inside me. I want you to do it like a little cock,' she ordered.

Tentatively he put his tongue inside her. Angie bucked in response, her buttock muscles clenched. The intensity of her response surprised her. His tongue was warm and slippery. Aroused and tender from her encounter with James, Jacob's exploration intensified her pleasure.

'Did I hurt you?' Jacob looked at her, confused.

'No. Do it again. I'm just so sensitive. I didn't expect it to feel so good.'

Jacob's expression brightened. He slid his tongue in her again. Angie moaned softly and closed her eyes. 'Oh, that's it. Slide it in and out. In and out.' She rocked her pelvis gently. Heat built inside her as she responded to Jacob's tonguing.

Clearly encouraged by her sighs, Jacob pushed his tongue in further until his warm lips met her entrance. Tiny prickles of hair from his chin brushed against her shaven lips, adding to the cocktail of erotic sensations.

She could feel the ice cubes melting against her warm buttocks. Her eyes still closed, she searched them out with her fingers, then rubbed the cool cubes over her nipples.

Jacob placed his hands on her hips. His tongue slid out of her, only to explore her tender shaven lips. He sucked, then nibbled, licking her from the base to the tip of her mound. Angie sensed his enthusiasm for his sensual task growing as he matched her every sigh with each firm stroke of his tongue.

The ice between her fingertips dissolved as she arched to meet his questing tongue and lips. 'Oh Jacob, don't stop. Keep licking me. Oh yes. Yes.' Opening her eyes, a thrill rippled through her. A dark man, his features partially obscured by the foliage, stood watching only a few feet away. Would he join them? Or would he stay a silent observer?

She closed her eyes, letting her fantasy take over. She imagined the man standing there in the bushes, his hand stroking his cock. First she would have Jacob. If his cock were as enthusiastic as his tongue, he would be sensational. But the thought of Jacob taking her did not stop her wanting the man as well. Once was never enough for her.

She could imagine the stranger walking silently towards them, opening the pool gate and standing just out of Jacob's line of vision. She wanted him to wait to take his turn. She did not need to know his name or to let him speak. Angie just needed the stranger to pleasure and please her until she could take no more.

A cool sensation on her clit made her cry out. Looking down, she realised Jacob had found the remaining ice. He slid it up and down her, following it closely with his tongue. His innovation surprised her. Untrained, he was good. As a student of her tutelage, he would be sensational. Too good to let go.

Jacob cupped his hands under her bottom. His questing tongue found her sensitive inner core. He teased her, putting the pointy end of his tongue in her clitoral ring and gently pulling.

Angie cried, a short, sharp gasp of excitement. She was so close to total surrender, she could no longer think straight. The combination of knowing they were being watched while Jacob tormented her with his lips and tongue was almost too much.

Impassioned by her cries, Jacob continued to stroke her until she arched and called out his name. Every muscle, every nerve ending she possessed tensed until she reached a pinnacle of ecstasy. Time stopped. She was aware of nothing but the electric intensity of her orgasm as Jacob's tongue oscillated on her most sensitive place. Pleasure streaked through her, then slowly subsided, leaving her fighting to catch her breath.

She pushed him away, unable to take any more of his insistent tonguing. She needed him to fill her but there was one other little game she had in mind. Though her legs were wobbly, she climbed off the deckchair. 'Take your clothes off,' she said.

Jacob did not argue. Instead, he rapidly peeled off his T-shirt and shorts, but Angie was too consumed with orgasm afterglow to laugh. Her little public display was not finished. Careful not to alert Jacob to their observer's presence, she walked over to the bar and leant her elbows on it. She rested her cheek on the cool bar top so she would be able to watch the stranger.

'I want you to spank me. Make my bottom pink the way you did before on the beach.' She turned to Jacob. 'Come on.'

Jacob followed her, his erection stiff, its end glistening. 'Angie, I can't wait. I can't think of anything else but taking you.'

'I will let you have me, but I want you to spank me first. You see, I like a little pain mixed with pleasure. It's my turn to be satisfied this time. So I want you to do things my way.'

'Angie.' Jacob groaned. 'I've waited –'

'Who cares,' she interjected. 'Spank me,' she ordered, not listening to his appeal. She knew her voice would carry across the morning silence, accompanied only by the sound of awakening birds. She steadied herself at the bar, sticking out her bottom. 'Do it!' It was time to give her voyeur the second act of her show. Just to warm him up enough so he felt compelled to join them in the finale.

The noise of Jacob's hand making contact with her bottom made a sound like a small clap. She turned, her eyes narrowed to a glare. 'Harder. I want to feel it.' She saw the reluctance on his face. 'Imagine your cock, filling me, sliding into me. If you want to feel how good that is, you'll do as I ask. Now hurry up.'

This time his hand made contact with a resounding thwack and she felt the tingles of delight on her bottom. She was too high with pleasure to feel pain. 'Again,' she ordered. Resting her head on the bar, her eyes scanned the bushes for her intruder. Thwack. Jacob continued to spank her. She wiggled in response. He ran his hands over her bottom, sliding his fingers down her crack. She bit her bottom lip when his fingers slid over her sensitive clit. 'Oh, that feels good.' She was open with wanting him. When Jacob was inside her, when he was too aroused to stop, she would call to the man and ask him to join them.

'God, Angie, you are slippery. I can't wait.'

'Keep spanking me.' She did not bother to turn her head. Jacob made a good slave even if he did protest occasionally. Anyway, she did not mind because she liked ordering him around. Thwack. Thwack. He spanked her, harder this time, his frustration showing in the timing. He rubbed her bottom with the palm of his hand, then slid his hand downward again, caressing her silky shaven lips, his index finger teasing her swollen bud. She could imagine his cock driving into her. Her legs trembled. Her eyes closed. She arched her back. Thwack. Thwack. It was enough to make her come again. She cried out, her fingers tightening their grip on the bar top.

Jacob wrapped both hands around her waist, his cock nudging her entrance. He slipped his cock up and down her slit and she parted her legs in response.

Angie braced herself, ready for him to slide into her, to stretch and fill her. Her breath held in anticipation, she looked for the man. What would he do as he watched Jacob taking her?

She could see him moving. She strained her eyes, trying to recognise him, but he kept moving out of her view. 'Shove it in me,' she called. What was taking Jacob so long?

A flock of brightly coloured parrots flew from the trees above the man, obviously disturbed by his movement. Feeling Jacob hesitate, she turned to face him. He was looking towards the greenery that bordered the pool area.

'Damn. I think someone is here.'

Angie stood and turned to look at him, taking his face in her hands? 'Do you want me? Do you want to put your cock right up inside me?'

'You know I do.'

'Then let whoever it is watch. That's the way I want it to be.'

'No, Angie. No.'

She saw a flash of uncertainty on his handsome face, but she leant forward, kissing him. Reaching down, she took his cock in her hand, caressing him. 'Do you like what I'm doing with my hand?' she whispered, her lips grazing his.

His answer was a soft moan. Jacob closed his eyes as she built up a steady rhythm. 'Imagine entering me. I'm ready for you. Let the man in the bushes watch.' Her action was enough to still his protestations because he gathered her in his arms, his cock pressing hard against her entrance. She could feel it pulsing.

'Stop right there,' called an authoritative woman's voice. Angie jerked her face from Jacob's, looking in the opposite direction to the man. Tahillia Ash walked towards them from the direction of the grotto pool. She stopped only a few feet away, her arms folded, her face a victorious sneer.

'I knew I only had to wait before I caught you breaking hotel regulations. Staff members are not allowed in the pool enclosure. Look at you both. Fornicating in full view of everyone.'

'Oh no,' groaned Angie. Where had she come from? She had been so busy concentrating on their intruder that she had not realised Tahillia Ash had been standing only a few feet away.

Before Angie could say anything else, she heard the pool gate open. She turned to see James step into the pool enclosure.

'I told you she puts on an entertaining show, Tahillia.' He walked towards Angie. 'I enjoyed it immensely, particularly the spanking.' He reached over and rubbed his hand over her bottom.

'Don't touch me.' She pushed him away.

'Leave her alone.' Jacob stepped between Angie and James. She noticed how Jacob's muscles clenched; a vein bulged on his forehead. He would fight to protect her, she realised, but she was not pleased about it. Gentle, kind Jacob was going to lose one of the best training positions in the hospitality industry because of her.

James just laughed. 'Your toy boy is getting possessive.'

'He is not my toy boy. He is my friend,' she countered. It was true, she realised. She liked Jacob and she would miss him if he were not around to torment and tease.

'Angie, you little slut,' drawled James, 'you just can't get enough. Did you tell your friend how much you enjoyed me fucking you in the grotto? Did you tell him how his tongue was licking where my cock has been?'

'That's a lie. She wouldn't go near an old bloke like you. Don't think I'm going to let you get away with insulting her. Angie's not a slut.'

James folded his arms and laughed. 'Oh, but she is. That is what I like about her.' He looked Jacob up and down, his gaze lingering on Jacob's now flaccid penis. 'I happen to know Angie likes older men. I don't lose my hard-on under pressure, do I, Angie? I can keep going and going.' He stopped to smile menacingly at Jacob. 'Don't think she would ever be satisfied with you.'

'Stop it, James.' Angie glared at him, furious at the way he was goading Jacob, but it only seemed to encourage him further.

'I can last the distance with this delectable slut. Only I don't let her order me about like a foolish, young pup. I call the shots. Angie knows I expect complete obedience.'

'You bastard.' Jacob took a step towards James, his fists clenched, ready to swing.

Tahillia Ash laughed, the high-pitched sound grating on Angie's nerves like fingernails dragged across a blackboard.

'That's enough!' said Angie to James. 'If you have a fight to pick then deal with me. Leave Jacob out of this.' From the look on James's face she could tell this was going to get nasty, but she did not want to drag Jacob down with her.

'And you stop it, too,' she added to Jacob, worried he would risk getting himself hurt to protect her. 'I can look after myself.'

'Is it true, Angie?' asked Jacob. 'Were you with him?'

She looked at Jacob. At twenty, his face was unlined; he still had dewy skin and soft lips. Life had not etched any pain. Surely Jacob must know that her being with James was a possibility; after all, he had seen her with Rick and Kate. He knew she was wild. He had said it himself. Yet when she looked into his eyes, she could see the potential for hurt that lay there and she could not bring herself to answer his question.

'Tell him, Angie,' ordered James. 'He wants to hear you say how you quivered at my touch. Describe to him what I did to you. Why don't you tell him how much you enjoyed my cock? Maybe he will learn something.'

Angie forced herself to breathe slowly, knowing James had got to her. She wanted to scream at him but she knew if he could see how upset she was, he would goad her further. She swallowed, forcing herself to face Jacob. 'I was with James in the grotto.'

'No!' Jacob looked at her in disbelief. 'He made you. He promised you a top job.' There was desperation in his voice. 'Angie, how could you? This guy is a creep.'

James laughed before turning on Jacob. 'She enjoyed every moment, you young fool. You loved what I did to you, didn't you, Angie?'

'No,' she answered. She was not going to let him score against Jacob. James had done enough damage already. 'I didn't enjoy it. Sex is all about power for you. You do nothing for me. I used you because you came along at a convenient time.'

'Lies. You begged me to take you. Admit it,' said James.

Angie noticed his face darken with anger and she was

181

pleased. Serve the manipulating bastard right. Jacob had been hurt unnecessarily and it mattered to her. He deserved better.

She maintained James's stare, determined not to back down. 'Don't be ridiculous. You were a convenience. Nothing more.' She glanced at Jacob, hoping her words eased his distress. Why did she have to develop a guilty conscience now? she wondered with annoyance. She had never suffered from one before.

But the answer was there, staring her in the face. She had been caught out due to her own sloppiness. A hunter had to remain cautious at all times. She had not realised that it was James hiding in the foliage. The danger of discovery had only served to fuel her lust. Jacob was an innocent victim who had finally relented in the face of her frenzied pursuit. Her determination to seduce him had over-ridden everything. She had played right into James's hands. No doubt he had invited Tahillia Ash to witness her unruliness. She would have to pay the price for her stupidity, but she did not want to drag Jacob down with her. He was the nicest man she had ever met.

Angie felt Tahillia's fingers dig into her shoulder. She turned to face her.

'I want you off my island,' said Tahillia. 'I took you on because James recommended you highly. But from the moment you arrived, I knew you were a useless tramp, not fit for anything except washing dishes. I will make sure you never get a job in the hospitality industry.'

'Come now, I think you are being a bit harsh, Tahillia,' said James. 'Angie won the Academy's scholarship. Without a good work experience report, it is worth nothing. I would like you to consider giving Angie a second chance. With a bit of guidance, I'm sure you will see a great improvement.'

Angie looked at James, surprised that he had come to

her defence. His dark eyes gleamed in the early-morning light. An uncomfortable feeling settled in her stomach. Things were never simple when it came to James. Whatever he had in mind for her, she was sure that it did not encompass her salvation.

'Oh. Is that right?' said Tahillia. 'Why should I give this filthy bitch a second chance? She has been trouble from the moment she arrived.'

'That is because she is young. You have trained many of my students. You know that some of them need firm guidance.' James pushed past Jacob and stood face to face with Angie. 'Watch, my dear Tahillia. I will show you what I mean.' James cupped his hand under Angie's chin. His fingers caressed her face. 'You want to keep your scholarship, don't you?'

'You know I do,' said Angie. She turned her chin to free herself. She liked it when he touched her, but she knew his caress always came with an emotional price.

Not put off by her rejection of him, James ran one of his hands over her breast and down her stomach until he reached her soft mound.

Angie shivered with excitement. Whether she liked it or not, there was something about him that aroused her. She dug her fingers into her palms, willing herself not to respond. She did not like James, nor did she want to believe that his hypnotic suggestions in the grotto had any influence over her.

James slid his fingers between her legs, stroking her tender lips. Angie clenched all her muscles, but she could not stop her legs trembling. She glared at him, hating him, furious with herself for wanting him at the same time. She knew Jacob would be watching her, not liking her response to James's questing fingers.

James located her piercing and slipped his little finger inside it. 'They use rings to tame bulls,' he said to Tahillia. 'They can lead them around, like so.' James pulled on Angie's ring and she stepped forward. She bit

183

her lower lip, trying to control her fury. He was not hurting her, merely demonstrating his power over her. If it had been anyone else, Angie would have retaliated, but James was a master of manipulation. She needed her scholarship. Courses were hideously expensive; she could never afford to pay.

'Let her go,' growled Jacob.

'Just shut up, Jacob. Stay out of this,' snapped Angie.

'I have no intention of hurting her,' said James, releasing Angie. 'I just wanted to give Tahillia a demonstration on how obedient Angie can be with the right amount of guidance.'

Tahillia laughed. 'James, you never cease to amuse me. I don't know how you come up with your ideas.'

'Then perhaps you should consider letting Angie complete her work experience because I am going to reprimand her. I don't like it when students let me down. It gives the Academy a bad name.'

'I don't want her here. I'll be glad to see the back of her.' Tahillia looked at Angie with real dislike.

'Now, Tahillia,' said James persuasively, 'I have thought of something that will delight and amuse you. I know how you like to be entertained. Perhaps you will reconsider when you see what I have planned.'

Tahillia smiled, her face alight with interest. She raised her eyebrows speculatively at James, appearing to consider his proposal. 'You may be right.' Her gaze moved to Jacob, roving over his taut, muscular frame before settling on his penis.

'Oh no,' groaned Angie under her breath. Though she knew she could cope with anything these two dreamt up, Jacob would not. She did not want Tahillia Ash corrupting him. The world was full of tainted men, but Jacob was different in his honesty. She wanted him to stay that way so she could enjoy him.

'I think these two should learn what happens when

staff break the rules at Hotel Desire,' said Tahillia, looking at Angie and Jacob.

James nodded his head in agreement. 'Most definitely.'

Then Tahillia smiled again, raising her top lip, which emphasised her prominent teeth, reminding Angie of a rat.

'I believe you have not had the pleasure of using the Room of Retribution for some time,' said James.

Angie's ears positively pricked up, her mood instantly lightened. The Room of Retribution. Now he was talking. James's idea of a reprimand sounded more exciting than Tahillia's punishment of endless dishwashing.

'None of our current guests seem that way inclined at the moment,' said Tahillia, sniffing. 'Unfortunately, they don't make rock stars like they used to. Nick Holt and his band are pathetic. Show them a whip and they run for their lives.'

Show me a whip and I would open my legs, Angie thought. She had already experienced James's idea of punishment in his office in Sydney and had enjoyed it immensely. The problem was she had been determined not to let James manipulate her again. Angie liked to call the shots, yet her career was important to her. For the moment she would have to do as James ordered.

'The Room of Retribution!' Jacob looked from James to Tahillia, his eyes bulging.

Angie would have laughed if Jacob's expression had not been so serious. He had barely said a word since he had found out about her and James.

'Forget it, you weirdos. We're not going to take part in any of your sick stuff. Come on, Angie. Let's get our clothes and pack. I don't want any part of this,' said Jacob firmly, but Angie stood where she was. She was not going to miss out on this for anything.

Jacob walked into the cabana and got a pool robe for

Angie, putting it around her shoulders. Then he gathered his scattered clothes and put them on.

'If you leave now, consider your course terminated,' said James, his hands on his hips.

'No, Jacob, wait,' said Angie. 'I don't want you to fail the course because of me.'

'It doesn't matter,' Jacob urged, taking her by the elbow. 'Don't listen to these two. We can still get jobs in the industry. I know people too. We don't need our diplomas to get a job.'

We need a diploma to get one in a good hotel, thought Angie. James's help and a great reference would make all the difference. If it had not been for her, Jacob would have had an excellent reference. She pulled away from him and walked towards James. 'I will cooperate if you let Jacob off,' she said to James and Tahillia.

'What?' Jacob looked at her with amazement. 'Angie, don't be stupid. You do not have to do what James says. He can't be much of a stud if he has to use his position to seduce students. I think he's pathetic.'

'Shut up, Jacob. You are making this worse,' said Angie.

'Why, Angie, how very unselfish you have become. I am disappointed. That is most unlike you,' said James, his voice dripping sarcasm. 'You both broke the rules. I have no intention of letting Jacob go unreprimanded. I don't want to disappoint Tahillia. She is rather partial to young men.'

Angie's spirit sank. She knew James intended to make Jacob pay for his remarks. Tahillia too, Angie realised, would enjoy exacting revenge on Jacob, who did not deserve any form of retribution.

'Forget it. I'm not letting that old bat near me,' said Jacob firmly.

Angie groaned and rolled her eyes. 'Oh God, Jacob, will you just shut up! Let me handle this.' Jacob was doing a great job of ensuring a whipping. While she would enjoy it, she knew Jacob would be horrified, yet he was not exactly helping his case. Tahillia, she guessed, was approaching the sensitive age of 40. Insulting her about her age guaranteed Tahillia would enjoy tormenting him. She could imagine her chaining Jacob until he could not move, teasing him, making him hard, and then sliding on to his cock.

She frowned, trying to clear her mind of the revolting image. There had to be some solution that did not involve Jacob. She did not want him to leave nor did she want Tahillia to have him. She looked at James and Tahillia, each a mirror image of debauchery. Then she thought of a rather exciting solution. If she were in luck, maybe James and Tahillia would agree. 'I'll do anything you want, but on one condition. I want you to do everything to me. Let Jacob watch instead. I don't want either of you to touch him.'

'No,' said Jacob, standing his ground. 'Either we both leave or we take whatever is coming together.'

Angie groaned. She did not want a hero. What she wanted was a virgin to seduce, and judging by the way Tahillia looked at Jacob, 'the old bat' had similar plans. Angie walked over to Jacob and took his hand. 'You won't cope, you idiot. Let's do this my way.'

Looking into her eyes, Jacob squeezed her hand. 'I'm not going to let you take the rap. It's not fair.'

'A touching performance,' said Tahillia, her eyes alight with malice. 'It is so romantic watching these two try to save each other.'

'I intend to reprimand you both. Make your choice. Leave or stay and take the consequences,' said James to Angie and Jacob.

'We will stay,' said Jacob.

Damn, thought Angie. Jacob would have to put up with Tahillia slithering all over him.

She, on the other hand, would have to accept James as her master. Tingles spread all over Angie's body.

Although she was more the hunted than the hunter, Angie was intrigued. She had lied when she had told James he was a convenience. James could excite and stir her like no other man. In the Room of Retribution, he would be at his best, and Angie could barely wait.

Chapter Ten

Thrilled and intrigued, Angie entered the Room of Retribution. She had never encountered a room dedicated to bondage before. The walls were washed the colour of a well-matured red wine. Although the room was dark, a light breeze blew in from the windows. She could see the sea, a sparkling brilliant blue, though at the moment life outside was a distant abstraction.

Solid brass rings, some with leather cuffs, were imbedded in the walls and floor. A chain hung from the roof; a leather harness attached to the chain swung slightly in the breeze. Angie bit her lip in excitement. She had never had the opportunity to try a harness before.

While she was looking forward to this, Jacob clearly was not. She noticed perspiration beading on his body. For him, she suspected, entering the Room of Retribution was like visiting an alien territory. His face was the colour of chalk and his gaze moved rapidly up and down from the walls to the ceiling as if trying to comprehend his strange environment. If his head swivelled any more he would be suitable for a lead role in *The Exorcist*, she thought with amusement. When his gaze finally stilled, she noticed he was staring at a stand containing whips, paddles and straps, plus the odd nipple clamp.

He should have stopped trying to be a hero, she thought. Jacob was way out of his depth.

'Strip her and put her in the harness,' ordered Tahillia. James pulled Angie's pool robe from her and lifted her into the harness. He strapped her arms and legs so that she could not move, then stood back to view his handiwork. His dark eyes shone with pleasure as his gaze roved over her. Angie's stomach clenched tight as she rode the waves of excitement combined with nervousness. Helpless and exposed, she could see James was savouring her with delicious intent.

She wriggled in the harness, testing her bonds. The leather harness, which supported her back and bottom, swung slightly. She tried closing her legs but the harness was designed for full penetration. Eventually her leg muscles cramped and her knees fell open. Vulnerability combined with the heady cocktail of arousal left her heart pattering in her chest.

Jacob stood watching as James secured her. His hands were bunched into fists. She could see every muscle in his lithe body was strained with tension. A vein pulsed on his temple. He was poised to fight, but the rules in this game were different.

'James, bring me some rope. I'm going to tie Jacob to the rings on the floor near the slave.' Tahillia motioned to Angie. 'It's time he saw what we do to disobedient students.'

'Anything to make you happy.' James smiled, his teeth wolfish in his pale face. He walked over to the stand and picked out some short pieces of rope that served as straps. It was clear to Angie that he was enjoying himself immensely, yet there was no tell-tale bulge in his pants.

He handed the straps to Tahillia. 'I will leave you to enjoy reprimanding your slaves.' He bent and whispered something in Tahillia's ear. She laughed. The shrill sound made Angie grit her teeth. Where was he going? Why was he leaving now? she wondered. She watched with confusion as James turned. His eyes narrowed as he looked at her, then he walked out of the room, closing the door softly behind him.

Jacob stood frozen, staring at Angie. He was beautiful, thought Angie with disappointment, wishing she were free to take him. He reminded her of a Greek sculpture.

'Take off your clothes and lie on your back.' Tahillia selected a thin riding crop from the stand and walked over to him. 'Didn't you hear me?' She ran the riding crop over his body, stopping to tease the lump in his shorts with the crop. Jacob wrenched the crop from her hands, holding it in his clenched fist.

'Don't touch me,' he growled.

Angie watched with fascination as Mr Virgin insisted on protecting the crown jewels. She would not have predicted that Jacob would have the courage to put up a fight.

'Give me the crop.' Tahillia held out her hand. 'Every moment you resist me, your fellow slave will pay.'

At the mention of Angie, Jacob looked at her, then he reluctantly surrendered the crop. Blood suffused his face, and she realised the moment cost him dearly.

'Take off everything. I want to see your cock,' ordered Tahillia.

Jacob glared at her, refusing to respond.

Tahillia raised the crop and whacked him on the bottom.

'Ouch!' shouted Jacob as he jumped in the air.

Angie noticed the creamy skin on his neck and throat stain with anger. 'For God's sake, Jacob, you agreed to this. Just get on with it,' she shouted. Angie could not bear the tension. Who would have thought Jacob would have such difficulty becoming a slave. He had been quite well behaved for her at the pool.

'I don't like to be kept waiting,' said Tahillia.

Jacob pulled off his T-shirt, dropping it to the ground. Tahillia flicked her long black hair from her face. Her pointy tongue protruded below her upper lip, slithering across her lips with anticipation. She stood a foot from him, watching his every movement with the intensity of a cobra. The base of her crop flicked up and down, click, click, click, as she tapped her thigh with impatience.

Desire gripped Angie. She had seen Jacob naked several times, but he still moved her. If only Tahillia would order him to finish what they had started by the pool. She remembered the silky warm feel of his bare skin on hers, the heat of his lips and tongue as he pleasured her.

Angie watched, barely breathing, as Jacob peeled off his shorts. His movements were slow with unwillingness. Yet his audience of two observed him as closely as they would a dancer performing a sensuous striptease. Jacob was delicious. He stood, naked, modesty covering himself with his hands.

Tahillia nodded with satisfaction. 'Now it's time to inspect what you are hiding. Put your hands by your side. I want to check whether you are big enough to satisfy me.'

'Forget it. I'm not interested.' His voice was deep and throaty with emotion. He dropped his hands and Tahillia circled him like a shark. His penis was thick but not erect. Jacob looked at Angie, his eyes signalling messages of distress.

'Don't worry,' she said to him. 'She can't have you if you don't get hard.'

'We shall see about that,' said Tahillia. She raised the riding crop and tickled him under the balls with the tasselled end. Though his fist remained clenched he did not try and stop her. Instead he looked down with dismay to see his cock swelling in response.

Angie leant forward, straining at her bonds until her muscles ached. She was wet with wanting him. 'No,' she said. 'Don't give in to her.' Jacob had will power. She hoped his cock would not dominate his brain like most men.

'Lie on the ground and spread your arms and legs. Get a move on,' said Tahillia.

He lay on the floor but looked at her defiantly. 'Don't think you are going to have me,' said Jacob. 'I have more control than you think.'

'Hmph! We shall see. I have never met a man I couldn't break.'

Holding several rope bonds, Tahillia stood over Jacob. She was wearing a lace-up leather bodice combined with a short black skirt and matching black, knee-high leather boots with high heels. She squatted, her knees apart, exposing herself to him.

Angie could see Jacob raise his head, looking straight up Tahillia's skirt. Angie had no idea if Tahillia wore underwear. But whether Jacob liked it or not, his view was having an effect on him. Angie noticed the head of his cock stir. 'Close your eyes. Don't look up her skirt,' called Angie. 'Think of something you hate.'

'Shut up or I'll gag you!' shouted Tahillia, casting her a nasty look. She tied each of Jacob's wrists to the brass rings. Then she reached for his cock, stroking it in full view of Angie. Jacob's penis thickened and stirred.

'"Old bat", indeed! It seems your cock does not agree with your point of view.' She laughed and Angie clenched her teeth at the irritating sound. Tahillia secured his ankles and stood to survey her handiwork.

The door opened and James entered the room. 'I see you have made the slaves ready for our entertainment,' he said.

'They make a beautiful pair,' commented Tahillia. 'I'll enjoy breaking this one,' she said, pointing to Jacob with her crop.

'If you think I'm going to let you have sex with me, then think again,' said Jacob to Tahillia. 'I don't want you.'

Would he ever learn to shut up? wondered Angie. Surely tied to the floor he must realise he was not in a position to argue.

James walked over to him, looking down. 'I will make a deal with you. You keep your cock flaccid, I won't let Tahillia touch you.'

'James, that's hardly fair. I have put no conditions on you and Angie,' protested Tahillia, her disappointment obvious.

Angie could not contain a smile. Serve the stupid bitch right. This was beginning to look interesting.

'Patience, Tahillia. I have promised to entertain you. Have I ever let you down?'

'No,' agreed Tahillia, though her tone showed reluctance.

'Do you agree?' James asked Jacob. 'If you are erect, then you agree to Tahillia doing whatever she wishes with you.'

'Sure. She won't get me hard,' said Jacob. He looked relieved and as relaxed as he was ever going to look in a room of bondage. He raised his head and looked down at his penis, ostensibly to check his cock had the same opinion. Though slightly swollen, it had not become any bigger. 'Don't let me down or that weird bat will get you,' he said.

Angie closed her eyes and groaned. Jacob had been so polite when she had met him. While she did not mind in the least being a bad influence on Jacob, this was not the time to show it.

James's eyes glinted as he watched Jacob. He had something planned, thought Angie. A feeling of unease fluttered in her stomach. Why else would he bother to bargain?

James walked to the stand, surveying the implements. 'We shall have to see what appeals to you. I don't want Tahillia to be disappointed.'

'You can forget that bizarre stuff. That isn't going to do a thing for me,' shouted Jacob.

James picked out a thin gold chain with nipple clamps on each end. Turning it over in his palm, he walked towards Jacob. He held one clamp, letting the other swing from its chain, back and forward, in front of Jacob's eyes.

'Listen, you pathetic creep,' said Jacob. 'Why can't you understand that you and your implements won't get me hard?'

'Actually, I was planning to use these on Angie. You can enjoy watching.'

'Oh no. Sorry Angie,' said Jacob.

'Idiot,' she replied, shaking her head.

When James attached each nipple clamp to Angie's breasts, her aureoles tightened in response. But though the clamps were tight, they were not painful. He tweaked the light gold chain. Angie's breasts jiggled in response. James stood aside so that he could observe Jacob. He played with the chain then caressed her breasts. The different sensations sent scintillating messages over the delicate skin of her chest. She opened her lips and moaned softly.

Jacob's eyes bulged then he looked down at his cock. 'Oh no,' he moaned, quickly closing his eyes. 'Don't look. Don't look. Don't look,' he repeated like a mantra.

Tahillia walked over, holding a dildo, and began sliding it over Angie's sex. Angie knew she was slippery and open after her night of frenzied passion. The dildo felt like a hard cock nudging her entrance, and she clenched down on it, gasping with pleasure as it entered her. James continued to strum the gold chain, and she writhed, biting hard on her lower lip, trying to keep silent. 'Oh God, Oh God,' Angie cried, her head thrown back and her eyelids fluttering as Tahillia and James tormented her.

'That's it. Cry out like you did by the pool,' said

195

Tahillia. 'Open your eyes, Jacob. Watch and see how this blonde slut enjoys me sliding this dildo in and out of her. Look at the way she is responding. See how her beautiful, firm breasts dance when James touches her. She loves what we are doing to her.'

Jacob squeezed his eyes firmly shut. 'No. No. Don't cry out, Angie. Please don't cry out,' he muttered to himself.

'You delectable slut,' crooned James. 'I know exactly what you like. I'm going to stroke you. Slide my fingers over your delicate pussy lips.' He reached over and teased her little bud. 'How swollen you feel. You want a real cock inside you. See the way Jacob is getting hard. You would like his cock, wouldn't you? Think of him pushing inside you.'

Angie arched to meet his touch. 'Yes, yes.' Her sighs filled the room. She was so sensitive after Jacob's tonguing she could not stay quiet.

'Angie, please!' cried Jacob, 'Stop it. Just stop.'

Looking at Jacob, she could see his head moving from side to side, his eyes clenched shut, but his cock seemed to be responding to her sighs of pleasure.

She squirmed, trying to avoid James's fingers, but as he had demonstrated so aptly in the grotto, he knew how to make her ache for his touch.

Tahillia increased the rhythm of the dildo, sliding it in and out as James stroked her. Trying to hold back her orgasm only made things worse. A flood of ecstasy surged through her. She moaned, writhing and bucking. A cry deep in her throat rose to a crescendo.

Throwing her head back as she arched, her whole body quivered like the plucked string of a violin, until at last she slumped forward, her blonde hair covering her face.

'What a wonderful performance,' said Tahillia. 'You couldn't resist watching this blonde slut come,' she said to Jacob.

Withdrawing the dildo, she walked over to him. 'Taste what you have been missing out on.' She slid the dildo over Jacob's lips. Angie's juices left a glistening trail. Jacob licked his lips and moaned. He looked down at his cock. 'Oh no,' he gasped. It was swollen and sitting on his abdomen.

Tahillia reached over and stroked it. 'He is not hard enough to mount,' she said to James. 'But he is close.'

She slid off her underwear. 'You liked what we did to her, didn't you? You wished you were inside her instead of this dildo.' She squatted over him. Putting the dildo aside, she took hold of his sac and cock in her hands. 'I will have you.' She slid the head of his cock up and down her pussy. Tahillia's eyes narrowed to tiny slits. 'I am going to make you fill me.'

Jacob looked at her in horror, then closed his eyes tight. 'No. No. Stay down. Stay down,' he repeated, his lips murmuring a private prayer to his penis.

'Patience, Tahillia,' said James. 'It is time for that special surprise I promised you. He won't be able to resist what I have planned.'

Tahillia stood and nudged Jacob's tight balls with the pointy end of her black boot. 'I do not like to be kept waiting by slaves. I need a cock in me.'

Angie raised her head, alarmed at the forceful nature of Tahillia's voice. She could see Jacob's chest heaving, his lips mumbling. Perspiration dribbled off him as he fought to contain his erection.

'Think of something you hate,' she said. 'Don't let her have you.'

'I'm trying. Oh God, how I'm trying. But she's been sliding my cock over her. It feels so good.' Jacob moaned a long, deep sigh. 'Then, when I open my eyes, all I see is you, pink and swollen. When I close them I can't stop the image of that dildo entering you. I can still taste you. Oh no!' The dismay in Jacob's voice rang out as he glanced down at his thick member.

'Then don't look at me, damn you. Keep your eyes closed. Try and think of something you don't like. Pretend it is Rod touching you. You know how gay sex turns you off.'

James's eyes gleamed at Angie's words. 'So he does not like men.' James looked at Jacob. 'I could have you myself.'

'You!' exclaimed Jacob, looking ill at the thought of James taking him.

'But seeing as I promised to entertain Tahillia,' James continued, 'pleasing her will have to come first, which means –' James looked at Angie '– you will have to see others pleasure themselves with Jacob instead.'

'Others?' repeated Angie, wondering what he meant.

'Come in,' called James, looking towards the doorway.

The door opened and in walked Isabella di Bellini. Angie's eyes widened in alarm. 'Oh no,' she groaned. So James did have something planned. She was not sure what it was, but she knew that if anyone could help crack Jacob's penile aversion to Tahillia Ash, it would be Isabella.

Angie surveyed Isabella, trying to find fault with her appearance but could not. Petite, with large breasts and a narrow waistline, Isabella personified sex on legs. Jacob liked her. No. What had his words been? Angie remembered what he had said about Isabella. Exquisite. That was the word he had used.

Isabella sauntered over to James, her hips swaying seductively. She flicked her dark, curly hair from her face and raised her eyebrows suggestively. 'What would you have me do, master?' she asked. 'How can I please you this time?'

This time! How many times had she pleased James before? Dislike rose like bile in Angie's throat. So Isabella had already been James's plaything. That did not surprise her. There was nothing Isabella would not do to get a placement at Desire.

Angie looked her over, realising the other girl was dressed to excite. She wore a microscopic gold skirt that started at her hips and ended just below her bottom. Her boob-tube top matched her skirt; its see-through Lycra material clung to her full breasts. A little gold bag complete with tassels hung over her shoulder. She knelt and kissed James's feet, the hem of her gold mini-skirt rising to expose the dark thatch between her legs.

Angie groaned when she realised Jacob was also looking at Isabella. If his erection grew any larger, Tahillia Ash would have him for breakfast.

'Come and see how we treat disobedient students,' said James, leading Isabella over to Jacob and Angie. Isabella stood in front of Angie, her lips curved into a satisfied smile.

'So, she has displeased you, master. I thought she was not suitable for the Desire placement. I wish you had sent me here earlier. I would never have disobeyed you or Ms Ash.' Isabella looked over to Tahillia and smiled obsequiously.

Angie glared at her, her fingers itching to take Isabella by the hair and shake her. 'If you crawled any lower, you would be a snake.'

'My, my, she does have a temper.' Isabella rolled her large dark eyes. James put his arm around her waist, his fingers stroking her flat stomach.

'Perhaps you would like to gag her,' said Tahillia, walking over with a leather gag. She handed it to Isabella.

Isabella giggled. 'I have been wanting to do that from the moment I met her.' She walked up to Angie, standing between Angie's open knees.

'Isabella, don't!' called Jacob. 'Don't let James and Tahillia manipulate you.'

'But I like pleasing James and Tahillia,' she said. She tried to place the gag on Angie's mouth, but Angie fought her, tossing her head from side to side.

Angie was exhausted, and her legs and arms ached, but she managed to close her legs, wrapping them around Isabella's hips so that their faces were inches apart. 'Leave me alone, you bitch.' She strained at her bonds, just managing to grab a handful of Isabella's glossy black hair and pull hard.

'Let me go!' screamed Isabella, digging her fingernails into Angie's hand. James circled them, watching, enjoying the catfight.

Isabella sank her teeth into Angie's wrist, forcing her to let go.

'You bitch!' screamed Angie, tearing her hand away with a fistful of Isabella's hair. 'Don't come near me unless you want more of the same.'

Isabella slapped Angie's face. 'How dare you touch me? Get your filthy legs away from me!' She dug her fingernails into Angie's thighs, forcing Angie to release her.

'Now, now, I did not bring you here to fight,' said James to Isabella, 'though I must say I enjoyed it.' He raised his eyebrows and leant towards her. 'You know what I want you to do.'

'Yes, master,' said Isabella, rubbing her head where Angie had torn out her hair. She brushed her dark curls from her face and rolled her hair into a knot that sat at the base of her neck. 'I will do anything to please you.'

James nodded. 'Do it.'

Isabella placed her hands around Angie's waist and shimmied her body against Angie's with the expertise of a professional belly dancer. 'Does this please you?' She looked at James. 'Is this what you want me to do?'

He nodded, smiling. 'Yes, but turn her so that Jacob can see everything you do to her. Tahillia is most disappointed. She wants to ride him. I'd like you to make that possible, any way you can.'

'I see,' said Isabella. 'Thank you, master. I am happy for the opportunity to serve you both. Watch, Jacob. See how I'm rubbing my body against Angie,' she said huskily, rotating her hips slowly and seductively against Angie's.

'Oh God,' sighed Jacob. His lips parted and his breathing quickened.

'You stupid bitch. How can you let them use you like this?' said Angie, struggling to get another handful of her hair, but Isabella was cautious this time and stayed out of reach of Angie's grasping hands.

'Here, give me the gag,' said Tahillia. 'Hold her face while I tie it. I don't want to hear another word from her.'

Though Angie struggled furiously, she could not fight the two of them. Deprived of her voice, she knew she could do nothing to stop Jacob from succumbing.

Isabella removed the nipple clamps. 'My, my, these must be uncomfortable. Look how erect your nipples are. I have something that will make them feel better.' She reached over and opened her little gold bag. 'Here,' she said. 'Strawberry lipstick.' She pulled off the top of the lipstick, turning the base. 'This will feel nice and it tastes delicious.' She painted Angie's nipples, the wet, warm lipstick turning them red.

'Let me suck your titties to make them feel better.' If she hated Angie for ripping out her hair she no longer showed it. Instead she eagerly licked then sucked Angie's sensitive nipples, her own lipstick leaving smudges on Angie's golden breasts. Angie's eyelids fluttered. She did not want to enjoy this, but the sensation of Isabella's tongue was so different from a man's. Her lips were softer, her tongue small and pointy, but just as potent. In spite of her dislike of Isabella, she thrust her breasts forward to be sucked. Her tender nipples, suddenly free of the clamps, responded urgently to the slippery lipstick and the hot caress of Isabella's tongue.

Tahillia slipped out of her black skirt so that she was

wearing only her leather corset top and long black boots. She walked over to Jacob and knelt close to him. 'You can't stop watching this, can you? You like seeing these young sexy women enjoy each other. Look at the way Isabella is sucking Angie. Watch as her fingers weave down to Angie's pussy. She is wet. Look at the way her sex is glistening. She may not like Isabella, but she responds to her touch.'

Tahillia reached over and took Jacob's cock in her hands, kneading it with her fingers. 'Imagine having them both wanting your cock.' She fondled Jacob, her fingers gliding the pre-come over the velvety end of his penis. 'You would like the two of them at once, wouldn't you?'

'No,' groaned Jacob, but his eyes bulged as he watched Angie and Isabella. His cock grew harder every moment he observed Angie squirm, her arms and legs jerking at her bonds, responding to Isabella's questing mouth and delicate fingers as they reached for her hard nub.

'Don't lie to me.' Tahillia slapped his face. Jacob looked at her in shock. His fists clenched and he struggled to free himself.

'Save your energy for pleasing me,' said Tahillia.

'Come here, Isabella,' ordered Tahillia. 'Angie has had enough attention. Strip for Jacob. He is just how I want him. Hard.' She weighed his cock in her hands. 'Perhaps he would enjoy you as well.'

'Hmmm, hmmm.' Angie struggled at her bonds. She shook her head furiously, glaring at Jacob, but when Tahillia knelt between Jacob's legs, her mouth devouring him, he gasped, seeming not to notice her protest.

Isabella sauntered over to Jacob and peeled off her top, freeing her breasts.

'Oh my God,' said Jacob, his voice hoarse. Isabella's breasts were full with dark nipples.

'I painted Angie's nipples with my lipstick. Would you like me to paint myself?' she asked.

Jacob nodded, his eyes glazing over as Tahillia's head bobbed up and down on his penis.

Isabella decorated her nipples with gold lipstick so that they matched her outfit, then slowly and seductively slid her gold skirt over her hips to reveal a neatly trimmed black thatch. 'Do you like what you see?' she asked him.

'Yes,' he croaked. Jacob's face and neck were flushed and the veins in his temples bulged.

'Don't come yet, sweetie,' said Isabella. 'I want you too.' She parted her legs for him, and slid her fingers over herself. 'Oh, I am wet for you.'

'I do not intend to let him come,' said Tahillia. She walked over to the stand and selected a small, studded leather device. Returning with it, she strapped it over where Jacob's cock and balls met, so that his balls were encased in leather. 'The biker look becomes him, don't you think, Isabella?' asked Tahillia.

'Very sexy,' Isabella sighed as she paraded around Jacob, her hips swinging seductively as she walked. She stopped and knelt near Jacob's face. 'Will you lick the lipstick off? I would like it,' she purred.

'Yes,' panted Jacob. 'Yes, yes.'

'Hmmm, hmmm.' Angie tossed her head from side to side. How dare Jacob give in to her enemies? After all the time she had spent hunting him, she would have thought he would have put up a better fight. So much for him wanting to feel something for the person he made love to. The man was a total pushover. She watched with fury as Isabella leant over Jacob, thrusting her gold-coloured nipples in his face. Jacob eagerly licked her teats until they stiffened, and the gold peaks left traces of colour on his lips. He moaned as Tahillia swirled her tongue over the head of his cock. Angie wanted him, but Jacob seemed to have forgotten her very existence.

James walked over to Angie. 'You don't want them to take him, do you?' He laughed as she glared at him. 'Unfortunately for you, you have no choice. You see, Angie, this is your punishment for your disobedience. You belong to me. In future you will be allowed to have sex when I tell you to, and only with whom I choose. I want you malleable like Isabella.'

Angie's fingers clenched into fists of anger. Damn James. Damn him, she thought, struggling against her restraints, wishing she were free. She had never felt more frustrated in her life, but James ignored her. The sensational show erupting in front of her eyes seemed not to have moved him beyond simple enjoyment. He seemed to have no erection and no desire to take her or to join Isabella and Tahillia. Instead he walked over to Jacob.

'Jacob. Remember our deal. Tahillia wants you and I have promised not to disappoint her.'

Jacob's gaze moved from Isabella's large breasts, then over to Angie, suspended in her leather harness.

'Hmmm, hmmm.' Angie shook her head. 'Hmmm, hmmm.'

'I'm sorry, Angie,' said Jacob. 'I'm dying here. I need release. I just have to have it.' He nodded to James and Tahillia. 'I agree. I think Tahillia's mean, but I want her.' He looked at Isabella and sighed. 'I want them both.'

Isabella giggled, stood, then knelt over Jacob's face, parting herself so that he could please her with his tongue. 'Oh, he is good at this,' she sighed. 'Thank you for training him for me,' she said to Angie.

Angie raged against her bonds. Tears of frustration spilt down her face. James, Tahillia and Isabella. She hated them all, and she wanted Jacob so much that it hurt.

Tahillia smiled; she turned to Angie, her look victorious. 'Watch, slut, and learn from your masters.' Then she lowered herself on to Jacob and his virginity was no more.

Angie could not get the memory of Jacob being taken by Tahillia and Isabella out of her mind. Both had insisted on taking turns to mount him while she was forced to watch. Jacob had lost all his virginal reserve and could not wipe the silly grin from his face.

Anger consumed her. She could not understand how he had managed to hold out on her for so long, only to lose his virginity to the two women she disliked most. The only good thing to come out of the incident was that she had finally escaped kitchen duty and was working in reception. Tahillia, who seemed in a remarkably good mood, forgave Angie all her past misdemeanours. It seemed to Angie that Jacob's silly grin was infectious to everyone except her.

To make matters worse, Isabella, with whom she shared a room, also worked on reception. Wherever Angie went Isabella tagged along, seeming to keep tabs on her every movement.

Tahillia had extended Angie's shift so that she had no time for hunting and, after several days, Angie was feeling the heat of frustration. However, if James thought he was going to dominate her by telling her who she could have sex with, he could forget about it. She was not made of soft putty like Isabella.

James prowled in and out of reception watching Isabella and Angie work. She forced herself to concentrate. Dressed in the hotel uniform of floral shirt complete with her trainee badge and khaki skirt, Angie was busy checking out guests and welcoming new arrivals. She knew she was undergoing assessment and she wanted to do well. No matter how frustrated she was, hunting would have to wait.

A woman wearing a zebra-striped jacket and matching

skirt walked into reception one morning. 'Big game,' said Angie under her breath as the woman walked towards her. Angie shook her head to clear her thoughts. She never hunted women. As a conquest women did not interest her. But this woman was glamorous like a modern-day movie star. The closer she came the more Angie tingled from head to toe.

A headscarf and large dark glasses framed the woman's face. She untied her headscarf and tucked it into her handbag. Her hair was beautifully groomed in a French roll and her magnolia cream skin was flushed with heat. 'Good morning,' she said to Angie, handing over her reservation slip. The woman's fingertips brushed Angie's. Tiny electric pulses threaded their way from Angie's fingertips up to her arms so that the hairs on her arms stood on end.

'Welcome to Hotel Desire,' replied Angie. She looked at the slip. Miss Carolyn Wolf. The name rang a bell. Wolf Publishing, she recalled. She recognised the woman's face from the society pages. Australia had its share of powerful multi-millionaires, but most of them were men.

'I need to change my reservation. My partner has decided to join me. She's flying in tomorrow. I want a double room overlooking the lagoon. Something private.' She took off her sunglasses and stared at Angie with the greenest eyes Angie had ever seen. 'I don't want to be disturbed,' she added huskily.

'I'll check the computer,' said Angie, looking to see what was available. Carolyn Wolf's frank admission of a female partner intrigued Angie. She wondered what it would be like to make love to a woman without the presence of a man. She was not sure she would be satisfied. Angie liked a cock. Liked one a lot. Well, more than one, if she was honest about it.

'Hello, Carolyn.' James walked over and leant on the counter.

Angie noticed the woman stiffen. 'James. It has been some time.'

He smiled and nodded. 'How is your sister?'

'Better now she has got you out of her system.' Carolyn Wolf's gaze hardened as she studied James.

James laughed. 'I warned her not to fall in love with me, but she could not help herself.'

'There is only room for one love in a relationship with you. Yourself! Hopefully she will be a better judge of character next time.'

James seemed unperturbed by Carolyn's insult. 'Cheer up – maybe some of your friends will convert her.'

'I don't think so. Unfortunately, she persists on chasing difficult men who let her down.' Carolyn shook her head, her lips pressed together in disapproval. She turned from James to Angie, obviously not interested in pursuing the conversation.

'Miss Wolf,' said Angie, who had been waiting for the right moment to interrupt, 'I have a double room available. Here is your keycard. Turn right past the dining room. Your room is at the end of the corridor. The porter will bring your luggage.'

'Thank you.'

James wore a half-smile watching Carolyn as she walked away. 'Pity to waste such beauty on another woman.'

'Did she turn you down?' asked Angie.

'Yes. She is angry with me for seducing her sister. I wanted her too. Both at the same time would have been delicious. But Carolyn has no interest in men, which I think is rather a shame.'

'Doesn't sound like she shares your point of view,' said Angie cheekily, thinking it would not hurt James to be knocked back for a change.

Isabella finished tagging a guest's luggage with a room number, walked over and joined Angie. 'Carolyn doesn't know what she is missing. She is crazy to refuse you.' She leant her elbows on the reception counter so that her large breasts pressed together and strained against the fabric of her uniform.

'Oh, please.' Angie rolled her eyes. 'Do you think you could stop grovelling to James? You have your Hotel Desire placement. What more do you want?'

James narrowed his eyes. 'Angie,' he barked. 'Remember you are representing the Hotel Desire. Save your catfights for somewhere private where I can enjoy them. I don't want to see a scowl on your face. You are on reception. Guests want to see a happy face, not a scowl.' He walked away, not waiting for a reply.

Damn, thought Angie, biting her lip. That would go against her in her work experience report. James was right, though, she thought. Guests did not want to see staff bickering. If only she could get away from Isabella and let off some steam. The woman irritated her. She wished she could pull out another chunk of her hair.

'You are just jealous because James favours me,' hissed Isabella when James was safely out of earshot.

'He's using you. James is a manipulator. He wants to pitch us against each other for his own entertainment. Why can't you get that into your thick skull?'

'Who cares.' Isabella shrugged her shoulders. 'James has promised me the position of assistant manager of Hotel Desire when I finish the course.'

Angie felt sick with envy. 'But what about Tahillia?' asked Angie. 'What if she doesn't want you?'

'James is a major shareholder in Hotel Desire. He told me he has been investing in the hotel industry for years. How else do you think he places his students? Besides, I get on with Tahillia. You should learn whom to suck up to if you want to get ahead.'

'Suck being the appropriate word,' said Angie, thinking of Isabella with her gold-painted lips pleasuring Tahillia after they had worn Jacob out. 'There is nothing you wouldn't do to get on the right side of Tahillia, is there?'

'Actually I enjoy making love to a woman. I like the way their bodies feel. Women know what other women like. I find making love to a woman exciting. It's not all over in ten seconds. Men are so fixated with getting their cock in, they forget how sensual a woman's body can be. Have you ever lain side by side with a woman, looking into her eyes, exploring her body with your tongue and hands?' Isabella's pupils dilated, and Angie could see her nipples hardening against the fabric of her uniform.

'But all that flirting you do.' Angie looked at her, surprised. 'You are not into men at all.'

'I flirt with whoever is useful, but if you must know, I prefer women.'

'But don't you miss a cock?' she asked, knowing that sex without a man with a big hard-on was a waste of time.

Isabella shrugged and tossed her curls away from her face. 'There are other things we girls like to use.'

Angie was about to ask for more details when the reception telephone rang. 'Reception,' said Angie, answering the phone. 'Just a moment, Miss Wolf. I will have a look.' Angie walked around the counter to the front of reception. She picked up the phone. 'Yes, Miss Wolf. You've left your handbag on the floor in front of reception. Would you like me to bring it to your room?' Angie put down the phone and turned to Isabella. 'I'm going to take Miss Wolf's handbag to her.'

'Don't be too long. James told me to keep an eye on you. He said you couldn't keep out of trouble.'

'I can do without you spying on me,' said Angie with a grimace. She picked up Carolyn's handbag and walked from reception to her room.

'The door is open,' said Carolyn. 'Bring in my bag and close the door behind you.'

209

Angie walked into the bedroom, closing the door behind her as she was asked to do. She could hear the splashing of water and realised that Carolyn was in the bathroom. Her suitcase lay open on the bed. Clothes were scattered on the bed, but what caught Angie's attention was the strap-on cock. Angie briefly wondered how it would look on the baggage X-ray at customs. Obviously Carolyn came on holidays prepared for pleasure.

Though Angie had never been interested in other women, Isabella's words stayed with her. 'Have you ever lain side by side with a woman, looking into her eyes, exploring her body with your tongue and hands?' She might not like Isabella, but she remembered the sensuous feeling of Isabella's body pressed against hers. Isabella's skin had been soft, the texture so different from a man's. Angie could feel her nipples hardening.

Carolyn came out of the bathroom wearing nothing but a towel. 'It's very steamy on the island, so different from Sydney.'

'Yes. Here is your bag,' she said, holding the black handbag out to Carolyn.

Carolyn took it from her. 'Let me find you a tip.'

Angie smiled and shook her head. 'It's just part of the service.' Her gaze roved over Carolyn. The towel did not hide much. Carolyn had beautiful well-shaped legs and petite feet. Even her toenails were painted in zebra stripes. Angie wanted to shake herself to stop the tingles working their way over her body. What she needed was a big, hard cock, she reminded herself.

'No. I insist. I think anyone who works near James Steele deserves a reward.' As she looked in her handbag the towel unravelled, exposing her breasts. They were petite with rosebud nipples.

Angie forced herself to look Carolyn in the eyes, but her gaze fell to Carolyn's breasts. Heat swelled in her loins. Carolyn looked thirty-something with a gym-toned body. She removed the towel and retied it around her hips. Angie licked her dry lips. She could imagine Carolyn wearing that strap-on cock, plunging into her. Maybe Isabella had a point. Angie bit her lip. Stay out of trouble. Stay out of trouble. Stay out of trouble, she repeated to herself.

'Here you are,' said Carolyn. Placing her bag on the bed, she held out a twenty-dollar note. 'It would have been very annoying to lose my handbag. I came here to relax and enjoy the sunshine. I'm told everyone goes naked on the beach here. Is that true?'

It would have seemed churlish not to accept the tip. Angie took it from her, but as her fingers touched Carolyn she shivered. 'Yes,' she said. 'Guests generally wear bathers in the pool area but not on the beaches. The island is a relaxed sort of place.' Her voice dropped an octave. 'You can do what you like on the beach. You can follow your desire.'

She could imagine Carolyn naked, walking along the yellow sand of the beach. She would like to walk with her then take her in her arms, feel her silky skin against hers and the rush of waves at their feet. Angie closed her eyes, momentarily fighting to get her mind off sex. She knew she was expected back on reception, yet her mind reeled with fantasies. James's deliberate deprivation of her sex life was getting to her.

'Stay a bit. I want to talk to you,' said Carolyn. 'You aren't busy, are you?' she asked.

'No,' Angie lied, wondering if Carolyn could sense how turned on she was. She should have said yes and left, but Carolyn was staring at Angie with the most incredible green eyes lined with black eyeliner. It felt odd being attracted to a woman, but this was no ordinary woman. She was sensational.

'Good.' Carolyn smiled, her gaze travelling up and down over Angie. 'You are very beautiful. Have you ever had a woman tell you that?'

'No.' Angie could feel her cheeks colouring, which was a strange feeling. Usually, she was in control, hunting and getting what she wanted from a man. This felt different. She wasn't sure what the rules were, but if she were honest with herself, she was enjoying the titillation of Carolyn's interest. It made her knees wobbly.

Carolyn motioned to the towel that covered her hips. 'Do you mind if I remove my towel? I need to unpack my things and work out what I'm going to wear. It doesn't embarrass you, if I am naked?' she asked.

Angie shook her head. 'No. We get used to that, working here.' She watched as Carolyn slipped the towel from her hips and dropped it to the floor. Though the rest of her body was hairless, her sex was covered with lush, brown hair. Angie longed to stroke it, to slide her fingers between Carolyn's legs. But instead she stayed where she was. She would have to wait until Carolyn made the first move, and the tension was killing her. So much for staying out of trouble.

'So, how is James treating you?' asked Carolyn. She pulled clothes from her suitcase and held them close to her body as if deciding what to wear.

'Pardon?'

'James. How is he treating you?'

Angie shrugged. 'OK, I suppose.' She did not want to discuss James. Instead, she wanted to unbutton her shirt, pull off her skirt and take Carolyn in her arms. She wanted to rub her tingling nipples against this sexy, suave woman. James and his dominance was not a subject she felt like discussing.

'I don't like the man,' Carolyn said bluntly. 'You are doing the Diploma in Hospitality,' she stated, looking at Angie's trainee badge.

'Yes,' Angie said, wondering why she wanted to know.

'My sister Eve did that course, too. Our father left us well off. Eve didn't have to work, but she enrolled because she insisted the Training Academy was the best school.' Carolyn's voice deepened with disapproval. 'That's when she met James.' Her lips tightened as if she had eaten something sour. She pulled another outfit from her suitcase, holding it against herself, then discarded it. She looked at Angie, her green eyes narrowing. 'James seduced her. Eve was so in love with him, she wanted to marry him. He broke her heart.'

'I'm sorry. James likes manipulating women. That's just the way he is.' Angie shrugged. The last person she wanted to talk about was James; instead, her gaze fell to the strap-on cock lying in the bag. She wanted to pick it up and run her fingers over it.

Seeing where Angie was looking, Carolyn nodded. 'Be my guest,' she said, handing the cock to Angie. 'Have you ever touched one of these before?'

Angie took it from her. Made of plastic, the cock was hard, but not unpleasant to touch. An elastic strap at the end of the cock for the wearer to slip around her hips and thighs held it in place. 'Very nice,' she said. She stroked her fingers along the width of the cock, wondering what it would feel like. She could imagine Carolyn strapping it on to her gym-toned body.

'Tell me,' asked Carolyn, taking the cock from her and placing it on the bed. 'Are you in love with James too?'

'Goodness, no.' She thought of how James seemed determined to control every moment of her life. The man was completely obsessive. She had lost Jacob to Isabella and Tahillia because of James. 'I can't stand the man. But I want a good job when I finish my course. James places most of his students in the industry. He's got that kind of pull.' Angie pursed her lips and shrugged. 'I guess I have to put up with him for now.'

Carolyn nodded. 'Some things never change. James knows that and uses it to prey on students.' She reached over and stroked one of her fingers along Angie's face. 'I know how James likes to control women. My sister told me.' She leant forward and placed her lips fleetingly on Angie's. 'But I think women should learn to rely on other women for what they need.' She kissed Angie again, this time more firmly. Angie closed her eyes, savouring the sensuous feeling of Carolyn's lips on hers.

Carolyn pulled away. 'I think we women should stick together. Don't you agree?'

'Yes,' said Angie, putting her arms around Carolyn's waist. She could not stop. Did not want to stop.

Carolyn unbuttoned Angie's shirt buttons, one by one, then peeled her shirt off her shoulders. She traced her index finger over one of Angie's nipples. 'You are a goddess.'

She leant forward and kissed Angie again, but this time she opened her lips, tracing her tongue over Angie's sensitive inner lips. Carolyn's mouth felt soft and lush. She pulled back and took Angie's face in both her hands.

'One day I'll find a way to bring James down,' said Carolyn. 'Teach him a lesson on how to treat a woman.'

Angie looked into her cat-green eyes. She wanted her. She wanted to lie alongside her, explore every part of her. A heavy feeling settled in her pelvis. 'Show me how you treat a woman, Carolyn. I want to know.'

Carolyn did not need any further encouragement. She pulled Angie to her, kissing her while she gently ran her fingers down Angie's spine. Angie felt her breasts squash against Carolyn's. Though Carolyn's breasts were smaller, Angie was conscious of a strange feeling of plumpness pressing against her chest. Intrigued with the difference of a woman's body from that of a man's, Angie held Carolyn close, exploring the fineness of her body. Angie traced her fingers down to Carolyn's waist, which was narrow, almost fragile like a baby bird.

Carolyn broke the kiss and took Angie by the hand over to the bed. 'Have you been with a woman before?'

Angie thought of Kate and Isabella. 'Not like this. Not

without a man around. This seems so different. I can't explain.'

Carolyn nodded. 'I remember the first woman I made love to. She was older and very experienced. She made the men I had been with seem rough. I was hooked. Men think women need them, but we lesbians know differently.'

She lay on the bed and patted it for Angie to join her. 'Take off your skirt. Come and lie with me. Let me explore you.' Carolyn reached behind her and pulled out her hair clips, so that her glossy, brown hair rolled out like a wave, spreading across the pillow.

Quickly, Angie slipped her skirt over her narrow hips, leaving it on the floor.

'Come.' Carolyn reached out for her.

Angie was conscious of Carolyn's liquid stare as she looked at Angie's shaven state, but Carolyn made no comment. Instead, when Angie lay beside her, she reached down and stroked Angie with her fingers. Her hands were small and slim. Angie liked her touch and the way she allowed her space. She did not paw her like a man.

She stroked Angie over her shoulder, then down over her spine. Angie could feel her fingers undulating over her until at last, her hand came to rest, holding her bottom. Carolyn's hand felt warm against her skin.

Leaning on her elbow and supporting her head on her hand, Angie reached over to caress Carolyn's tight cherry-like nipples. She traced her finger over the peaks, feeling them contract further in response to her touch. But what she really wanted to do was to stroke her fingers through the luxuriant curls between Carolyn's legs.

She brushed her hand lightly over Carolyn's warm pussy. Carolyn sighed and arched towards her hand, her eyes heavy with pleasure. Her pubic hair was soft, not wiry like a man's. Angie slipped her fingers between

215

the oyster-like ruffle, finding what she sought between her legs.

'Oh yes,' sighed Carolyn, as Angie slid her fingers up and down. Carolyn lay on her back, pulling Angie close to her and nibbling at her throat and neck. 'Yes, yes,' she sighed, and Angie, encouraged by her sighs of pleasure, slipped two fingers inside her. She was wet.

Angie moistened the ball of her thumb, rubbing it over Carolyn's clit while dipping her fingers deep inside her. She could feel Carolyn trembling, her muscles gripping her fingers.

'That is just heaven,' whispered Carolyn, her words slurred. She closed her eyes and ground against Angie's seeking fingers. Soon she was arching, crying out, her sighs rising until they matched the call of the bright parakeets that flourished on the island.

Finally, as Carolyn's breathing settled, she looked at Angie, a small smile creasing her lips. 'I was supposed to be introducing you to the ways of loving a woman.'

'There's still time.' Angie sucked her fingers that had so recently treated Carolyn to the intricacies of pleasure, and was surprised at the clean yet tangy taste of her.

Carolyn looked at her, her eyes hooded. Casually she stroked Angie's breasts, then leant over to suck her nipples. Despite being sated, Angie sensed that Carolyn wanted to please her. Angie savoured the pleasure she saw reflected in Carolyn's eyes. Her touch sent messages like tiny tingles from her breasts to her stomach and downward. She lay on the pillow enjoying the rich scent of Carolyn's hair as it draped over her. Carolyn rose to a kneeling position between Angie's legs, spreading her wide, her long hair tickling the inside of Angie's thighs. But instead of feeling charged with adrenaline as she did when she hunted, Angie felt languid, savouring every ounce of pleasure Carolyn gave her.

She circled Angie's hot little anus, slipping in her index finger. Then she pushed her thumb between the wetness of Angie's lips and fucked her like a little cock. Angie pulsed to meet her, teasing her own nipples with her fingertips. Her skin was tender and sensitive and she knew it would be soft to Carolyn's touch. Her eyes shut tight, Angie tensed her bottom and legs as Carolyn increased the pace, adding her lips, licking and sucking where Angie needed her most. Unlike a man, Carolyn knew exactly where to go. Days of frustration soon had Angie arching against Carolyn's mouth, shuddering and crying out until her body went limp. When at last Angie could open her eyes she saw that Carolyn had strapped on the cock.

'I know you are used to a man. I wouldn't want you to leave disappointed.'

'Oh,' said Angie, too short of breath to talk.

Carolyn supported herself on her elbows as she slid into Angie. Angie could feel the tips of Carolyn's nipples rubbing against her breasts. She closed her eyes again, letting heaven take her. Carolyn nibbled and sucked on the white of Angie's exposed throat. Angie wrapped her legs around the slender woman's hips, savouring the softness of her body rubbing against her own. All the while the cock slid in and out until Angie cried out, her song of pleasure overtaking the cries of the beautiful parakeets. This was pleasure in its most pure state, and Angie wished as she floated back to earth that she could stay forever in Carolyn's tender embrace.

A knock on the bedroom door brought her back to reality. Carolyn pulled a wrap from her bag and walked to the door, but did not open it. 'Yes. Who is it?'

'It's Isabella di Bellini from reception. I'm looking for Angie, the girl who delivered your handbag.'

Angie tensed. Trust Isabella to come looking for her. James had probably sent her. She leapt from the bed, her head spinning, and struggled into her uniform.

'She was here,' said Carolyn, 'but I sent her to buy me

some cigarettes. I'll tell her you are looking for her. I'll send her straight down when she returns.'

'Oh, thank you,' said Isabella, but her voice sounded none too pleased.

'Thank you,' whispered Angie. 'You probably just saved my skin.' She looked at her watch and groaned. 'I had better get back.' She smoothed the wrinkles out of her uniform, then looked in the bedroom mirror to tidy her hair. She could see from her reflection that her eyes were unusually bright. Her fingers seemed to be all thumbs and she was aware her hands were shaking. Never had she dreamt that being with another woman would be so good. She had not expected it.

Carolyn strolled over and put her arms around Angie. 'Here, let me help you,' she said, and kissed her softly on the lips. She stroked Angie's hair away from her face and twisted it into a French roll similar to the one she had been wearing. 'Any time you would like to join me again, you are welcome.' She walked over, picked up her handbag and pulled out her business card. 'I work in the city. My office is just around the corner from the Academy. Here's my card. Keep it with you.'

Angie smiled, reached for the card and slipped it into the pocket of her skirt. 'Thanks.'

'My company publishes about ten magazines a month. If you ever need a job in publishing, let me know.'

'I'm hooked on hospitality. All my life I wanted to manage a hotel like this one. The only bad bit about the course is James.'

Carolyn took hold of Angie's hands. 'He is evil. Don't let him hurt you like he did my sister.'

'I won't. Don't worry. I am tougher than you think.' She squeezed Carolyn's hands. 'I'll call you when I'm in Sydney.' She leant over and kissed Carolyn briefly on the lips. 'I'll definitely call.'

And she would call Carolyn. Though at the time, Angie had no idea why.

Chapter Eleven

'*I*'ve been invited to an orgy.' Isabella looked at Angie, her expression smug.

Angie dropped the reservation sheet she had been holding. Trust Isabella-The-Lesbian to get an invite to an orgy while she Angie-The-Sex-Starved did nothing but work. Several days of long hours and no pleasure thanks to James and Isabella had made Angie agitated.

James had tormented her with his sexual suggestions, and it had taken all of Angie's will power to knock him back. This, combined with Isabella following her every movement so she couldn't hunt, was sending her crazy. She was not going to let James manipulate her again, nor was she going to give in to him.

Curiosity overcame her dislike of Isabella. Taking a quick sweep of reception to ensure she was out of guest earshot, Angie hurried over. 'When? Where? Who by?' The questions tumbled from her lips so quickly that Isabella laughed.

'Tonight. I knew you would be interested. It has been such a beautiful afternoon the orgy is going to be held on the little island in the lagoon. You know, where they have the sculpture garden. James and Tahillia organised everything to celebrate my coming appointment as assistant manager.'

Angie bit her lip, forcing herself to remain calm by mentally counting to ten. Isabella obviously could not resist lording her coming appointment over her. Now she was invited to an orgy. Angie could not stand it. She felt hot and frustrated and her hands trembled with agitation. 'I don't understand why you want to go. You don't like men,' said Angie.

'I didn't say that. I said my preference is for women. Anyway, there will be some women there too. Kate, the red-haired waitress with the huge boobs will be there with her boyfriend Rick; Cole and Rod, the guys who run the shark boat; plus guests that are into that sort of thing. Oh, and Tahillia told me she has invited that spunky pop star Nick Holt now that he has sent his wife home. Not that he interests me. I can't wait to get my hands on Kate. She really does it for me. That big bust of hers is sensational. Ooh, this is making me hot.'

Isabella's face glowed with arousal. She lifted her black curls from the back of her neck with one hand, fanning herself with the other.

'I think I might turn up,' said Angie. She would like to catch up with sexy Nick Holt again. The heated sensation between her legs made her breath quicken. She thought of Cole and his giant penis and knew she just had to attend.

'Sorry,' said Isabella, not sounding the least bit sorry. 'It's invite only. So you can't come.' She raised her dark eyebrows. 'It's James's show. You have to be invited by him. He probably hasn't included you because you can't do what you are told. You know how he likes to dominate everyone.'

Angie groaned at the mention of James's name. 'I don't understand James. Look how he manipulated everyone in the Room of Retribution. We all ended up doing what he wanted, but he didn't join in. That's totally weird.'

Isabella brushed an imaginary bit of fluff from her skirt. 'Who cares. I don't bother trying to understand James. Once, when I wanted to get this Desire placement, I waited in his office totally naked. I had decorated myself with strawberries and mango. There I was lying on his desk like a ripe fruit salad, waving off the fruit flies. You know what he did when he discovered me?'

'What?' asked Angie.

'Nothing! He told me to come back at the same time tomorrow.'

'That's bizarre,' said Angie. 'Then what happened?'

'I did what I was told. I came back the next day with the fruit. We had great sex. He organised the Desire placement.'

Angie shook her head puzzled. 'There is something wrong with that guy, but I can't work out what it is.'

Isabella made a dismissive gesture with the wave of her hand. 'Who cares. You should learn from me. If you obey James you will get what you want.' Isabella clasped her hands together. 'I couldn't be happier.'

'I can't suck up to James and Tahillia the way you do. I just can't.' Angie's voice was brittle.

Isabella's dark eyes sparkled. 'It doesn't bother me one bit. Anyway, if you had bothered to "suck up" to James and Tahillia, you probably would have had the assistant manager's job. So I guess I'm glad you didn't. I couldn't stand you when I first met you. I rather like you now.'

Angie sighed and crossed her arms in front of herself. Isabella's sycophantic style of friendship she could do without. 'James does not have the right to tell me who I can and can't have sex with,' she said passionately.

'It's just his way of controlling you. Not that it works.' She leant close to Angie. 'You don't fool me. I know what you were up to with Carolyn Wolf the other day. I could hear you coming from the corridor. She must have been good.'

'Don't be ridiculous,' said Angie. 'You know I don't go for women. Anyway, I can't believe you are such a spy.'

Isabella shrugged and smiled smugly. 'I'll do whatever it takes to get a job here. I've got what I want now. Isabella di Bellini, Assistant Manager, Hotel Desire. That has a great ring to it, don't you think?'

Angie bit her lip to stop her reply. Isabella di Bellini, Assistant Crawler, was more like it. Still, she had a point. Isabella had been offered the plum job that Angie wanted.

'Oh, look,' said Isabella. 'Here comes my replacement on reception. I'm off. I want to get ready for tonight. I'm so excited. The orgy theme is "come as your favourite historical character". I'm going as Lady Godiva. I have heard that one of the guys who works on the shark boat is the size of a horse. Pity you are not coming.' Isabella giggled. 'You would have liked that.'

'I'm sure I would,' said Angie, her voice flat with disappointment, watching Isabella leave. She knew most of the people going to the orgy and she wanted to go. Would Jacob be there too, since he had joined the Silly-Grin-Club? She had barely talked to him since he had betrayed her by giving in to Tahillia and Isabella. He had caved in to their demands so easily; she could hardly believe it. So much for his waiting for the special person.

Several hours later, Angie walked to her room. Her feet ached and she sat on her bed massaging them. The floor of her bedroom was dusted with gold specs. Isabella's cosmetics littered the dressing table. She was probably having a wonderful time, thought Angie with frustration. Then Angie had an idea. Though she may not be invited to the orgy, there was no reason why she could not go and watch. She would let the darkness hide her.

Angie showered, dressed in a tight black top and pants and headed along the staff quarters corridor, making her way towards the lagoon. She was walking so fast she nearly bumped into Jacob exiting his room.

'Hi there,' he said, putting his arms out in front of him to catch her. 'Where are you going so fast?'

'I'm surprised you don't know. Don't tell me Tahillia didn't invite you?'

Jacob looked at her, his expression bemused. 'I don't know what you are talking about.'

She pushed past Jacob. 'Tahillia has organised an orgy. I'm going.'

Jacob grabbed her arm. 'Are you crazy? After what that weird woman put us through? Stay away from her.'

Angie put her hands on her hips. 'Put us through? Excuse me! Am I hearing this right? I was the one who suffered watching you pleasure Tahillia then Isabella. You haven't been able to wipe that silly smile off your face.'

'So that's why you haven't spoken to me for the last few days. You're jealous.' Jacob put his arms around Angie's waist and tried to pull her close. 'Angie, you of all people should know I am not interested in Tahillia. I made an agreement with James. I kept my end of the bargain.'

'And thoroughly enjoyed doing it,' said Angie indignantly.

Jacob groaned. 'I tried not to, but I couldn't help myself. When Isabella entered the room, I had no chance. What man can refuse her? She would have to be the sexiest woman I have ever seen.'

Jacob's enthusiastic endorsement of Isabella was the end. She brushed away his hands from her waist. 'For your information, you are wrong on two counts. One. I am not jealous. Two. Isabella does not like men.'

'You could have fooled me,' said Jacob with disbelief in his voice. 'She was sensational.'

'I'm not sticking around to hear this. I have to work with the woman all day. That's bad enough.' She stalked away, shaking her head.

'Boy, what has got into you? You are positively caustic,' said Jacob, catching up with her.

Angie stopped and turned on him. 'Nothing! That's the problem.'

'Angie, don't do anything wild.' Jacob reached over and gently stroked her hair. 'Stay with me. There's a full moon. It's a beautiful night. Let's go for a walk on the beach.'

She looked at Jacob in disbelief. Trust him to be thinking of something sickeningly romantic when what she wanted was some hard, fast sex. 'In case you haven't worked this out, let me make it perfectly clear,' she said through gritted teeth. 'I don't want to walk. I don't want to talk. I want a big, hard cock. Now quit following me.' She pushed him aside and marched out the exit door on to the lush grass.

A pleasant breeze brushed her face and she took in a large breath of fresh air. Angie knew Jacob was right about her mood, and she also knew exactly what would make her feel better. Some women resorted to chocolate. She hunted. Barefoot, she walked across the lawn to the bridge which linked the small island with the sculpture garden to the shore of the lagoon. When she crossed the bridge she could hear voices mingled with moans of pleasure. She stopped, transfixed by what she saw. The soft uplighting of the sculpture garden illuminated the orgy participants.

The first man she spotted was James. Whether she liked it or not, the man had an electricity that made her draw breath. He was naked except for a dark cape that would have looked ridiculous on anyone else. He stood on an imposing rock-slab altar. Isabella knelt before him, taking his huge phallus into her mouth. Her gold-painted body gleamed in the night.

A tingle raced up Angie's spine and her nipples tightened. She watched as Isabella sucked him, fighting the urge to join them. James's hands were entangled in Isabella's hair, his muscles tense and his breathing fast and shallow. He was strong and magnetic in his appeal. Angie's breath quickened. Her own hunger for him surprised her. It spread throughout her like an intoxicating but deadly poison. Angie wanted James, but she hated him too. Her juxtaposed feelings did not make sense. She had managed to refuse every offer he had made since the Room of Retribution, but seeing him naked aroused her intensely.

Realising she would be seen if she stayed near the bridge, Angie quickly walked over to hide behind one of the several large sculptures in the sculpture garden. There she could watch unobserved. She forced herself not to look at James and Isabella, fighting the irresistible pull he seemed to have over her.

Instead, she turned to see Cole and Rod dressed as centurions. Cole's enormous cock was erect. Rod held it like an offering as various women took turns trying to mount Cole. Amused, Angie's mouth twisted to a grin as she watched Kate try to mount him. Rick wrapped his arms around Kate's waist and lifted her on to Cole's cock. Within minutes, Kate vigorously shook her head, pushing hard against Cole's chest, her face a picture of disappointment. Rod, however, was smiling, and Angie suspected he would use Kate's lack of success to his advantage.

Just near them on the ground, Tahillia, wearing a Zorro-style mask, had tied Nick by the wrists at the base of one of the sculptures. She knelt over his face like a jockey, undulating as he licked her. Crying out with pleasure, she ground herself on to his face. Occasionally, she hit him on the thigh with the small whip she held in her hand. Angie could hear her telling him to lick her faster and harder. She could easily imagine the rock star's long tongue with its stud exploring her secret place. The thought made her hot. Lucky Tahillia, she thought enviously, to have Nick as her prisoner.

Nick's erect penis jerked every time Tahillia hit him. Angie realised he was enjoying his treatment. Tahillia had managed to convert him to her kinky way of thinking after all.

Soon Tahillia was screaming, gyrating above him. Her cries of pleasure attracted interest. Rod walked over to join them. He fondled Nick's cock in his hand, stroking it up and down. Tahillia, intense on her own ecstasy, held Nick's face so he could not see who was touching him. Rod parted his butt cheeks, then lowered himself on to Nick's erect shaft, his eyes shining with delight.

Though she did not want to watch James and Isabella, like metal to a magnet, Angie's gaze soon returned to them. James thrust himself vigorously into Isabella's mouth. Dark and swarthy in his black cape, he made Angie shiver. He looked like the devil he was.

Isabella, still kneeling at his feet, continued to work her mouth vigorously along James's shaft. James grimaced, his teeth bared in a snarl as he climaxed. Finally he released her, stepping back, his broad chest heaving with exertion. Isabella continued to kneel at his feet until he waved her away with the flick of his hand. He stood on the altar surveying the scene, his hands on his hips.

Angie looked with fascination as somehow he managed to stay erect. She had heard rumours that a man could orgasm and keep his erection but in all her hunting days she had not encountered the unusual phenomenon. Then James's gaze turned to where she was hiding. Angie froze. Perhaps he could sense her presence, Angie did not know, but the compulsion to join him grew until she dug her fingernails into her palms. Every nerve ending she possessed was alive with desire.

Yet she had sworn he would not dominate her again. She could not understand her attraction to him. Perhaps it was her own inability to control him. She did not know.

James's gaze turned from her and Angie expelled a large breath. He had not seen her. She followed the line of his gaze to see Isabella, who had brought Kate over to stand in front of him. Isabella pulled Kate into her arms and kissed her. They were beautiful together. Isabella's dusky gold skin sparkled in the moonlight, a contrast to Kate's paler form. Their bodies were pressed together, a sensuous contrast of beauty.

'Oh,' sighed Kate, her eyes wide. 'Oh, that feels good.' Isabella had moved from Kate's lips to her breasts. She cupped Kate's large breasts in her hands and began sucking each one in turn. Her pink, pointy tongue oscillated over the tips of Kate's nipples. Kate caressed Isabella, her hands weaving through Isabella's black locks. When Isabella moved lower, Kate parted her legs in anticipation.

Angie reached under her top, caressing her own nipples. Pinching the tips, she remembered what it felt like to have Isabella rubbing her body against hers. While her feelings of dislike for Isabella had not changed, Angie had been awakened to the ecstasy of having a woman. She wanted to share in their sensual softness. But she knew she could not. The moment she gave in, James would use it as an opportunity to dominate her. He watched, his eyes gleaming as the women pleasured each other in front of him.

Isabella pulled Kate on to the soft grass. Isabella's face was alive with lust as she opened Kate's legs to explore what lay between. Soon she was tasting her. Kate moaned softly, raising her hips. This delicious scene attracted the attention of several men. They circled the women. Watching. Waiting.

Finally content, Tahillia finished with Nick and left

him to the mercy of Rod. She walked over to the women, her face flushed with arousal.

Free of Tahillia, Nick looked down to see Rod enjoying him. 'Get off me!' yelled Nick, when he saw who possessed him. Rod only laughed and continued.

'Finish him off,' said Tahillia to Rod. She laughed, the high-pitched sound as irritating as ever. 'Enjoy him.'

Nick's eyes opened wide with horror as Rod moved up and down on his cock, savouring every inch of him. Cole and Rick circled the women. Cole stroked his enormous erection, his expression wishful.

'Is this pleasing you, James?' asked Tahillia. He nodded. 'Yes.' He watched Kate writhing in front of him, as Isabella urgently claimed her with her mouth. Isabella pinched the top and bottom of Kate's clit, exposing the sensitive bud, and vigorously licked until Kate arched and screamed. James's eyes gleamed.

Angie noticed James's erection had lost none of its power. He stepped off the altar and moved towards Isabella and Kate. 'Leave her,' he said to Isabella. 'I want her.'

Isabella looked up at him, a frown creasing her forehead, but she did as James ordered. Angie knew from Isabella's sulky expression that she was disappointed. Just when she had made Kate pliant, James had demanded her for himself.

James pulled Kate to her feet. 'Put your hands on Isabella's shoulders. I want her to watch while I take you.'

James stood behind Kate, guiding his cock inside her. 'Oh, I like that,' sighed Kate. 'Oh, that feels so good. I'm so close. Oh, so close again.' Kate reached between her legs with one hand, stroking herself. Angie watched as Isabella glared at James, clearly furious that he had spoiled her pleasure. She had wanted Kate for herself.

Cole moved behind Isabella, obviously hoping to join the exciting display. Isabella took one look at the size of him and her eyes widened and she quickly slapped him away.

James smiled at her response, his white teeth wolfish. Angie realised as she watched that although Isabella had been made assistant manager, she would always have James as her master. Though she had claimed she did not care about doing James's bidding, Angie realised this was not the case. Isabella's face darkened as she watched James possess Kate. She looked furious.

Angie watched as Kate trembled, her auburn hair flicking back and forward over her face, following the movement of her body. James possessed her with a passion that was frightening. He gripped her, one arm around her rib cage, his hand full of her breast, the other hand between her legs. She looked pale and insignificant as he owned her with his body. He strummed her expertly, his fingers matching her rhythm. Soon Kate was calling out with pleasure, excited by what he could do for her.

James was an expert. He could maintain his erection. He knew what excited a woman. But after him, would Kate ever be satisfied with a gentle guy like Rick? Angie did not think so.

James was like a tidal wave, Angie realised. He surged in carrying all in front of him with his will, but he left wreckage behind. Yet even though she knew how James operated, that did not stop Angie wanting him. He could satisfy a woman like no other man. That was his power. Angie ached for him. She yearned to be satisfied as she listened to Kate's impassioned cries. She remembered her time with him in the grotto. She wanted to feel his strong arms binding her, his magnificent cock inside her and his fingers touching her. He knew instinctively what she wanted and how she liked it. Only James could do that.

She watched as he stiffened and shuddered. A deep growl left his lips and his powerful arms tightened, holding Kate still, and then he finally released her. Kate fell forward into Isabella's arms. Isabella tried to kiss Kate but, sated by James, Kate turned her face away, gasping for breath.

Kate staggered to sit at the base of the altar and closed her eyes. As she recovered, her legs flopped apart. Isabella looked longingly at those parted thighs. James smiled – amused, Angie thought, at Kate's rejection of Isabella.

James stood, his hands on his hips, surveying all before him, his cock still erect. Angie watched, unable to understand how he could keep hard for so long. He could not possibly maintain an erection, unless he faked his orgasm. Her need for him intensified. She wanted to know how he did it and the only way to find that out was to try him herself. Though she had no wish to be dominated by James, Angie had to have that wonderful feeling of satisfaction. She could not bear to watch all these people having sex while she had so little. The effects of her passion with Carolyn had long worn off. No-one could do it for her like James.

James turned in her direction, as if he sensed her telepathic need. Angie could feel the hypnotising pull of his gaze. She could not bear it. Every part of her tingled with desire. The hairs on her arms and legs stood on end. Her nipples were painfully tight. She wanted to feel his hot mouth on them, sucking her. She wanted to feel him pushing inside her, filling her until she could take no more. She needed him.

He held out his arm in her direction. 'Come out, Angie,' he called. 'I saw you at the bridge. I know you are there.' He raised his voice. 'I order you to come.'

All the reasons why she shouldn't go to him crowded in her mind. She hated him. He used his power for the wrong reasons. He did not respect women. And yet her traitorous body tingled urgently with wanting him.

She knew she had vowed not to give in, but she

needed the sheer feelings of pleasure only he could give her. She also realised she would regret it afterwards, but even that did not stop her. The man was addictive. She came out from her hiding place behind the sculpture, and walked towards him.

'No! Angie. Stop!' called a voice she recognised. She turned to see Jacob running over the bridge. 'Stay away from him. You know he will only humiliate you.'

James walked towards Angie. His hand caught her wrist in a steel-like grip. The pain of his grip snapped her out of her sensual fog.

'Let me go!' she cried pulling away from him.

Jacob ran towards her. 'You heard what she said. Let her go.'

'What will you do if I don't?' asked James, his voice a sneer.

Jacob, his hands bunched into fists, walked over to James. He was shorter by a head but he was strong and wiry. He had been prepared to lose everything for her once before, Angie thought. Why was he doing this? Why did it matter to him what she did?

'You heard what I said. Let her go. She doesn't want you.'

'Oh, she wants me.' James jerked Angie towards him. He reached down and slid the palm of his hand over her tight black pants. Angie shuddered at the caress of his hand. His touch was hot, even through the fabric. He rubbed his hand back and forward. The heat he generated seemed to sear her skin, increasing the intensity of her desire for him.

'She's wet,' said James, looking at Jacob triumphantly. 'She's ready for me. You liked watching me, didn't you?' He let go of her, not bothering to wait for Angie to reply. Instead, he stared down at Jacob, taking a menacing step forward, so they were only inches apart. 'She knows sex with me is better than with any other man. She wants me.'

Angie looked at James. Hate for him flamed in her chest. Yet it was not enough to stop her wanting his thick cock inside her. As much as her feelings for James did not make sense, Angie knew that she did not have to like a man to enjoy sex with him. She wanted those powerful multiple orgasms she had been dreaming of for days. James would deliver. She knew that with a certainty that reached her soul.

'Damn it, Angie. Don't just stand there!' shouted Jacob. 'Tell him you don't want him.'

Angie looked at Jacob. His handsome face was suffused with blood. He was a man who cared about women, and had been raised in a large family of females whom he loved. Standing opposed to James, his goodness shone through. But Angie wanted great sex, not a do-good boyfriend. 'I want you to leave,' she said to Jacob.

'What?' Jacob turned to her, his eyes wide with disbelief. 'Angie, you can't mean that.'

'She wants my cock,' said James. 'No matter how much I humiliate her. She is prepared to do anything to get it. You young pup,' he said condescendingly, pushing Jacob hard against his chest with the flat of his hand, 'you have no idea what it takes to satisfy a woman.' James raised his face to the inky sky and laughed. The sound was chilling, almost a howl of victory. Then Jacob hit him and he went down like an undignified sack of potatoes.

'Oh my God!' screamed Tahillia. 'Oh my God! Look what you have done!'

Angie watched, amazed, as James lay flat on his back groaning. Intimidating Jacob had been a mistake. James covered his nose with his hand. Blood seeped through his fingers. Suddenly, as if a spell had been broken, she saw James for what he really was – a lecherous, 40-year-old man who preyed on young women in order to prove his virility. But perhaps the most ludicrous sight of all was his still-erect penis, pointing to the moon.

Angie shuddered. She did not want him now. He looked ridiculous.

'Come on,' said Jacob, taking her by the hand. 'Let's get out of here.'

'So you think I can't satisfy you?' said Jacob.

'I know you can't,' teased Angie. 'I saw how long you lasted with Isabella and Tahillia. They had to satisfy each other.'

'Give me a break, you demanding woman. It was my first time. I have been practising ever since.'

'Oh yeah? Who with?'

Jacob looked rather shamefaced. 'Well ... um ... myself.'

Angie rolled her eyes. 'Oh great, and that's supposed to do it for me.'

'Come with me,' urged Jacob, taking her by the hand. 'I'll prove it to you. But I want it to be special. You know ... you and me together. Our first time.' He took her hand and they walked along the beach. The moon lit their way.

Angie was amazed that none of the orgy participants had tried to stop them leaving. In the background they could hear voices from the sculpture garden, but as they made their way along the shore, the voices faded until they were alone.

'Where are we going?' asked Angie. She stopped to catch her breath.

'To a special place where that weird lot won't find us. It's not far now. Have you been to the rock pools?'

'No.' She shook her head. 'I've been working double shifts. I haven't had time to explore.'

'Good,' said Jacob. 'They are beautiful. I want to be the one to show them to you.'

Angie smiled, glad that the partial darkness hid her

face. Jacob was such a romantic. One day he would make a fantastic husband. The thought was not too repulsive. She could just imagine him at his wedding, with her beside him tossing confetti at him and his bride, while she surveyed the other guests, working out who would be her prey.

She sighed, realising she had not had the opportunity to hunt for a long time. James had made her stay suffocating. Tomorrow, she and Jacob would leave for Sydney and she was glad. Hotel Desire had not turned out to be the jewel she had expected. Not with James and Tahillia on the island.

They picked their way over some boulders that separated the main beach from a little cove. When they climbed down, they came to several rock pools filled with seawater. The crystal pools shimmered in the moonlight, full of reflected stars. The water was the colour of midnight. Jacob was right – the pools were beautiful. There was only the sound of the sea in the distance, rushing in and out. She walked to the edge of the largest rock pool and dipped in her toes. The water was still warm from the sun.

Angie shook her head as she stared at the water. Things had not worked out as she had planned. James had got to her, though she had thought she could control her desire for him. The thought of sex with him was exciting, but his dominance made her shudder. Jacob had come just at the right time, only she was sure he would pay the price for his actions. 'You do realise you will be tossed out of the course for hitting James,' she said, turning to Jacob.

He shrugged, picking up pebbles and tossing them in the rock pool. 'Not necessarily. I haven't broken any rules. I just defended myself. Anyway, if I do get chucked out, I'll make him justify why. I'm not prepared to let him get away with bullying me. And I wasn't going to let him bully you either. I'm glad I hit him. I happen to think you are worth protecting.'

Jacob turned to Angie and kissed her with a passion that surprised her. His mouth was sensuous and Angie met his kiss, teasing his tongue with hers. She held him close, enjoying the lithe yet subtle strength of him. Jacob was full of surprises. She would never have thought he would have had the courage to hit James.

'Oh Angie,' he said, looking into her eyes. 'It feels like I've waited all my life for this moment.'

Angie groaned quietly. Surely he was not going to get all romantic on her again? Quit talking. Just get on with it, she thought. Just hurry up.

He slipped his hands under her T-shirt and pulled it over her head. He stroked her breasts and Angie bit her lip, resisting an urge to rip every shred of clothing off him and throw him on to the sand. She knew he needed time to worship every inch of her. That was the problem with him.

'When I first saw you,' he said, his voice hoarse, 'I thought I had found perfection. He stripped off her pants, then rapidly removed his own clothing. 'That time on the beach with Rick and Kate, I thought I would go crazy with wanting you. I still feel that way.'

And I'm going to go crazy if you don't stick your cock in me, thought Angie. She pulled him close and kissed him again to stop him talking. She thrust her tongue into his mouth, claiming him as her own. Things were so much better when he was silent. She explored the smooth muscles of his back with her fingers. His skin had that same erotic, silky feel she had come to know. But best of all was his cock throbbing at the apex of her sex. She parted her legs, wanting him inside her.

'No, wait,' said Jacob.

'Jacob,' she said warningly. 'I'm not waiting.'

He laughed and held her hand, leading her into the

largest rock pool. The water was warm and she liked the feel of the soft sand beneath her feet.

Jacob lay in the water, his head resting against one of the smooth rocks that surrounded the pool. 'Come on.' He reached out his hand and pulled Angie on top of him. 'Let's make love here. This feels like heaven to me.'

Angie resisted rolling her eyes at his comments. There was no point insulting him when she was so close to her goal. A good hunter was patient. However, there was no way she would tolerate any more foreplay. The erotic sight of the orgy had aroused her to fever pitch. She knew exactly what she wanted, and she was determined to get it. Angie parted her legs and reached for his cock. It was smooth and swollen with a big, thick knob. She slid it in, closing her eyes as she sighed with relief. The feeling of Jacob's cock parting her, the heat of him pushing up inside her, was sensational.

His thick pubic bush tickled her shaven lips. She leant forward so that she could rub her clit against him. She pushed herself down on to him, building her rhythm. Soon, she was rocking her hips backward and forward. This was what she needed; hard, fast, satisfying sex.

Jacob groaned as he thrust into her. 'Oh God, Angie. I've wanted this. You are such a tease. I've never met a woman who loved sex like you do.'

'You have been mixing with the wrong sort of women,' she grunted. She squeezed her pubic muscles as she slid up and down on him, enjoying the thickness of his cock.

Leaning forward, she pushed her breasts towards his mouth, determined not to let him start talking again. There was only so much romance she could handle in one evening, and Jacob had just about filled her quota.

He licked and sucked on her swollen teats. His tongue teased the springy plumpness of her nipples. The pointy end probed the eye of her nipple. It made her hot and close to coming. But she wanted to keep this moment for ever. He pleased her. She loved the way he wanted to please her.

'Oh God, Angie,' he cried. 'I have to come. I can hardly stop.' He squeezed his eyes shut.

'Don't you dare,' she ordered. 'You have teased me long enough. You can damn well last until I let you come.'

'OK.' He nodded, his eyes still tightly closed. 'I'll try to think of something I hate, but it's so hard with you milking my cock.'

'Well, think,' she urged.

'Bats,' he said.

'What?' asked Angie, slowing her pace.

Jacob opened his eyes. 'Bats. I don't like them. They give me the creeps.'

'Oh, just shut up.' She gripped Jacob's shoulders, rocking her hips, rubbing herself against his pubic bone. He was just delicious. She loved the way he tried to please her. She could hear him murmuring to himself. 'Bats, bats, bats.' If she weren't intent on her own orgasm, she would have laughed.

She could feel it building and growing like a lighted wick attached to dynamite. She squeezed her eyes shut, her breathing ragged, hips jerking as she came. Her orgasm swept over her like the sea, its heat spreading up her spine, over her sensitive breasts, finally encompassing all of her. She cried out, releasing her passion, her voice intermingling with the rush of the waves at the shore.

'That's it, that's it,' groaned Jacob. 'Oh God, Angie. That's it.' He grabbed her hips as he thrust up into her until he cried out, his own orgasm consuming him. His gentle face stared up at her, his soft lips parted in pleasure until finally he was spent.

She lay on him, staring at him, her breath hot and fast. He put his arms around her, drawing her close. The warm water covered them like a protective womb. She wanted to stay in his arms, drinking in his generous warmth. Jacob was special, she thought, with misgivings.

She lay on him, listening to the roar of the sea and the thumping of his heart. He cuddled her. 'I dreamt of bringing you here,' he said. 'I wanted you to be mine. I knew I could make you happy.'

He stroked her hair from her face, staring into her eyes. 'I did please you, didn't I?' he asked, tenderness written across his face.

Angie looked at him and sighed. Sex with Jacob had been fresh and exciting. Her whole body tingled with delight, he made her feel so good. However, she could not afford to get attached to him. He would only end up getting hurt, and he did not deserve that.

Things were getting serious. Never in the past had she allowed a man to get so emotionally close. Soon Jacob would be taking her home to meet his mother, she realised with horror. 'This is the last time we can be together.'

She saw the confusion in his eyes. 'I don't understand,' he said. 'I thought you enjoyed it.'

'I did. That's why I don't want to do it again.' She pushed him away and walked out of the pool. Standing at the edge of the rock pool, she picked up her top, brushed it over herself to wipe away the water, and pulled on her clothes.

Jacob followed her out. 'I don't understand you, Angie. I know you like me. Why don't you want us to be together?'

She realised it seemed ridiculous that, after hunting him for so long, she would have to stop seeing him. When the course finished she would walk away and never see him again. She liked her life as a loner. The thought of being a couple made her feel caged. She would have to give up hunting, and that was too great a sacrifice to make.

'Is this another of your games?' he asked.

She turned from him, not wanting to talk any longer. Jacob was so different from her. He had been brought up on relationships while she had never known her parents. He would never understand that a conventional relationship would never work for her. It was time to return to the hotel.

'Damn it, Angie, I have to know.' Jacob took her by the shoulders and swung her around to face him.

'This isn't a game,' she said, brushing his hands away. 'You have never understood me. I don't want a boyfriend, and I don't need rescuing. I warned you once before. I'm not some delicate princess you need to save. Don't put me on a pedestal. It's not what I want.'

'I couldn't help it. I couldn't let James have you. You deserve better.'

Angie sighed, realising she had not got through to him. It was so easy when she hunted. She did not know the prey. Their feelings did not matter. Jacob was different. She liked him; cared about what he thought and felt. But if she did not stop him now, he would be planning their wedding. 'Don't fall in love with me, Jacob. Just don't.'

She saw him stiffen. He swallowed as though a huge lump was blocking his throat. Jacob looked away, then stooped to pick up a handful of pebbles. The first few he sent skimming across the pool, then he tossed in the rest with one ragged sweep of his arm. They landed in a splash, breaking the serenity of the pool. 'It's too late for that,' he said. 'I fell for you long ago.'

Angie crowded with the other students, trying to see her name on the examination results board. The past few weeks back in Sydney at the Academy had been spent in lectures, followed by a major exam. She had studied late into the night, determined to do well. The work experience placements made up 40 per cent. Though she

239

had passed, her pass rate had been low. Angie was not surprised. Her ambition had been surpassed by her desire to hunt. At least James and Tahillia had not failed her. The theory exam was worth 60 per cent of the course, and she had worked hard to pick up her marks.

She knew she had done well yet an urgent tightness throbbed in her chest as she looked for her name. She scanned the list until she found it. 'Masters,' she read. 'High Distinction.'

Angie jumped in the air with happiness. She knew she had blitzed the exam. James had said he would help place the best students in a job in a good hotel. Hotel Desire was definitely out – Isabella already had that job – but there were some new hotels in the city. Angie liked the city. Anonymity when hunting suited her. Unable to wipe the smile from her face, she walked past Jacob, who was looking unusually gloomy. 'Hi there,' she said. 'What's the matter with you?'

Jacob looked at her, his blue eyes narrowed. 'That bastard failed me.'

'Pardon?' said Angie, too surprised to take in his meaning. Jacob never swore.

'James failed me,' repeated Jacob. He frowned. A muscle ticked in his jaw. 'Tahillia and James passed me with a distinction for the work experience, but then James failed me on the exam. I know I did better than that. I know I passed.'

Angie felt a sinking feeling that made her stomach muscles clench. 'I knew James wouldn't let you get away with hitting him. This is his way of punishing you. He let you think you would pass by giving you a good work experience report – not that you didn't deserve it,' she added quickly.

Jacob paced up and down in front of Angie. Finally he stopped and looked her in the eye. 'I'm not going to let him get away with it. I'm going to demand he organise a re-mark of my exam by one of the tutors.' He crossed his arms in front of him. His face was suffused with blood. 'Gosh, I'm sorry, Angie,' he said a moment later, his expression gentling as he studied her. 'I'm so concerned about myself, I didn't even think to ask how you went.'

She nodded and smiled. 'I did OK,' she said, not wanting to big note herself.

'Good. I knew you would,' said Jacob. 'You're smart and beautiful. A dangerous combination.' He walked over and kissed her lightly on the cheek. 'Congratulations.'

Angie sighed and looked at him. Sometimes she thought he was so nice she did not want to stop seeing him. Angie shook herself. What a ridiculous way to think.

Isabella walked past them. 'I passed with High Distinction. Topped the course,' she boasted. 'I can't wait to get back to Desire. I'm going to put my stamp on that place. James said I make excellent management material. The best ever.'

Yeah right, thought Angie. Material to be managed by him. Hardly an excellent arrangement.

'Well done,' said Jacob. He flashed her a grin. 'Have a great time. Hope you enjoy your new job.'

'Oh, please,' Angie groaned as Isabella walked away. 'Do you have to be so sweet to her? You know she slept her way right through this course.'

Jacob raised his eyebrows. 'I seem to remember there's a saying about people in glass houses –'

'Forget it,' interjected Angie, 'I don't want to hear it. Anyway, Isabella couldn't care less who she slept with providing she got what she wanted. At least I enjoyed myself.'

'I enjoyed it too,' said Jacob softly.

Angie looked at him warningly. 'Don't start going all romantic on me. I meant what I said at the rock pools on the island. I'm not interested in a relationship.' Her heart twinged when she saw his expression. The man was enough to make her feel guilty. She must be losing her touch. Since when did hunters feel guilt? 'What are you going to do about James?' she asked, changing the subject.

'I'm going to confront him now. I'm not going to let him cheat me.'

'I'll come with you,' said Angie.

'No! Stay out of this. This is my problem,' said Jacob firmly. He stopped her following him by taking her by the shoulders. 'I mean it. Don't follow me. This is my problem, and I want to solve it man to man.'

'Great,' murmured Angie as she watched him go. 'Now you are really going to stuff things up.' She was certain that James would enjoy having power over Jacob. He would relish failing him. She glanced at her watch and decided to wait ten minutes. If Jacob did not come out, she would have to go and save him.

She did not normally involve herself in other people's problems, but she owed Jacob. He was in this mess because of her. The feeling of wanting to look after a man was new to her. Angie sighed with irritation. Hunters devoured their prey; they did not save them. God, she was getting soft. She looked at her watch again. Eight minutes had passed. A crash from James's office sent her heart thudding.

She raced to James's office and stopped at the door. Instinct made her pause and listen. A good hunter surveyed her territory before she entered a dangerous situation. She could hear male voices, one low and aggressive. 'So you want to pass, do you?' growled a voice Angie knew to be James's. His tone had a particularly unpleasant ring to it.

She opened the office door and stepped inside, closing it behind her. Her breath caught in her throat when she saw what James was about to do. Only he would stoop so low. James had forced Jacob to lie stomach first on his desk. Jacob's clothing had been ripped from his body. James, the bigger and stronger man, lay naked on top of Jacob, pinning him to the desk with brute force. The office was a mess. Evidence that Jacob had put up a struggle.

'Get the hell off me,' choked Jacob, his face purple with rage.

But James, his expression alive with sardonic pleasure, forced Jacob's wrists to the desk. 'I see we have a visitor,' said James. 'Angie has come to watch me deflower you. I like to be the first. A man's arse is tighter than a woman's sex. Think how it will feel when I shove my cock up you.'

'Stop, James. You can't do this,' said Angie, her voice loud with alarm.

'On the contrary, I can do what I like. I shall enjoy sliding my cock into this young buck. Especially after you informed me in the Room of Retribution of how much Jacob hates the idea of a cock up him.'

James leant forward, pressing the whole of his body weight on to Jacob. 'This will teach you to hit me. Can you feel my hard cock waiting to take you?' he said, his lips pulled back in a sneer. 'I've been waiting for you.'

'Get off me, you crazy bastard,' growled Jacob, struggling fiercely. His wrists were red from James's iron grip. Though he fought to release himself from James's possession, he could not budge the stronger man.

'I need assistance to hold him,' said James to Angie. 'I want to prise him open. Take my time so that he never forgets what I have the power to do.'

'Forget it,' replied Angie, walking over to James. 'You are sick. You have gone too far. Get off Jacob or I'll call the police.' She noticed as she reached James that he was sweating with the exertion of holding Jacob. He smelt sour.

'No, you won't. You'll help me to get what you want,' said James confidently.

Angie shook her head. 'Forget it. I passed my course. I can get a job without your help.'

'I'm offering you the position of assistant manager of Desire.'

'Don't listen to him,' urged Jacob. 'Don't let him manipulate you. Please, Angie. Don't help him.'

Angie frowned as she looked at Jacob. Lying underneath James, he stared beseechingly at her. She could hear his hoarse breath as he sucked air in and out.

'What about Isabella?' asked Angie.

'I'll find something else for her,' replied James.

Angie nodded, pleased at the thought of replacing Isabella. 'It would serve that haughty bitch right. I'd like to take that job from right under her nose,' she said slowly.

James laughed. His eyes gleamed. 'You and I are similar creatures. You will betray anyone to get what you want. In my antique Korean chest, I have handcuffs. The chest is locked. The key is in the drawer of my desk. Get the key and unlock the chest. Bring the handcuffs over and put them on him. Then come and watch me take him.' James laughed maniacally.

'Angie, don't do this.' Jacob struggled furiously. Sweat poured off him as he writhed under James, but that only seemed to excite James further.

Angie walked purposely around the two men to the front of the desk and opened the drawer. Picking up the key, she looked into Jacob's eyes. He was a beautiful, gentle soul, but she did not want him. She could not bear being worshipped by him. It was as bad as being controlled by James. She had had enough of guilt. That was how Jacob made her feel because he was so good. She held up the key in front of James.

'That's the one. Get the cuffs,' he ordered.

'Not so fast,' said Angie. 'I want my share of Jacob.' Hunters, after all, thought Angie, occasionally worked together and shared the spoils.

'You can do whatever you like with him,' James puffed in his effort to hold Jacob down. 'Now hurry with those cuffs. I have had enough of this struggle.'

'No, Angie, no!' cried Jacob. 'You don't have to do this.'

She looked Jacob squarely in the eye, thrilled to be hunting again. A hunt did not get better than this. Raw lust fuelled her body until she was tense with arousal. 'Yes I do,' she said.

Angie walked over to the chest and unlocked the door. A variety of scents assaulted her nostrils. The chest smelt like a Chinese herbal shop. Several sets of handcuffs lay on one of the shelves. She picked two sets up, and checked to see whether the cuffs were open and ready to attach. Then she caught sight of the other oddities in the chest.

'Quickly, bring those cuffs over now,' urged James.

'Stop, Angie,' called Jacob. 'Don't give in to his manipulation. I love you.'

'I told you once before. I never wanted your love,' replied Angie, her mind on what she had discovered in the chest.

'You are naive,' James sneered at Jacob. 'She wouldn't want you. She is too wild for you. Angie is like me. That is why she can't resist me. You were no more than a fuck for her.'

Angie looked again in the chest. James's posturing bored her. The voices of the two men faded as she reeled with understanding. James had a veritable factory of lotions, potions and pills for male impotence secreted in the chest. She recognised some of the manufacturers' names on the pill bottles. Others she had never heard of. The unexpected sight hit her like a thunderbolt. So now she finally knew how he managed to keep an erection for longer than other men.

She fought the urge to examine the goods. It was time to use the handcuffs. She had always been partial to bondage. The thrill of binding a man aroused her intensely. Slavery was always sexy providing she was not the slave.

'Hurry, Angie,' growled James. 'I can't keep him still much longer.'

Angie walked towards the men, swinging the cuffs casually in her hand. Her whole body tingled with pleasure from the ultimate thrill of the hunt. She could barely wait to trap her prey.

'Click one cuff to the leg of the desk,' urged James. 'This desk weighs a ton. He won't be able to budge it.' He forced Jacob's hand close to the corner of the desk.

Angie clicked one side of the cuff in place. It fitted the round leg of the heavy wooden desk perfectly. The cuff had an extra long chain, and she suspected it was purposely selected for this type of bondage.

'Now click the other side to Jacob's wrist,' ordered James.

'Oh God, Angie, don't do it,' cried Jacob, his voice hoarse. Angie looked at his hand. It was purple with the pressure that James applied to keep him still. Then she looked at James, remembering the pleasure he took in humiliating her. In one swift movement she clipped the other side of the cuff to James's wrist.

Both men looked at her in disbelief.

'Damn you!' screamed James as he aimed a swipe at her. Jacob, seizing his opportunity to escape, quickly struggled free from underneath James.

'Get his other hand,' urged Angie, her heart racing. 'Help me cuff the other one.'

James fought like an animal but the two of them managed to secure him. 'Get these off me.' He snarled at them, a caged lion, dangerous but contained.

Jacob leant against the wall, breathing with exertion.

'Come, Jacob,' Angie took his hand, 'you can't rest now. There's something I want to show you.' She led him to the Korean chest and pointed to the assembled concoctions. Jacob picked up a tube of cream. 'Potency Cream for Erectile Problems,' he read with disbelief. 'Oh my God, Angie. There's everything here. He held up one file of shrivelled brown nut-like objects. 'Deer testicles.' Jacob screwed up his face. 'Yuck.'

'Get away from there, damn you!' screamed James.

'Help me,' said Angie gathering up the bottles, creams and lotions. 'Here, bring them over to James.'

'What are you doing?' James asked. Don't you dare touch those or I'll –'

'Or you'll what?' Angie stared at James. 'I think it's time you stopped bullying people to get your way. You went too far this time. You think I would help you rape Jacob?' She shook her head vigorously. 'Rape disgusts me. I'm not like you. Not at all.'

James glared at her, but did not attempt to continue with his threat.

The pieces of the puzzle began to fit into place. James was not the stud he claimed to be. He could not get an erection without chemical help. Now she understood why James used the handle of the whip on her in his office. It also explained why he had initially refused Isabella with her fruit salad, and had told her to come back the next day. He needed time to prepare for sex. Even when Jacob had hit him on the island, he had still maintained an erection thanks to his lotions, potions and pills.

Angie strode over and stood in front of James. 'You can't get it up without help, can you?' Angie asked. 'No wonder you can keep going and going as you boast.'

'Wow, these things do work,' said Jacob, peering at one of the bottles in his hand. 'I'll have to try these.'

'Cut it out,' said Angie to Jacob. 'One total fake is enough.'

She looked at James and her eyes narrowed. 'I know someone who would be very interested to learn your pathetic secret.'

'Who?' asked James, though his face had blanched to the colour of bleached toilet paper.

'Carolyn Wolf.' Angie let the name roll softly from her lips, watching James's reaction. 'I think I'll telephone her and tell her to come over. She would love to see you like this.'

James's normal sardonic expression faded as the realisation of what Angie intended hit him. He looked ill. 'God, no! Not that ball-crunching lesbian.'

'She has never forgiven you for what you did to her sister. Just imagine if I rang her, and asked her to send a photographer down. This would make a wonderful picture for *Wild* magazine. A picture of you decorated with all these would look great.' Angie shook the bottles vigorously in James's face before setting them on the floor. 'Your reputation would be ruined.' Tingles spread through Angie's body. She had finally landed big game. The thrill of the hunt was intoxicating. It was payback time.

'What do you want?' asked James. 'I'll give you anything. You wanted management of Desire. You shall have it. I'll give you Tahillia's job.'

'Tahillia's job!' Angie looked at him in surprise. He must be desperate to offer her Tahillia's job as manager of Desire. But James *was* desperate. She could see him tremble though he tried to hide it. 'Now that would be interesting. I would be Isabella's boss.' Her eyes shone with excitement. This was the prize she had been seeking. Double revenge and a good job too.

'Don't do it,' said Jacob. 'Don't let him bribe you. You will never be free of him on Desire. Once he's free it will be your word against his that he is impotent.'

She looked at Jacob, wanting to tell him to leave, but Jacob had failed the course because of her. She owed him. Angie sighed. She hated the feeling of guilt, and Jacob had the irritating ability to get under her skin.

'I'm a wealthy man,' said James, his voice cutting into

her thoughts. 'I can pay you, too. I'll do anything. Now get these cuffs off me.'

'Jacob didn't fail his exam, did he?' asked Angie, ignoring his monetary offer.

James looked at her in surprise.

'No. I wanted to punish him for hitting me. I couldn't let him get away like that.'

'I knew I passed,' said Jacob. 'I knew I blitzed that exam.'

'Let me go.' James looked from Angie to Jacob. 'The graduation certificates are in my filing cabinet. I only have to sign them.' James nodded at his filing cabinet. 'If you let me go, I'll sign your diplomas and give you both the best references. I'll find you a great job, too,' James said to Jacob.

'Forget it,' said Jacob vehemently. 'I don't want your help.'

'No, wait a minute, Jacob,' said Angie. 'You worked hard for your diploma.' She walked over to the filing cabinet, pulled it open and extracted two certificates. 'I'll uncuff one of your hands to sign these,' she said to James. 'If you try anything underhand, I'll open your office door and call in some students. I'm sure they will be interested in your impotency concoctions.'

'Don't do that. I'll sign,' said James. Angie walked to the chest, took out the key and removed the cuffs from one of James's hands. She gave him a pen and the certificates to sign. 'Here,' she said to Jacob. 'Take these certificates.'

'Now let me go,' said James.

'Beg me,' ordered Angie.

'Like hell I'll beg you,' James said furiously.

Angie walked past James and picked the telephone off the floor where it had landed after James and Jacob had tussled. She picked up the receiver and started dialling.

'No!' screamed James. 'Don't ring Carolyn.'

Angie walked towards James with the telephone in her hands. 'Beg me not to call her.'

She could feel her nipples tightening with pleasure as she brought this once powerful man to heel. He deserved every bit of torture after what he had put her and Jacob through. Her body called out for pleasure. James had a magnificent erection despite his bondage and it put her in the mood. She was hunting, and she was at her best.

'I beg you,' growled James through gritted teeth.

'Not good enough. I want Jacob to hear you. Say it loudly.'

'You dominating bitch,' James said, his dark eyes black with anger.

'Really, James, that is not good enough.' She put the telephone down and walked over to the Korean chest again. Pulling out the tasselled whip, which James had used on her, she returned to stand near him, stroking the whip in her hands.

'Angie,' said Jacob, shocked, 'you can't use that on him.'

Angie rolled her eyes. 'Just shut up and watch,' she snapped at Jacob. Saving him was the one good deed of her life, and it made her feel antsy. She was sick of men telling her what to do. 'I have finished this course, and I can damn well do as I please. I don't want to hear what I can and cannot do from either of you.'

'Now you,' she said to James, her voice low with authority, 'get on your knees and beg me not to call Carolyn.'

James, with one hand still chained to his heavy wooden desk, slowly got down on to his knees. Angie looked at him. Every muscle in his body was tensed. He was the most dangerous of prey she had ever hunted. She could feel her sex moistening. It had taken her quite some time to bring this man to his knees, and she intended to enjoy every minute of it.

'Beg me,' she ordered.

'I . . . beg . . . you,' said James through gritted teeth.

Thwack! Angie hit James on the side of his rump with the tasselled whip.

'Fuck you!' screamed James, climbing to his feet.

'Maybe,' said Angie, standing just out of his reach. 'But only if you please me enough. Get back on your knees. I want you to lift my dress and pleasure me with your tongue.'

James, his fists clenched, reluctantly got back on to his knees.

'Now beg me again. I like to hear you say the words,' said Angie.

'I beg you,' said James, his voice trembling.

'Good. Now please me,' ordered Angie.

She stared down at James, enjoying the feel of his firm hands on her thighs as he pushed the skirt of her dress up her legs. James was made for pleasing a woman. His problem was he liked power too much, but then, so did she. She sighed, almost closing her eyes as James's tongue tickled the outer lips of her sex. Opening her legs further, she allowed him to press his hot mouth against her.

'Jacob, come over here and take off my dress.'

'Pardon?' said Jacob.

She looked at him. It seemed such a shame not to use Jacob for her pleasure as well – although from the frown on his face, it was clear he did not approve of what she was doing. But that did not stop Angie wanting him too. She could see his sex swelling as he watched James.

'You heard me. Come over here and take off my dress. I want you to stroke my breasts.'

'No,' said Jacob. 'I want you, but not while he is touching you.'

Trust Jacob to put up a fight. Angie sighed and hit James with her whip.

'Damn you,' said James angrily. 'What did you do that for?'

Angie pouted. 'No reason. I just felt like it.' James glared at her. Angie stared down at him and raised the whip. Quickly he parted her with his thumbs. His pointy tongue slid over her clitoris. It felt hot and wet as it oscillated over her. Angie arched towards him, burying one of her hands in his thick dark hair.

'You know, Jacob, you don't have to do as I ask, but if you don't, I'm going to order James to take me while you watch. I'm going to let one of you fuck me. I haven't decided who it is yet.'

'It's not going to be him,' said Jacob, his tone jealous.

'He won't satisfy you,' said James, raising his head. His dark eyes narrowed as he watched Jacob approach.

Their animosity delighted Angie. She hit James with the whip. His body jerked. 'Did I tell you to stop?' she asked.

'Bitch!' James snarled.

Angie nodded. 'Yes. You got that right.'

James opened her further, sliding his tongue inside her. Angie's legs began to tremble. 'Oh God, that is good.' Small waves of pleasure spread up inside her.

Angie smiled to herself. She liked Jacob, but he would have to learn that she could take whoever she pleased. If he had any lingering thoughts about her being his girlfriend, this would change them.

Jacob was already hard. He walked over, glaring at James, who continued to lick her.

'Good,' she purred as Jacob unbuttoned her dress and pulled it over her head. 'Hmmm, I like that,' she sighed as he stroked her breasts. She could feel his erection pressing into her back. She had both men doing what she wanted, and it made her want to come. Her nipples ached and pleasure pooled in her womb. She knew a fat cock would relieve her tense excitement. She was in her element. This was the most exciting hunt she had ever experienced.

'I want you inside me,' she said to Jacob. James tried to stand, but Angie pressed both hands on to James's shoulders. 'Get down,' she ordered. 'I like the real thing.' She glared at James. 'You can keep pleasuring me with your tongue. I enjoy having you at my feet. It is where you deserve to be.'

Jacob tilted her slightly, and thrust into her. She was wet from James's delicious exploration. Jacob held her firmly by the hips and increased his rhythm. Two delicious men thought Angie. One good, the other bad. Both worth the time she had put into hunting them.

Soon she was arching as Jacob held her tightly, thrusting more and more of his cock into her. Her fingers held James firmly by the ears as he sucked her small nub, his tongue rapidly caressing the tip. It did not get better than this. She had both men where she wanted them, and she was free. Free at last from the course, and free to hunt.

She cried out as she came. The heat that centred inside her spread outward until it ran like hot lava through her nerve endings, reaching her fingertips. She arched, moaning as both men pleasured her. James sucked her, sliding his tongue over and over her while Jacob drove himself into her. Jacob's fingers pinched her nipples, driving her excitement further. She had achieved everything she had wanted. Her heart pumped with excitement. This was the pinnacle of ecstasy for her. She wanted to stay there for ever, but slowly her orgasm ebbed.

She could feel Jacob shudder his release. He held her, his arms around her, breathing heavily on to her neck. His warm breath made the delicate skin of her neck pucker. Trembles of satisfaction coursed through her. Slowly, her breathing slowed. Needing them no longer,

Angie pushed both men away and picked up her dress. She watched as they stood glaring at each other.

'Let me go,' said James to Angie.

Angie shook her head. 'No. You see, James, I'm no longer interested in the management of Desire. It's too small. I don't like to feel caged. Anyway, I don't want to work in a hotel that has an association with you. I'm not like you at all. I love sex. I enjoy seducing men. I like manipulating them, playing with them, but I don't condone rape. Look at you with your fake erection. I happen to think you are pathetic.'

Angie walked over and picked up the telephone that had been knocked to the floor. She dialled a number.

'Who are you calling?' asked James, his face alive with horror.

Angie ignored him. When the beast was wounded, and at his most dangerous, the hunter went in for the kill.

'Hello, Carolyn. It's Angie Masters here. If you are not too busy, could you come around immediately to the Academy with a photographer? I'm in James's office. James has something interesting to show you.'

Epilogue

'You gave up the management of Desire for me, didn't you?' asked Jacob. 'I thought you really wanted that job.'

Angie turned to him. They were leaving the Academy for the last time. Carolyn was delighted to have James at her mercy, though Angie had had enough. She had left them together. Trapping James had been her greatest hunt, yet she was left feeling curiously hollow. She had thrown her chance of a great job away.

Angie frowned at Jacob, knowing he was to blame. His irritating do-good attitude was starting to rub off on her. 'I couldn't let James take you, nor cheat you of your diploma. You worked hard for it.'

'So did you,' he said.

She shrugged. 'I guess it's not worth as much without a reference from James.'

'Oh, I don't know,' said Jacob cheerily. 'I happen to think you could get a great job without James's help.'

Angie looked at Jacob, resisting the attraction she felt towards him. He was always so cheerful. Somehow he had managed to get under her skin.

'Did you mean what you said in James's office?' asked Jacob.

'I said a lot of things in James's office.' She sucked in her breath, and hoped he was not going to tell her he loved her again. She had told him she did not love him, but she wasn't sure whether he believed her.

Jacob looked at her. His brown hair was ruffled and his blue eyes shone earnestly. 'The bit about you wanting to work for one of the big hotels.'

'Oh!' said Angie, breathing a sigh of relief. 'Yes, I did. I don't expect I'll get anywhere though. Especially after setting Carolyn on to James.' Angie let out another sigh and shrugged her shoulders. 'I'm not sure what I'm going to do now.'

'Remember I told you my family work in the hospitality industry?'

'Yes, you did mention it. They run some small place, don't they?'

'Not exactly small. My father owns the Hamilton in Double Bay. Oh, and the Hamilton Hotel in Brisbane and Melbourne, too. He is looking for staff. That is, if you are interested.'

Angie stared at him, her eyes wide with amazement. 'But they are the most exclusive hotels in Australia! I'd love to work in the Hamilton in Double Bay! I had no idea you were part of that family. You never told me you were rich.'

Jacob ran his hand through his hair. 'I didn't want to say anything. People suck up to me when they know my background. I didn't want someone to be after me for my inheritance.' He smiled at her. 'I know you don't care about money. You threw away your job offer for me. I would like to offer you another.'

Angie stared at him as he looked at her earnestly. 'That doesn't change things between us. You know I can't stand the idea of being someone's girlfriend.'

'I know,' replied Jacob quietly. 'I accept that, but what

I want to know is would you consider a business relationship? Would you come and work with my family and me? We need a front office manager. You'd like that position.' He raised his eyebrows and grinned. 'You would get to see everyone who comes into the hotel, plus access to all the bedrooms.'

'Yes,' she said, looking at Jacob. 'Yes, I would.' She reached out and touched his cheek. 'Thank you.' Happiness swelled in her heart. Jacob finally understood that she could not abide a conventional relationship. She had never met a man before who could accept her for what she was – a hunter of men.

She could not believe her luck. Moments ago, she had thought she had thrown her career away. 'Front office manager would be great,' she said with excitement, thinking of the hunting possibilities.

Jacob took her hands and gave them a squeeze. She laughed and kissed him. 'You know I would miss you, even though I wouldn't want to. I really enjoy tormenting you.'

Jacob's eyes shone with happiness. 'I know. I'd miss the torment. I'd miss that a lot. You've changed my life, Angie.' He flushed and Angie suspected he was embarrassed by his effusive admission. In some ways Jacob was full of youthful enthusiasm, yet when it came to goodwill, he was the most generous and mature person she had ever met.

'Well, see you soon,' said Jacob. He fished in his pocket for his wallet. 'Here's the number for the hotel. Call me. I want to introduce you to my parents. My sisters are keen to meet you too.'

Angie groaned and rolled her eyes. 'I just knew I'd end up being presented to your family. Just don't get any ideas, OK?'

'Bye, Angie.' Jacob leant forward and kissed her again. His kiss was tender. She wrinkled her nose appreciatively, liking his fresh, manly scent.

'Bye,' he said again softly, squeezing her hand. 'Call soon.'

Angie nodded. She watched him walk away. Things had a way of working out, she thought. Jacob was kind of cute in a do-good sort of way. She guessed she could put up with him worshipping her for a while.

When Jacob was out of sight, Angie started to walk. It was morning, and the city was crowded. She breathed in. This was freedom. This was exactly what she needed. Anonymity. Then a certain tingle rushed up her spine. She spotted a man walking past her. He wore jeans and a white T-shirt. He stood out in the city where men and women dressed in suits. He was tall and lanky with dark hair. Just how she liked a man to be.

She followed him, keen to catch up with him. Soon she was striding beside him. He turned and looked at her, then stopped. Angie smiled and saw her smile reflected in the stranger's eyes. Her nipples tingled. It was time to hunt.

Visit the Black Lace website at
www.blacklace-books.co.uk

LOOK OUT FOR THE ALL-NEW BLACK LACE BOOKS – AVAILABLE NOW!

All books priced £7.99 in the UK. Please note publication dates apply to the UK only. For other territories, please contact your retailer.

BARBARIAN PRIZE
Deanna Ashford
ISBN 0 352 34017 7

After a failed uprising in Brittania, Sirona, a princess of the Iceni, and her lover, Taranis, are taken to Pompeii. Taranis is sold as a slave to a rich Roman lady and Sirona is taken to the home of a lecherous senator, but he is only charged with her care until his stepson, General Lucius Flavius, returns home. Flavius takes her to his villa outside the city where she succumbs to his charms. Sirona must escape from the clutches of the followers of the erotic cult of the Dionysis, while Taranis must fight for his life as a gladiator in the arena. Meanwhile, beneath Mount Vesuvius, there are forces gathering that even the power of the Romans cannot control.

Coming in March

CAT SCRATCH FEVER
Sophie Mouette
ISBN 0 352 34021 5

Creditors breathing down her neck. Crazy board members. A make-or-break benefit that's far behind schedule. Felicia DuBois, development coordinator at the Southern California Cat Sanctuary, has problems – including a bad case of the empty-bed blues. Then sexy Gabe Sullivan walks into the Sanctuary and sets her body tingling. Felicia's tempted to dive into bed with him . . . except it could mean she'd be sleeping with the enemy. Gabe's from the Zoological Association, a watchdog organization that could decide to close the cash-strapped cat facility. Soon Gabe and Felicia are acting like cats in heat, but someone's sabotaging the benefit. Could it be Gabe? Or maybe it's the bad-boy volunteer, the delicious caterer, or the board member with a penchant for leather? Throw in a handsome veterinarian and a pixieish female animal handler who likes handling Felicia, and everyone ought to be purring. But if Felicia can't find the saboteur, the Sanctuary's future will be as endangered as the felines it houses.

RUDE AWAKENING
Pamela Kyle
ISBN 0 352 33036 8

Alison is a control freak. There's nothing she enjoys more than swanning around her palatial home giving orders to her wealthy but masochistic husband and delighting in his humiliation. Her daily routine consists of shopping, dressing up and pursuing dark pleasures, along with her best friend, Belinda; that is until they are kidnapped and held to ransom. In the ensuing weeks both women are required to come to terms with their most secret selves. Stripped of their privileges and deprived of the luxury they are used to, they deal with their captivity in surprising and creative ways. For Alison, it is the catalyst to a whole new way of life.

Coming in April

ENTERTAINING MR STONE
Portia da Costa
ISBN 0 352 34029 0

When reforming bad girl Maria Lewis takes a drone job in local government back in her home town, the quiet life she was looking for is quickly disrupted by the enigmatic presence of her boss, Borough Director, Robert Stone. A dangerous and unlikely object of lust, Stone touches something deep in Maria's sensual psyche and attunes her to the erotic underworld that parallels life in the dusty offices of Borough Hall. But the charismatic Mr Stone isn't the only one interested in Maria – knowing lesbian Mel and cute young techno geek Greg both have designs on the newcomer, as does Human Resources Manager William Youngblood, who wants to prize the Borough's latest employee away from the arch-rival for whom he has ambiguous feelings.

DANGEROUS CONSEQUENCES
Pamela Rochford
ISBN 0 352 33185 2

When Rachel Kemp is in danger of losing her job at a London University, visiting academic Luke Holloway takes her for a sybaritic weekend in the country to cheer her up. Her encounters with Luke and his enigmatic friend Max open up a world of sensual possibilities and she is even offered a new job editing a sexually explicit Victorian diary. Life is looking good until Rachel returns to London, and, accused of smuggling papers out of the country, is sacked on the spot. In the meantime Luke disappears and Rachel is left wondering about the connection between these elusive academics, their friends and the missing papers. When she tries to clear her name she discovers her actions have dangerous – and highly erotic – consequences.

Black Lace Booklist

Information is correct at time of printing. To avoid disappointment
check availability before ordering. Go to www.blacklace-books.co.uk.
All books are priced £6.99 unless another price is given.

BLACK LACE BOOKS WITH A CONTEMPORARY SETTING

☐ SHAMELESS Stella Black	ISBN 0 352 33485 1	£5.99
☐ INTENSE BLUE Lyn Wood	ISBN 0 352 33496 7	£5.99
☐ ON THE EDGE Laura Hamilton	ISBN 0 352 33534 3	£5.99
☐ LURED BY LUST Tania Picarda	ISBN 0 352 33533 5	£5.99
☐ THE NINETY DAYS OF GENEVIEVE	ISBN 0 352 33070 8	£5.99
Lucinda Carrington		
☐ DREAMING SPIRES Juliet Hastings	ISBN 0 352 33584 X	
☐ THE TRANSFORMATION Natasha Rostova	ISBN 0 352 33311 1	
☐ SIN.NET Helena Ravenscroft	ISBN 0 352 33598 X	
☐ TWO WEEKS IN TANGIER Annabel Lee	ISBN 0 352 33599 8	
☐ PLAYING HARD Tina Troy	ISBN 0 352 33617 X	
☐ SYMPHONY X Jasmine Stone	ISBN 0 352 33629 3	
☐ SUMMER FEVER Anna Ricci	ISBN 0 352 33625 0	
☐ A SECRET PLACE Ella Broussard	ISBN 0 352 33307 3	
☐ THE GIFT OF SHAME Sara Hope-Walker	ISBN 0 352 29935 1	
☐ GOING TOO FAR Laura Hamilton	ISBN 0 352 33657 9	
☐ THE STALLION Georgina Brown	ISBN 0 352 33005 8	
☐ SWEET THING Alison Tyler	ISBN 0 352 33682 X	
☐ TIGER LILY Kimberly Dean	ISBN 0 352 33685 4	
☐ RELEASE ME Suki Cunningham	ISBN 0 352 33671 4	
☐ KING'S PAWN Ruth Fox	ISBN 0 352 33684 6	
☐ SLAVE TO SUCCESS Kimberley Raines	ISBN 0 352 33687 0	
☐ SHADOWPLAY Portia Da Costa	ISBN 0 352 33313 8	
☐ I KNOW YOU, JOANNA Ruth Fox	ISBN 0 352 33727 3	
☐ THE HOUSE IN NEW ORLEANS Fleur Reynolds	ISBN 0 352 29951 3	
☐ DRAWN TOGETHER Robyn Russell	ISBN 0 352 33269 7	
☐ VIRTUOSO Katrina Vincenzi-Thyre	ISBN 0 352 32907 6	
☐ FIGHTING OVER YOU Laura Hamilton	ISBN 0 352 33795 8	

BLACK LACE BOOKS WITH AN HISTORICAL SETTING

BLACK LACE ANTHOLOGIES

To find out the latest information about Black Lace titles, check out the
website: www.blacklace-books.co.uk or send for a booklist with
complete synopses by writing to:

> Black Lace Booklist, Virgin Books Ltd
> Thames Wharf Studios
> Rainville Road
> London W6 9HA

Please include an SAE of decent size. Please note only British stamps
are valid.

Our privacy policy
We will not disclose information you supply us to any other parties.
We will not disclose any information which identifies you personally to
any person without your express consent.

From time to time we may send out information about Black Lace
books and special offers. Please tick here if you do <u>not</u> wish to
receive Black Lace information.   ☐

Please send me the books I have ticked above.

Name ....

Address ....

....

....

....

Post Code ....

Send to: Virgin Books Cash Sales, Thames Wharf Studios,
Rainville Road, London W6 9HA.

US customers: for prices and details of how to order
books for delivery by mail, call 1-800-343-4499.

Please enclose a cheque or postal order, made payable
to Virgin Books Ltd, to the value of the books you have
ordered plus postage and packing costs as follows:

UK and BFPO – £1.00 for the first book, 50p for each
subsequent book.

Overseas (including Republic of Ireland) – £2.00 for
the first book, £1.00 for each subsequent book.

If you would prefer to pay by VISA, ACCESS/MASTERCARD,
DINERS CLUB, AMEX or SWITCH, please write your card
number and expiry date here:

....

Signature ....

Please allow up to 28 days for delivery.